Amid Summer's Nightmare

Season of the Witch, Book Three

ISBN (Paperback): 978-1-62251-042-9

Cover artwork by Fairytale Design

Interior Layout by Jennifer Carson

Edited by Trisha J. Wooldridge

Summary:
While searching for her missing best friend, teen fire witch Summer Wormwood faces her nightmares and discovers herself.

First Edition: December 2018

Published by Bellatrix Press, an imprint of Prince & Pauper Press

Amid Summer's Nightmare: a novel by April L Wood

Amid Summer's Nightmare

Season of the Witch, Book Three

April L. Wood

Also by April L. Wood:

Winter's Curse, Season of the Witch Book One

"Wood springs the extraordinary on you in the most ordinary of ways, slipping it in-between the action. From slushy tears to segregation curses to broom flying contests to pennyroyal oil tea, Wood's imaginative talent shines through..."—Literary Fiction Author K.P. Ambroziak

Spring in Summerland, Season of the Witch Book Two

"April L. Wood has a gift. She conjures up real magic with words, breathing life into a world full of love, laughter, ancient witchcraft, and color. I see color when I read her books. I don't know how she does it, but I see everything that she describes in vivid detail and astounding shades of greens, blues, violets, pinks. I don't know of many authors who can do that, I truly admire the few who can. Ms. Wood, thank you for your characters. Thank you for your stories. Thank you for sharing your magic."—YA and Horror Author Jacqueline E. Smith

For those who chase after
their dreams...

1

"Would you like to try our new herbal Green Witch Tea?"

"Nope. An iced caramel macchiato, please," I reply to the caffeinated barista. She raises a pierced eyebrow, eyeing my best friend's broomstick and shooting me a puzzled look before spinning around to prepare my drink. I'm accustomed to the reaction. She isn't the only one who finds my lack of witch culture mystifying.

"Why don't you ask her to pour it into a hollowed-out avocado instead of a cup?" Aspen Widow-Tears remarks, wearing a self-satisfied grin. He leans against the rustic counter, and his messy blond hair spills across his forehead, falling across his lavender eyes that almost look sparkly under the exposed lightbulbs of the trendy coffeehouse.

I roll my eyes. My best friend and former foster brother has a hipster joke every time I drag him here. I'd think he would've run out by now, but nope, they just keep coming.

They say one can tell a lot about someone from the type of coffee they drink. I suppose it says even more that I pass the Witches Brew—my neighborhood coffeehouse—on my way to the Coffee Cuties. Then again, there's flavored coffee here with whipped cream, shaved chocolate, and drizzled caramel. Plus, rainbow cupcakes, mustache cookie pops, and other artificial sugar-laden sweets one doesn't find at the

Witches Brew that specializes in herbal teas, savory bread, and cauldron stews.

The regulars of Coffee Cuties are your run of the mill, stylishly-scrubby sophisticates who peer through black-rimmed glasses at laptop screens for hours on end writing speculative fiction, memoirs, and other works of literature. Dreamy chillwave music pulses through the air, and the baristas wear hot pink aprons over unadorned, dreary black uniforms.

What Coffee Cuties doesn't have a lot of are witches.

The barista returns with my drink, and I pass her several crumpled bills dug out from my overstuffed, lime-green backpack. Aspen walks ahead, eager to leave the non-magical establishment. He holds open the door and twirls his broomstick impatiently. I take a sip of the sweet drink.

"Mm. I'll take this over a wheatgrass-chamomile-cauldron-sludge tea any day," I say, with vanilla, sugar, and cream at the tip of my tongue. He shoots me a puzzled look and I shrug my shoulders. "Hey, I'm just enjoyin' my last bit of freedom before Charm School…" I sip. "Deep in the woods of Elwood…" I take another sip. "Where nobody'll be able to hear us scream… I fear it's hardly a coincidence."

"Please," he scoffs, as we step outside into the heat and humidity. He leans his broom against the brick building, then crouches on the crumbling sidewalk to tie his shoe. "In just a couple weeks, you'll be crafting your own herbal tea blend in a cauldron and stirring it with a broomstick. I just hope you won't want to fly to the opposite side of town for a damn beverage anymore." He rises to his feet, grinning.

"I'm not making any promises." I shove him playfully—a bit harder than I intend—and he steps off the curb's deteriorating edge, stumbling backward into traffic. Cars slam their brakes and drivers honk their horns. I tell Aspen I'm sorry several times; my voice taking on a higher pitch with each apology. He finds his footing, laughs it off good-naturedly, and we hop on his ride and split. I hold onto his backpack strap and my beloved iced drink for dear life, squeezing the broomstick handle with my thighs as we fly through the sky.

"You better be enjoying that macchiato, *heavy hands*," Aspen says smartly over his shoulder.

We soar over the city of Springfield, the tips of ages-old hemlock trees and pines brushing against my ankles and sandaled feet. The wind stirs my long black hair, lifting it mercifully off my neck, shoulders, and back. We rise higher and cut through streaks of clouds, startling a flock of noisy grackles.

"I think one just swore at me," Aspen says, regarding the birds.

"I think he was warnin' us to turn around. You know, I'm already looking forward to the day when it's time to pack up and I hop on a broomstick and shout, '*see ya later, witches*,' leaving Headmistress Starwort in a cloud of dust."

"It might be fun, like a summer camp," Aspen suggests.

"I'm just gonna go through the motions—adopt a pet toad, craft a bubbling potion, or whatever *authentic* witches do—and hocus pocus I'll be done, and I can graduate on time," I shout over the roar of the wind.

"Uh huh," he replies flatly, half listening.

We dip under a large oak tree within the forest of Elwood. My sandaled feet hit the dirt ground with a solid thud. My hair is a bit tangled and windblown; I finger-comb it the best I can with my free hand and hop off the broom.

We step onto a well-worn path. Branches have been thinned for ease of access. The dirt trail winds through the forest and leads to Camp Bitter Tonic, where Headmistress Starwort's Charm School is held for the summer season.

The pathway is edged with large smooth rocks. Wild ferns and deep-green moss have taken over the forest floor, where it basks in the dappled shade alongside the dirt trail.

Soft, green fronds brush against my calves as I pass. A lady slipper flower pokes through a bed of fallen leaves.

"Whaddya think would happen if we didn't show up?" Aspen asks with a sly smile. He pulls a bottle of water from his backpack, uncaps it, and takes a swig.

"I'm more worried about what will happen if we *do* show up. I imagine the High Priestesses getting together and forcing us inside these individual cauldrons, where they bathe us in the bathwater of the Elders to infuse us with witchy goodness. Then, they'll have us drink glorified herbal tea before forcing us all to dance under a full moon in only our underwear."

Aspen raises an eyebrow. "First of all, I hope so. And second, that's probably a *little* dramatic," he says as he makes a motion of swatting me with the broomstick.

"But that's where my brain goes," I remind him, stepping out of the reach of his broom.

We weave around pine and oak trees, stomping over pine needles, acorn shells, and fallen leaves. A twig snaps under my foot. It's unbearably hot, even for me, a fire witch, but voices are ahead, so I know we're getting close. A trickle of sweat rolls down my chest, disappearing behind my floral-print babydoll top. I set my coffee down momentarily and gather my thick hair at my neck before rolling the elastic tie off my wrist. It snaps on my finger and I mutter a curse. I stuff the broken tie into the pocket of my lace-trimmed denim cutoffs to discard later.

"I can feel my freedom slipping away from me with each step forward," I whine as I pick my coffee up from the forest floor and peel pine needles from the bottom. I take a sip and chew on the straw nervously.

"You better finish that coffee before we get there, or Headmistress Starwort Wormwood will give you the herbal equivalent of having your stomach pumped."

I stop dead in my tracks. "You mean, no coffee at all?" I blink.

Aspen laughs through his nose, approaches me, and ruffles my hair. "It'd do you some good. All that sugar and artificial flavoring is garbage. It's not the coffee itself, it's all the crap and chemicals added to it."

I step away from him, off the trail and into a patch of wild fern. "How are you so calm?" I ask. "I feel like my heart is about to bust my ribcage open."

Aspen smirks as he holds back a branch, letting me pass first. "How bad can it be? It is what it is." His gaze dips to my drink. "Also, I have no sympathy for you when you're suckin' down hipster caffeine juice."

As I roll my eyes for the umpteenth time today, something peculiar catches my eye. Above the trees are fluttering ribbons in gold, red, and fiery orange. They drop, disappearing behind the foliage. With a gust of wind, the twirling ribbons are propelled back toward the sky.

We come around a bend to investigate and reach a forest clearing. The ribbons we spotted are attached to a welcome banner that's strung between two giant fir trees. On the banner is the Charm School crest of antlers, twisted green vines, and red poppy flowers. Below the banner, a Wormwood witch with wavy, shoulder-length black hair is seated at a small folding table. She reminds me of my late grandmother and all the puzzles we'd do together on a similar folding table, and my sister, who cheated by cutting the pieces of the puzzle to fit when she'd get frustrated. The memory makes me smile. I hope my sister will be alright at home this summer without me. Knowing her, she'll be out a lot with her friends.

The witch at the table is armed with stacks of paper, pens, and a clipboard. Another student from high school, Azalea Devil-Claw, hands her documents.

"Well, I guess this is it. Are you ready?" Aspen asks.

I remove the lid from my iced drink and finish it in one gulp. I dump the ice and drag my hand across my mouth, flatly responding, "Nope."

"C'mon," he says with a throaty chuckle, crushing my cup in his hands before hiding it in his backpack. He wraps his arm around my shoulders, dragging me with him to the registration table. He smells like freshly mown grass and the cinnamon gum he's chewing.

I met Aspen many years ago in a temporary placement home. I think he liked me, in that immature way where boys hit girls to show their interest, but we were of separate bloodlines and for a short time shared a foster mother. The Segregation Curse of Old was active and strong, so we focused on friendship and he became like a big brother to me. He might tease me, but *whoa buddy* if someone else did, he'd rip their tongue out. Aspen's always had my back. He's the one constant in my life. As annoying as he is, I can't imagine not having his friendship.

The line clears. The woman behind the table calls me forward, gesturing to me with a wave of her hand. Her long fingernails are natural and there's not so much as a hint of makeup on her face. She's dressed in all black and her badge identifies her as Mistress Aster Wormwood.

"Your name?" She readies the clipboard and her pen.

"Summer Wormwood." I step forward.

She runs her finger down the small list, then nods as she discovers it, and checks off one of several boxes beside my name. She sets the pen down and holds out her palm. "And do you have your consent forms and signed waivers?"

I swing my lime-green backpack forward and dig the envelope out from a zippered compartment. I pass it to her dutifully.

After affirming the signatures are present, she points to a trail leading to a lesson area. "You may proceed now. Please follow the path and await further instructions with your fellow peers. Orientation begins shortly."

I hang back, waiting for Aspen, which earns me a piercing glare from Mistress Aster. I walk ahead a bit, and I soon hear his footfalls behind me.

We follow the trail around a curve and arrive at a good-sized clearing in the forest where five girls from my high school are gathered and cloistered in two groups. There are boulders, stumps, and cut logs positioned before a wide stump at the clearing's edge; the lectern, I suppose. Above it, a painted wooden crest with real deer antlers, carved flowers and greenery, hangs from a tree behind the lectern. Thick smoke billows from a large black cauldron. The air smells of sunscreen, pine, and campfire smoke, like summer should smell like.

The Wormwood girls, fire witches Amaranth and Petal, chat while they balance on a long log, beside Azalea, a water witch of the Devil-Claw clan, who picks at her nails, sitting on another log to their left. The Widow-Tears girls, air witches Fern and Hyacinth, perch on stumps behind them, chatting together in hushed voices, giggling ever-so-often.

"Fern," I shout, happy to see my friend. She looks over her shoulder and waves to me, flashing me a million-watt smile before returning to her private conversation with Hyacinth.

"It's an outdoor classroom," Aspen says with amusement. "And I'm the only dude here. Coolness."

"Oh, no way!" a male voice says from behind us.

"Or not," I say.

Aspen claps his hands with elation as he spins around. The owner of the voice is his friend, Rugosa Rose-Thorne, an earth witch who's immigrated last summer to the Forest Park neighborhood from the icy, terrestrial north pole.

"You got a letter too?" Rugosa asks, coming up the trail. He smells like a wintry mix of pine, peppermint, and fir trees. He's buzzed his long scarlet hair down for the summer. As he approaches, I rub my palm over the barely-there red bristles. "Easiest fix to dandruff, ever," he says with a grin.

"Oh gross." I retreat, dragging my palm against my denim cut-offs.

"Summer got a letter too, dude." They bump fists and we commiserate over our placements in boarding school during summer vacation.

"Hate to interrupt your little social gathering." Mistress Aster approaches us, reaching for Aspen's broomstick. "I neglected to take this during registration and will be needing it now."

Defensive, he steps back from her, white knuckles wrapped around the yellow handle. His grin falls from his face, replaced with a scowl. "From my cold dead hands, maybe. Whaddya want with it?"

She explains she needs to secure it in the broom shed, which he immediately protests because his broomstick is his baby. As he argues with her, I'm reminded of an incident he's still mad at me for, when a wayward buckle on my boot scratched the brand-new yellow finish. We were twelve years old.

He still hasn't forgiven me.

"While on campus, you aren't permitted to leave. You won't need it. Don't make this difficult," she says, losing her patience. "It's just a ride," she adds, holding her palm out and wiggling her fingers.

"That broomstick is more to Aspen than *just* a ride," I say. "It's symbolic of his freedom, craftiness, and hard work. He constructed it himself as a preteen for a school wood project and colored the handle yellow with onion skins to symbolize the sacred color of the Widow-Tears clan. He doesn't want anything to happen to it. That's all."

"Thank you, Summer," Aspen says, calming down some.

Mistress Aster convinces him it will be perfectly safe, and for peace of mind, he follows her to the broom shed to check it out for himself. I sit upon one of the rocks, sliding my backpack from my shoulders, and free a small stone wedged between my sandal and foot.

"I've heard the Headmistress is stern but kind. Just make a good first impression on her, and you'll cruise," Rugosa says. He sits beside me and dumps his canvas bag between us. A cloud of dust rises from the ground, triggering me to sneeze. I quickly turn my head over my shoulder, sneezing all over the bare feet of Headmistress Starwort.

The Headmistress shrieks as her toes curl into the dirt.

"I'm so sorry," I croak. Silence falls over the group. I hastily dig through my overstuffed backpack, pulling out a pair of wrinkled, pink pajama bottoms. My hair hangs over my face, hiding the shame that colors my cheeks. Well, that's it for me. I'll never graduate on time. I'm doomed! May as well pack up, return home and face it: I'll be held back while the rest of my friends receive their diplomas next summer from Springfield High. I ball the clothing up in my hands and pat her bare feet with the stretch-cotton fabric.

"What on Mother Earth are you doing, my lovely?" she asks.

I halt abruptly, my gaze lifting timidly from her feet to her face. Her green linen dress billows around her ankles as the wind blows. Her skin is dark, and her hair is silver, plaited in two long braids that hang over her bare shoulders. Her hand is poised over her heart and she's shaking her head. I apologize again for—I have no idea what—then I stuff the clothing back into my bag.

I could just jump into that smoking cauldron here and now.

"Well, as charming as that clearly was…" She clears her throat and someone giggles. "It isn't my health I'm worried over. I'm concerned about yours. You appear to be suffering from an allergy to Nature, just as your teacher, Priestess Anna

Devil-Claw, suspected. It's a good thing you are here," she says, centering her pendant necklace.

"Wow, Summer. That was slick," Rugosa says with a smirk when the Headmistress is out of ear-shot.

"Shut up," I mutter under my breath, my ears and cheeks flaming.

I haven't much time to register how an allergy to Nature and attending an outdoor boarding school can be mutually beneficial before a familiar melodious laugh rings out behind me. My head snaps up and my body stiffens.

As I look over my shoulder, my worst fear is confirmed. Joining us is Dahlia Devil-Claw—the girl my ex-boyfriend dumped me for, only days ago.

2

Three Days Earlier

The final bell rings, jolting me upright at my desk. Chairs screech across the linoleum, and classmates bolt to the door. It's the last day of school at Springfield High; students rush out of the classroom, eager to begin summer break.

"Summer, can you hold up a sec?" Priestess Anna Devil-Claw asks before I step out the door. I turn on my heel slowly, puzzled by her request. She presses an envelope into my hand and frowns. "Have a nice summer." I blink and leave the classroom, stuffing the envelope in my backpack to check out later. Now, I just want to find my boyfriend and go home to get ready for his show tonight; he has his first art exhibition at the local community center and I can hardly wait.

There's a lot of excitement, but also some uncertainty in the air, as graduating seniors stream through the corridors and out the high school doors to embark on new journeys. A rollercoaster of emotions from my fellow classmates surrounds me. Friends clutch one another and say tearful goodbyes for the summer. Locker doors slam shut. The atmosphere is cheery and hopeful, but my thoughts are troublesome because my boyfriend is being *so* weird today.

I'm hoping he's just nervous about his art show tonight—a lot of people will be there, witches and non-magicals alike—but I can't help but wonder if it's something else... Could it be *me*?

He didn't meet me between classes, and if that wasn't strange enough, when I tried to kiss him this afternoon, he turned his face! If those aren't the warning signs of an impending breakup, I don't know what are.

Most high school romances don't lead to tying the handfasting knot at a mystical, woodland ceremony. Nevertheless, I thought I could beat the odds with a carefully crafted love spell.

I gathered the biggest, reddest strawberries I could find from the farmer's market in the Rose-Thorne territory of Forest Park. And later that night under a full moon I carefully engraved our names into the ripe fruit with a pin and planted them in the pot. I chanted the love spell letter-perfect, and on the following full moon, at Petal Wormwood's Esbat, he asked me to be his girlfriend. Now, only a couple months later, our romance has decayed—much like I imagine those strawberries in the pot have.

How will I get through another breakup? Oh, I know, another ice cream binge. Broken hearts and fudge brownie ice cream are synonymous. I have a nagging feeling I'll be stuck home tonight, in my bedroom, scraping my spoon across the bottom of a pint or two... when I should be out celebrating my junior year graduation, hanging out with friends at the show tonight, supporting my boyfriend.

I weave my way around sweaty, flushed students. The school is overcrowded from a recent influx of refugee witches, and the exit is practically jammed. I was born in Elwood; I've lived in Springfield all my life. I haven't had to seek refuge from the witch hunters of my southern homeland, as my family did before me, thank the Gods, but that doesn't mean my life has always been easy.

Somebody slams into me from behind, sending me into the massive wall that is the frozen solid back of classmate Rugosa Rose-Thorne. He grunts, and I mumble an apology to the icy witch. The frost of his shirt from sweat melts quickly on my hot skin.

The humid air in the corridor smells of gym socks, musty textbooks, and intermingled perfumes, deodorants, and hair products. My friend Fern Widow-Tears pops out of the crowd. Her golden hair is short and spiky like a pixie, smattered with pink and silver glitter. She thrusts her yearbook and purple permanent marker in my face, insisting I sign it. Her vibrational energy feels caffeinated. She practically buzzes. I write a quick message and draw a heart around my name. As I'm passing the yearbook back to her, I ask her if she's seen my boyfriend.

"Oh, yeah... just saw him in Mrs. T's," she says, pointing down the hall with her marker. "She was hyping him up for later. You going tonight?"

I blink. "Why wouldn't I be?" I stand on tiptoes, peering over her and down the crowded hallway. "Sorry, gotta run," I say in a rush when I catch sight of him by the exit. Fern frowns. "I'll see you later!"

"You know, Summer, I'm sick of you ditching me for him!" she shouts back in a strained voice, but I keep going.

I nudge several people out of my way, zipping down the hallway to Mrs. T's art class. A teacher scolds me for pushing students; I apologize. Spotting my boyfriend, River, I shout his name, but he doesn't react.

"There you are," I say, slightly out of breath, throwing my arms around him for a hug once I approach him. His body tenses in my arms, like I'm his annoying aunt who insists on a hug and a kiss at family get-togethers.

"C'mon," he says to me sharply, nodding toward the exit. His short golden-brown hair spills over his forehead into his dark blue eyes. "I'll catch up with you guys in a bit," he says to his friends who pat him on the back and wish him luck.

"Good luck with what?" I ask, but I don't receive an answer. I know it isn't for his art exhibition; it isn't until much later. The fire within me prickles beneath my skin; hot indigo blood rushes through my veins, warming me from the inside out in nervous anticipation.

He steps ahead of me, running his fingertips through his short fade as he checks himself out in the reflection of the window he passes. I frown and take a deep breath. His aura is so shady that I have a strong urge to smudge him with sage, but the last time I did that on school grounds, someone thought it was weed and the police were called.

As we exit the double doors a summer breeze touches the warmth of my cheeks. In the green sun-drenched courtyard below, witches straddle riding brooms, ready to leave campus. Each broom represents its owner's personal style and clan. Some have ribbons woven within the stiff fibers and others display thorny stems and crooked twigs. Handles are stained in a rainbow of colors, from beets, onion skins, berries, grasses, and the leaves of rudbeckia and chamomile. Non-magical students step into long yellow buses parked in the lot.

River squeezes my upper arm. He jerks me out of the stream of traffic. I stumble into a sloped, landscaped garden beside the concrete steps. Sharp gray stones roll beneath my feet and cut through the soles of my strappy leather sandals.

"Um…What's up?" I ask when I find my footing. His inky blue eyes dim behind drooped eyelids. My heart sinks in my chest because I'm *definitely* being dumped. And he's doing it here, in front of all these people. This is *actually* happening.

"Yeah, so." He shuffles his feet and stuffs his hands in the pockets of his olive-green cargo shorts. Rocks roll down the gardened slope. The tall pines surrounding the school crack, bending with the wind.

"River, if you don't say something soon, my head will blow up. Like, it will actually explode. So, just spit it out."

"I think we should go back to being just friends," he says in a rush.

My mouth gapes open like a fish, at a loss for speech. His words are like a forest fire through my heart.

"Don't cry," he says condescendingly.

"I'm not," I retort, my voice cracking with emotion.

Amaranth Wormwood giggles as she passes us down the stairs. Hyacinth Widow-Tears tags after Amaranth. Her blonde head snaps to the side as River says to me, "Stop it. You're making a scene." His eyebrows draw together.

His friends holler for him. River tightens his jaw before shouting irritably over his shoulder, "Chill out for a sec! Damn."

I drag the back of my hand across my eyes. I wish desperately that he would wipe away my tears for me, like in every romance novel on my bookshelf at home. I want him to tell me he's sorry, that he didn't mean it. That the pizza he ate for lunch today had moldy cheese that's bringing him to hallucinate... Except, he says none of those things or even anything at all. He just stands there, looking like he has something better to do, and I'm holding him up with my pesky heartbreak.

Two fresh strawberries, a flower pot, and one pin. That's all it took for River Devil-Claw to fall in love with me. If only keeping him interested was as easy.

"You told me you loved me. What's changed?" I ask, biting my bottom lip to stop it from trembling.

He closes his eyes briefly, exhaling sharply through his nose. "I don't know," he says. "I'm just not feeling it anymore."

"What?" I ask, shaking my head, but the truth is, I know. I know better than he does. It's the weak love spell I crafted. I didn't plan for what I'd do after I nabbed him. My charm wasn't enough to keep him interested. Nor were my push-up bras, apparently.

"We probably won't see much of each other over school break, with how needy Meadow is." He fidgets with the straps of his tattered khaki backpack, covered with watercolor stains and splotches of acrylic paint.

"She's totally *not* needy." I sniff, rubbing my nose with the back of my hand. "She just needs me around for things."

"Mm, needy, like I said, and I'm not fightin' with you." He wags his finger at me and I make a biting motion. "It's too complicated, you and your mother. My parents don't really like me hanging out at your house, because, you know… but if you want, we can stay together…" he pauses.

I brighten.

"—and see other people."

And there it is. The good ole *"we should see other people"* line. A passive aggressive way to say, *"I wanna see if someone better comes along."* My ears ring momentarily, drowning out the roar of bus engines and other commotion. My long black hair prickles against my scalp like static—my inner fire energy brimming. The smell of sulphur fills the air, emanating from the tips of my long tresses.

"Calm down," he says, bringing his hand to his nose.

"I can't believe you'd really suggest that, River Devil-Claw—"

"Oh, spare me the lecture, Summer." He folds his arms and stares off into the distance. His expression hardens.

"Who is it that you want to see?"

River throws his palms up in mock defense. He opens his mouth but shakes his head, saying, "Nope."

"Who?" I demand again with a stomp of my foot; a sharp stone cuts into the sole of my sandal. It's only seconds before I have my answer.

Approaching behind River is Dahlia, a water witch of the Devil-Claw clan. She's one of Mrs. T's prized pupils, having already had several art exhibitions for her watercolor paintings at the community center. Her flip-flops *thwap* against the concrete as she climbs the steps, matching the pounding of my heart. Her cinnamon-colored curls twirl and undulate in the wind. Her gaze meets mine briefly.

Dahlia's eyes—like all water witches of the Devil-Claw clan—are a startling blue-black. Her ebony eyelashes are curled and caked with layers of mascara. Her frilly red plaid miniskirt is accented with completely useless studded spike suspenders hanging off her hips. She looks like a groupie; the only accessory she's missing is a mattress strapped to her back.

"River! Comin'?" she calls in her sickly-sweet, saccharine voice. He motions for her to wait with his finger. I take a deep breath, exhaling it slowly through my nose. I'm certain my pale green eyes are colored the emerald of the proverbial green-eyed monster.

This is so much worse than I imagined. I'm gonna need a lot of fudge brownie ice cream to deal.

Dahlia retreats; her shiny curls bounce with each step down to the courtyard. She joins his friends who step aside, welcoming her into the fold. Funny, they were never so accepting of me, but I suppose I could never fit into River's technicolor world, to begin with. I'm not an artist—I'm not even remotely creative. I shake my head and gesture to Dahlia.

"Is that who? Dahlia freakin Devil-Claw?" I ask.

"Don't be so melodramatic. So, we cool? I gotta get down there." He hooks his thumb over his shoulder.

"Fine." I shrug, adding, "We're done. Go hang out with Dahlia and your art dorks. You can all finger paint together—"

"You know what, Summer." He averts his gaze and chuckles, gripping the straps of his backpack. "This is *exactly* what I mean. I tried to be nice. You've never supported my art. Maybe if you had a passion of your own, you'd understand, but you insist on being boring and doing nothing with your life. And your emotions... you're too intense—"

"I'm a Wormwood. A fire witch," I interrupt. "I'm not a go with the flow water witch, like Dahlia. What'd you expect, River?"

"And I liked it, at first. You're sizzling hot." His gaze rolls down my body. "But, girl, you've burned me out."

And with those final words, he steps away, strutting down the steps toward his friends and Dahlia. "Just had to handle something that was long overdue," he shouts to his friends for me to overhear. Over macho guffaws, Dahlia's girlish giggle echoes across the courtyard. He wraps his arm around her waist and pulls her to his side, making it clear he's moved on and has chosen her over me.

"Talentless hack! William Blake wannabe," I shout, stepping out of the rock garden. I trip on a stone in my haste, lurching forward and nearly falling on my face. "Stupid sandals," I mutter under my breath. The giggles and snickers add to my humiliation, making me feel even worse. I weave around students and stomp across campus, wishing I could spontaneously combust.

I dip under the shelter of trees at the woodland edge, following the path leading to my clan's neighborhood sanctuary—Elwood. The lobed leaves of an oak tree snap at me angrily in the wind. I crouch to pass under a low hanging branch of a hemlock.

The wind blows through the wood, but it isn't enough to dry my tears. Tree branches creek as they brush against one another. The lingering scent of River's dark, musky patchouli oil wafts up from my top. Fiery hot tears slip off my cheeks as I trudge forward through the forest on my way home. That is the absolute last love spell I'll ever do. It's never real; it's not love. It's only enchantment. I swear to myself right here in this forest; I will never cast another. I renounce my magic. I'm just not good enough—the proof is in the failed spell.

The front door of my home groans in protest as I push it open. Scraps of flaked purple paint dust the black threshold. "Meadow?" I bring my hand to my nose; a smoky odor overwhelms the small kitchen. A trio of mice skitter across the dirty floor, seeking shelter beneath the refrigerator.

"What," my mother barks testily, tying her robe as she emerges from her bedroom. She closes the door behind her. "I'm surprised to see you here. Isn't your boyfriend's art thing tonight? I thought you'd stay out with your friends, but I gotta say I'm kinda glad. I need help with these." She gestures to the cluttered countertop as she approaches the sink to wash her hands.

I roll my eyes, closing the purple-painted wooden door behind me. Beside the sink loaded with dirty dishes on the scuffed Formica countertop are herbs, pendants, and a list of uncompleted Love Charm orders. Moon water sits in a row of mason jars on the window ledge above the sink. Nothing has been done since I left for school this morning.

"Did you get *any* of the orders completed?" I ask, irritated, not wanting to hear one iota about love spells.

"Mhm, guess not." Her eyelids droop as she runs the water and garbage disposal. She makes room in the sink, rinsing curdled milk and bits of food down the drain. I glance at the calendar on the wall; an appointment is scheduled in blue ink for her today.

"Hey'd you know you have an appointment today with your shaman—"

"I canceled," she hollers over the roar of the garbage disposal, waving me off with a quick flick of her wrist. She turns off the tap and flips the switch to the garbage disposal, silencing it.

"You *have* to go." Frustrated, I tighten my grip on the straps of my lime-green backpack.

"Well that's the problem, isn't it? I'm agoraphobic; I *can't* leave."

"Why can't we just have your shaman come here? Can we see if that's possible?" I suggest.

"I'm fine, Summer. Don't worry about it." Her eyebrows knit together as her lanky arms drop to her sides. "Your energy is on fire…and what's wrong with your face?"

"River dumped me," I respond sullenly, letting my hair fall over my face to partially cover my puffy eyes and flushed cheeks.

"Oh, that's why you're home early." She tosses an empty milk jug from the counter into the toppling recycling bin in the adjoining room. She returns, twiddling her thumbs. "How long did this one last?"

"Two whole months," I answer.

She blinks. "Summer, I've had longer blind dates than that."

I narrow my eyes, holding back the urge to respond, *yeah, but mine aren't paying customers*. It's an automatic slap across the face to bring up her other side-business.

She approaches me for a hug, wrapping me up in her lean arms. She smells awful, like sulphur and soot. Earthy smoke perfumes her hair, kind of like sage, but a little different. Witches who rarely bathe have peculiar body odors that reflect their element. Fire witches wear their moods like perfume. Lack of sunshine on a cloudy day can wreck a fire witch, and my mother's fear of leaving the house for days, weeks, sometimes even months at a time has rendered her depressed.

Her long black hair is uncombed, knotted in tangles. The ends of her tresses are split from a combination of fire energy and stress. She's so thin because she swallows more herbs than food. Her sharp angular bones poke through her ratty blue bathrobe. I wish she would keep her appointments. I hate to see her like this.

"What's this you got?" she asks, her hand in the pocket of my backpack.

I squirm out of her skeletal embrace as she digs something from my bag; it's the envelope Priestess Anna Devil-Claw handed me on my way out of her classroom. I snatch it back and tear it open.

It's an official document, with an odd crest of antlers, red flowers, and leaves at the header. "It's requesting my attendance to Headmistress Starwort's Charm School," I answer incredulously.

Attached is a brochure for Camp Bitter Tonic, a spiritual-based campground nestled within the secluded forest of Elwood, where a unisex summer boarding school for witches is held. It's signed by a Wormwood Elder.

"My attendance is mandatory," I add, frowning. "If I don't attend, I won't graduate Springfield High on time with my class... Oh my Gods! It begins in only a few days!"

My mind races in what feels like a million different directions. I'm angry at River and with my boarding school placement. And I'm fed up with my mother who can't keep her head straight. My little sister and I have been back with her for about a year now. Things were going well at first, but the same mental illnesses that prevented her from caring for us properly have manifested their ugly heads once again. I'm left to pick up the slack. Because of that, I'm tired all the time, and my grades have suffered.

I read the planned activities, calming down a bit. The better ones include camping under the stars, swimming, magical gardening, and arts and crafts. It sounds better than anything I'd be doing this summer, like crafting fake love spell pendants for non-magicals. Elemental cleansing, witch etiquette, and nature adaptation sound like things I'd hate, so I'm not super looking forward to those, but the rest isn't terrible.

My mother snatches away the document. A flash of anger sparks in her absinthe-colored eyes. "Wait a moment here. I know what this is *really* about—"

"Oh boy, let's get out the tinfoil hats…" I prepare myself for one of her infamous conspiracy theory speeches. She gets twitchy as she's about to gear up for one, and judging by the rapid involuntary blinks, this one should be a gem… I roll my eyes as my chin drops to my chest.

"—It's those social justice warriors who think they know what's best for us and our children yet live as far away as possible from witches because Goddess forbid their children see a little diversity. Nuh uh. Not interested in this charity handout for us *poor, at-risk* witches," she says bitterly. She abruptly slaps the letter down on the counter, startling me. "Tell them I said no!"

"Meadow!" I bemoan, snapping my head up. "It's not like that *at all*. I think it could be fun, in a weird sort of way."

"Fun?" she asks, her mouth twisting around the word as if she's biting into a lemon. "Could it be that you want to escape from something? Or someone? Like, watercolor boy?"

I clench my fists, briefly close my eyes. "If I don't go, they're saying I won't graduate on time. It has nothing to do with social justice whatevers or River."

"Mhm. I'm your mother. I know things and I'm always right." She reaches for the brown-stained glass carafe and pours herself a cup of coffee. She sets the carafe down with a loud *thunk* and black liquid splashes on the counter. "Even if I weren't totally offended by the social justice warrior charity handout, you know I need you, Summer."

I avert my gaze to the floor, guiltily. The ratty edge of her bathrobe covers all but her yellow, overgrown toenails.

"I know, but what if—"

Her bedroom door swings open, startling us both. In a cloud of earthy smoke, one of her repeats steps out. He's a Wormwood witch named Ash, and out of everyone she *entertains*, I hate him the most.

He has long salt and pepper hair, a full silver beard that gives him the appearance of a wizard, and a large potbelly. He's about twenty years her senior, supplies her with herbs in addition to cash, and is totally disgusting. He stumbles to the fridge and yanks it open, stroking his ratty beard as he inspects what little food we have—soda, neon orange macaroni and cheese leftover from last night, a rotten apple, a limp celery stalk, and an old box of baking soda.

I shoot my mother a look. "Really?" I mouth, disgusted. It's just another reason to add to the growing list of why I should run, not walk, to Headmistress Starwort's Charm School.

She cradles the steaming mug of coffee in her hands and averts her gaze, ashamed. "I'm sorry, Summer. I know you want to talk about this and other stuff, but I have company," she says under her breath.

"I want to talk about this *now*. It's in exactly three days. That barely gives me enough time to pack. Maybe you can help me get things together and we can talk?" I lower my voice, adding, "Maybe Ash can take a hike for an hour?"

She raises an eyebrow and shakes her head, blowing on the steaming coffee.

I sigh, completely frustrated. "I really don't think you're being fair!"

"I'm not signing anything. I need you around here—"

"You got me, baby girl. I'll take care of ya," Ash interrupts with a chuckle, waggling his eyebrows and cupping his crotch. He then scratches his round belly and pulls a two-liter bottle of grape soda out of the fridge.

"You gonna replace that?" I snap at him. He snickers as he twists the cap and tips the bottle of my favorite soda back to his lips. "Pig," I mutter under my breath, earning a glare from my mother.

As I watch him, I worry about what could happen if I leave. I fear that Meadow will lose her Love Charm business altogether if I go to boarding school, and that would mean more men coming through here. I can't handle that. I can barely handle how things are now. The pig gulps my favorite drink loudly, draining it. I feel like he's doing it just to irritate me and show me who's boss. It gets on my last nerve. My scalp prickles with electricity and my hair comes alive, perfuming the air with the scents of smoke and sulphur.

"Just because you think you're entitled to my mother doesn't mean you can also have your way with our fridge!"

The familiar hot sting of my mother's hand across my cheek sends me reeling back. My ear pops painfully. Ash chuckles in amusement. Meadow stomps away on the heels of her flat, bare feet. Her blue bathrobe trails behind her on the floor in tatters. The bedroom door slams, rattling the small house followed by the sudden, loud applause from a daytime talk show. She increases the volume.

I storm past Ash, rubbing my smarting face and jaw.

In my bedroom, I dump my book-bag on the old beige carpet, marked by River's spilled paint, candle wax, and dirt. I crumple the document into a ball and toss it across the room where it lands in one of the many heaps of dirty clothing that litter my floor. I throw myself on my twin-sized bed and scream my frustration into the mattress until my throat hurts.

Today has been an absolute nightmare that I can't wake up from.

I never thought I'd think this, but I'd rather be back in an overcrowded foster home than here. All those nights I spent tossing and turning, crying, and wishing I were back here was for nothing. This isn't a home, it's merely a house. I longed for a mother that didn't exist. Meadow will never change.

I roll over, gazing up at the yellow, water-stained ceiling. I can't wallow around here all summer, tethered to this house and my agoraphobic, codependent mother, feeling sorry for myself over a stupid water witch while a revolving door of perverts enter the house and I'm stuck at the kitchen table making fake love pendants. I reject love spells—real or fake—especially after what happened today.

I scoot off my bed and cross the bedroom to my overstuffed bookshelf. I run my fingers across the bindings of teen romances and untouched herbal dictionaries and spell books—their spines never cracked. I love reading fiction. Books offer me a much-needed escape when things get tough. I wish I could live within the pages of these novels. Through the wall, my mother's TV blares, "You are *not* the father!" The audience goes mad in response. A woman screams in dismay. I shake my head. Gods, what is so interesting about parenthood results?

River's presence is heavy in my bedroom. His watercolor paintings of magical, enchanted forest settings hang on my walls. One is half acrylic and half watercolor. The top is dark and ominous, featuring malevolent forest creatures with red coals for eyes, while the bottom is light and hopeful, of a young woman bathing in a green mist, oblivious to the darkness above her. It's always freaked me out.

I yank down a watercolor painting above my bookshelf, titled Blue Lady. The voluptuous woman sits cross-legged on a stump in a pastel-colored forest, surrounded by glittering golden mushrooms. Her eyes are round and innocent, like a baby fawn. I tear it in half, right between her stupid eyes, tossing the pieces onto my bed in anger.

I dig a pillowcase from my dresser drawer. With one good sweep of my arm, I remove framed photographs of him and me from the dresser; they fall into the sack. I accidentally knock over two small vials of rosewood and sandalwood essential oil, sending them rolling to the floor. Another falls into my sack. I rescue a bottle of jasmine oil from the pillowcase, setting it back on my dresser with my red candelabra.

Makeup pots and hair brushes are strewn haphazardly across the dresser. I sift around and discover the cedar box containing pressed flower petals from a wildflower bouquet he picked me. I lift the latch of the box and dump the dried petals into the pillowcase.

It all needs to be burned in the cauldron out back; After, I can pretend he never existed. He'll be as good as gone.

I grab the torn Blue Lady painting, stuffing it into my pillowcase. I tear his art off my wall, adding to my collection. I pull his hoodie out of my closet, packing it into the sack. Lastly, I reach for my diary and pen. Two months of our relationship are written in sickening detail. I flip through the pages one last time, feeling the ache in my heart. Every trace of River Devil-Claw will be purged from this room.

By the time I'm through, my walls are mostly bare. Other than my candles, essential oils, beauty supplies, and books, my personality barely shows in this room. I've always filled my space with mementos of my relationships, surrounding myself with the essence of the person I love.

Is that all I am? Am I *just* somebody's girlfriend? Is this how I identify myself? The blank walls suggest as much.

Perhaps River is right; I'm boring. It's no wonder he'd dump me for the beautiful, ultra-creative, watercolor artist extraordinaire, Dahlia Devil-Claw.

I sling the sack over my shoulder, passing my mother's room. The door swings open. "Running away?" she asks with a nervous chuckle. "I still need your help, you know." She gestures to the countertop, cluttered with uncompleted Love Charm materials.

"Just doing a little spring cleaning first," I reply with attitude over my shoulder, inadvertently getting an eyeful when I gaze upon Ash, shirtless and sprawled across her bed watching daytime talk TV, elbow deep in a potato chip bag. He laughs with the audience, spraying potato chip crumbs. I roll my eyes and stop to rifle through the junk drawer in the kitchen. I find matches and use my hip to close the drawer.

"Since when do we have cable," I ask her. "He rig that?" She steps back into her room and closes the door without responding.

Great, so I guess we're stealing cable now.

We haven't had cable TV since my father has been around, many moons ago. It's too expensive and per Elder ruling, we aren't allowed the internet either, so no streaming movies or TV shows. It supposedly takes us away from our element because the technological world is non-diverse and non-magical. In other words, it's more *who's the baby daddy* daytime talk TV, and less *cauldron stew recipe* cooking show.

I exit the house, stepping out into the oppressive heat. The air is thick with humidity and the honeyed scent of summer-blooming flowers. I round the house, following a winding sandstone pathway. It's bordered by fluffy pink peonies and straggling ground cover. The grass has been freshly mowed. Green clippings litter the ground. It's been a while. Usually, one of our neighbors helps and takes care of our small yard for us. Sometimes this house looks like an abandoned property. For once, this isn't one of those times.

Bumblebees dance across tall patches of pink clover at the edge of a garden. As I step off the path, a bee buzzes past my ear. Out back, hanging from a rusted iron hook over a pile of charred wood and coals is my late grandmother's cauldron.

A window opens with a loud screech; my mother waves a long pair of tongs and clicks them twice. "Hey! You'll need these!"

I jog to the window, grabbing the tongs. "Thanks. Uh, you're not gonna watch, are you?" I nibble my bottom lip. She frowns. Hurt, she slams the window shut.

I return to the cauldron and set the silver tongs in the tall grass. I strike a match and light up one of his watercolors. The pastel edge blackens as it burns. I drop the canvas into the cauldron.

The window squeals open again and my mother bellows sharply, "Use the tongs!" It bangs shut.

"Use the tongs," I mimic under my breath, sticking out my tongue. I sift through the pillowcase and create a bed of kindling using some of River's paintings to feed the fire. Black smoke swells from the pot. It crackles and pops. I step back. Embers shoot into the sky and ash settles in the grass.

I dig into the pillowcase, finding my favorite photograph of us. It's from school, in the lunchroom. Petal Wormwood took the picture. We reenacted the scene from Lady and The Tramp, using an orange gummy worm instead of spaghetti. My vision blurs; a hot tear trickles down my cheek.

I tear the photo in half and toss the pieces into the cauldron. Black smoke billows from the pot as it burns. I turn the sack upside down over the cauldron. The flames quickly consume the paintings, dried flowers, and other mementos. I stand watch until everything is reduced to char and ash.

How bad could a boarding school in the middle of the woods be? At least, I won't have to watch River and his new girlfriend sucking face at all the local hang-outs. I'll be nice and secluded, with no risk of running into them, completely isolated from all the nonsense of River and Dahlia, and my mother and Ash. Charm School might even be like sleepaway camp.

It's time to forget River and begin anew. Perhaps, without a boyfriend, I'll be able to figure out who I *really* am this summer. Maybe I can discover my own interests. That'll show him... I'm not as boring as he thinks I am. Perhaps I can uncover my inner fire witch and stop being such an utter failure at magic. Possibly after this experience, I'll wear less denim. I'll return home wearing a beautiful crushed-velvet robe, pointy boots, and wildflowers within my hair. I'll adorn myself with necklaces and bracelets of semi-precious stones and carry an athame like a real witch. Headmistress Starwort's Charm School is just the fresh start I need. I will rise from the ashes of this heartbreak.

But first, I'm gonna forge my mother's signature and drown my feelings in a tub of fudge brownie ice cream… if Ash hasn't gotten to it first.

Present Time

"Hey, Dahlia! Over here!"

Azalea Devil-Claw waves her friend over and pats the log she sits atop. Dahlia dashes through the group and perches beside her. She drops her overpacked satchel to the ground with a thud and wraps her arm around Azalea's thick waist for a hug. As she does, her curly hair falls forward, revealing an unsightly love bite on her neck.

The sight of it breaks my heart. I touch my neck—my fingertips brushing against the fading hickey he left on my neck merely a week ago—and tears sting the back of my eyes.

I was crazy to think this would be a breeze. I was wrong to think this might be like summer camp. I just wanted to get away from the nonsense for a little bit, but I've been tossed within the thick of it. I'll never be able to focus on my magical studies when I'm reminded daily of my ex-boyfriend.

Azalea whispers into her friend's ear and Dahlia peers back through thick tarantula leg-like eyelashes. Her blue eyes go wide as her gaze falls upon me, and she swings her legs forward. They speak urgently in hushed tones.

I'm so fixated on my ex-boyfriend's absolutely perfect new girlfriend, I barely register the crunching of leaves behind me. As the footsteps come closer, the aromas of pine, cauldron fire, earth, and sunscreen are overwhelmed by the musky, intoxicating scent of patchouli.

Please no.

My ex-boyfriend, River Devil-Claw, strides past me without so much as a sideways glance and joins the log with Dahlia and Azalea. He unholsters his khaki backpack from his shoulder, letting it slip to the ground.

No.

Aspen returns from the broom shed, sidling in on a sitting rock between me and Rugosa. He takes a second look at me as he sits, concern etched in the grooves of his forehead. "What's wrong?"

"No!" I accidentally shout aloud, slapping a hand over my mouth.

Aspen reels back in confusion, his brow pinched. "What's your frickin problem?"

"Where do we begin?" Rugosa asks, running his palm over his freshly buzzed scalp.

I point to the offending couple and Aspen's jaw drops.

I grimace in pain as our group is silenced by the sudden shriek of an animal horn that is hardly necessary for a gathering of twelve people. The Headmistress clears her throat and passes the horn to Mistress Aster, then takes her place on a wide stump at the head of the seating arrangement. Behind her, the Charm School crest, a large wooden emblem with real deer antlers, green vines, and red poppy flowers, is tacked onto a tree. From where she stands, it appears she has horns; I wonder if she realizes that. It gives me something to focus on, other than River and Dahlia, holding hands.

"Merry meet and blessed be. I'm Headmistress Starwort, of the Wormwood clan. The ten of you sitting before me have been chosen for a special summer program tailored specifically to help you graduate on time while meeting your magical needs. A respected member of the community has raised concerns that you may be at risk for Nature Deficit Disorder—a pervasive ailment that strips elemental witches of their physical, emotional, and spiritual attributes. She feels this ailment may be preventing you from doing your best within your magical studies.

"It's the intention of Mistress Aster and myself to have you reclaim your wild nature, align yourselves with the lunar cycles, and discover your inner magic. It's become our mission to prevent Nature Deficit Disorder and protect our clans. It's vital to get in touch with your roots if you wish to harness your inner magic and the best route is through direct exposure to Nature. It's not only essential for the clans, but for your health and well-being as a witch. Does anyone have any questions?"

Several hands shoot up and Amaranth Wormwood is called on. "Uh. Why am *I* here? I haven't done anything wrong." She bats her eyelashes, tossing her long black hair over her shoulder.

"It's what you're *not* doing right that has put you at risk for Nature Deficit Disorder," Headmistress Starwort Wormwood responds, earning a blank stare from Amaranth. "That's why I've brought you all here. However, don't look so relieved. Other than falling behind in magical studies, most of you have other offenses that have paved the path to Nature deficit."

Mistress Aster passes a document, rolled and tied with a silky red ribbon, to the Headmistress. The parchment uncurls as she pulls the tie. She calls students forward in alphabetical order, beginning with Amaranth. She is accused of shoplifting beauty supplies from Winter's Cures and Curses. She then calls Aspen forward.

"Aspen Widow-Tears, your symptoms of Nature Deficit Disorder derive from poor grades in magical subjects, including alchemy and divination." She pauses for breath and he uses the opportunity to interrupt her.

"Where's your proof? What are these symptoms?" He scratches his nose before erupting into a sneezing fit, effectively answering his own question.

The Headmistress rolls the parchment as she steps down from her stump. She approaches Aspen, her face stern. "I will not have you talk out of turn. Where is your decorum, young man? Do you have any witch etiquette?" she asks.

"I'm sorry, Headmistress Starwort," Aspen answers contritely, wiping his nose on the short sleeve of his tee-shirt. "I'm not big on structure, but I don't want that Nature detention disease, or whatever."

"Nature *deficit disorder*," she corrects him, enunciating the words. Students stifle their giggles. On return to her platform she tosses out, "We have our work cut out for us, Mistress Aster."

She resumes reading the scroll of offenses. Aspen reclaims his seat on a boulder; his shoulders hunch forward and his eyelids droop.

I pat him on the back. When that doesn't get a reaction, I lean in and whisper, "Don't worry. I'm on her crap-list too. I sneezed on her feet when you were gone."

Aspen chuckles. "Good. I hope it was extra snotty," he says, his gaze never leaving the ground. Azalea Devil-Claw is called to stand next.

Azalea hops to her feet, awkwardly stating, "I'm present!" She fidgets with her hands before clasping them together behind her back.

She's wearing a sleeve of wire bracelets with small charms. Most of her chubby fingers are adorned with polished stone rings. She's of the Devil-Claw clan, with the trademark indigo colored eyes, and reddish-brown hair that hangs loose in soft waves. She's quite pretty, but her beauty is lost on most of the boys at school because of her size. Goddess forbid they date her and become labeled "chubby chasers" by their peers.

"Azalea, your offenses include harboring a cell phone— something the Elders strictly disallow— and endangering yourself with an inner technological world of non-magical influence. What do you say to this?"

Azalea shrugs. "To be honest, I just wanted to take selfies."

The Headmistress purses her lips as her students snicker and giggle. "The lens doesn't reflect your true self, my precious water witch. The true reflection of your self can only be viewed in rivers, streams, lakes, and oceans."

"If Azalea makes a duckface at a pond, the ducks might adopt her into their raft," Rugosa remarks smartly, earning him the laughter of those around him.

"Nah, man. Fish-gape is the new selfie trend now," says River, turning around. His inky-blue gaze sweeps from Rugosa to Aspen, finally falling on me. He blinks, his lips parting upon recognizing me. For an awkward few seconds, we lock eyes.

"Enough!" shouts Headmistress Starwort over unrestrained laughter. A hush falls over the small audience. She calls Dahlia next. River returns his attention forward. I resume a somewhat normal breathing pattern.

"Dahlia, you have been accused of vanity and poor attendance at Sabbats. What do you say to this?"

Dahlia rises, her nose up in the air. "I see nothing wrong with wanting to look my best."

"And you do, baby," River chimes in, earning him the glare of Mistress Aster beside them.

"Gross," I mutter.

"The Sabbats are always held so late. I need at least eight hours of beauty sleep. Plus, the food sucks, and the rituals are the same every year," Dahlia adds in a whining tone.

"Is that so? Well, perhaps the upcoming Sabbat will be more suitable for you, then, my dear. High Priestess Violet Widow-Tears has invited us for an early morning service to welcome the Sun on its longest day of the year. Since you are opposed to the menu, Dahlia, you can make your own potluck dish to bring and share."

Dahlia drops to her seat between River and Azalea, defeated. Her boyfriend snakes his arm around her back, pulling her toward him. She slumps into his body, falling into the crook of his arm. I roll my eyes and shake my head.

Fern, Hyacinth, and Petal are called forward next. They are accused of much of the same, poor grades in magical subjects, disrespect to Elders, and vanity. River is called up as Petal takes her seat.

He rises, running his fingertips through his short fade before folding his arms over his chest.

"River Devil-Claw, you have narcissistic tendencies that darken your aura."

He waves her off and takes his seat before she finishes speaking, crossing his legs at his ankles. As Rugosa Rose-Thorne is asked to come forward, I feel strangely joyous to have witnessed my ex-boyfriend getting called out. That feeling vanishes when my name is spoken. I rise, wondering what my offenses will be. My wobbly knees threaten to betray me.

"Mistress Aster, the pot, please." The Headmistress extends her arm. From a green crossbody bag, the school mistress exposes a small terracotta pot dirtied by soil. It only takes a moment for me to recognize it's the one I planted for the love spell.

My dirty secret is about to be revealed…to not only my rival and my peers, but to the person I cast that spell on.

I panic and make a split-second decision to fake a medical emergency.

I close my eyes and crumple to the ground. Aspen lunges forward, misunderstanding that I'm only fake passing out, and grabs my arm to stop me from falling. I jerk away from him and my shoulder slams into a sitting rock. I scream in pain. Eleven pairs of eyes are boring into me. A cloud of dirt in the air from my impact with the ground triggers a bunch of us to have a sneezing/coughing allergy fit.

The Headmistress—who undoubtedly realizes I staged this little show—has no sympathy. She clucks her tongue and shakes her head as the dust settles. "You're all doomed," she says, regarding our symptoms.

I clutch my shoulder and rise to my feet. "Sorry," I mutter, frowning and gazing downward.

"Mm. As I was saying, Summer Wormwood, this was discovered in your backyard by a concerned neighbor when landscaping for your mother."

My eyes snap open. It then dawns on me: the grass was mowed, and the flowers were tended to when I returned home on the last day of school. The gardener must have unearthed the pot earlier that day, nullifying the love spell. Admittedly, I didn't bury it super deep, but in the jungle that was my backyard, it didn't seem to matter. I don't know whether to be relieved to be done with such a jerk like River or depressed that I lost a relationship I desperately wanted for the wrong reason—to feel whole.

"Summer?"

"I've never before seen it in my life," I respond to Headmistress Starwort in a rush. She raises an eyebrow, piercing me with her absinthe colored eyes before turning over the pot. I take a breath. Soil spills out onto the forest floor in a large clump. She gives it another shake and two dirty, yet perfectly ripe and beautiful, strawberries roll onto the forest ground.

Well, I'll be damned; they aren't even rotten. My magic isn't half bad. Perhaps there's hope for me yet. This better not get back to Meadow, or she'll be expecting me to craft actual *authentic* Love Charms for her clients.

Headmistress Starwort stoops to the ground, retrieving the berries. She blows the dirt from the fruit and peers at each one, before tossing them to her assistant. Mistress Aster is swift; she catches the berries single-handedly.

"Read those to me, please," demands the Headmistress.

I take a deep breath and close my eyes. I'm so screwed if her squinty eyes can make out those names.

"This berry has the name Summer inscribed." She rolls the other one in her hand. "And this one says River."

"Why does it say my name?" River asks, swinging around to face me. My lips move but words fail to form. "Hey! I'm asking you a question."

I think I might really pass out this time…

"I… I… It's true, I crafted a love spell on River Devil-Claw," I croak to Headmistress Starwort.

Amaranth and Hyacinth burst into a fit of giggles. They clutch their abdomens and double over. Fern Widow-Tears looks on, her lavender eyes round with pity, and Dahlia appears surprised. She blinks several times, a slight smirk on her face.

"You did frickin what?" River asks, clenching his fists. A water witch, his dark blue eyes are stormy and turbulent.

Aspen rises, squaring up. "Sit down before I make you," he threatens River, pointing his finger.

The Headmistress commands them *both* to take their seats with warnings of expulsion and delayed graduation. My heart pounds in my chest, and I can feel my hair prickling. Sulphur perfumes the air. Blood courses through my veins like lava, warming me from the inside out. My cheeks and ears heat. I'm mortified; they all think I'm pathetic. I look to my friend Fern for support; she quickly glances away, confirming my fear. I bow my head, ashamed of my actions.

It's one thing to harbor a cellphone, or steal from Winter's Cures and Curses, and quite another to place a spell of black magic to strong-arm someone to fall in love with you...

Once everyone is seated, she returns her focus to me. "Proper witches never use magic to coerce another's free will. Not only is it unethical, but it's also dangerous," admonishes Headmistress Starwort. Several students nod.

"Yes, Headmistress," I respond solemnly, wiping a tear from the corner of my eye with my finger. I return to my seat, feeling like the sludge at the bottom of a cauldron.

River mutters under his breath to Dahlia, "Knew she was a damn psycho."

"So pathetic," she whispers, nodding in fierce agreement.

"You put a love spell on that jerk?" Aspen asks, his face twisted with disgust. We argue in hushed tones as Headmistress Starwort discusses something privately with Mistress Aster. We snap back to attention at the mention of a bag inspection.

Under the watchful eye of the Headmistress, Mistress Aster requests students to empty their backpacks. Amaranth Wormwood—arguably the most popular and prettiest girl in my grade—is the first to protest the bag search. She loses the argument with Mistress Aster. With a huff, Amaranth unzips her floral print backpack and turns it upside down, angrily dumping her belongings onto the forest floor. A slew of glittery makeup pots, a pink tube of mascara, bug spray, nail varnish, and a bottle of hair gel spill from her bag, along with socks, underwear, and other items. Without warning, the school mistress chucks her beauty products and other material items into the campfire. Amaranth's shrill scream cuts through the forest, sending frenzied birds from their perches within the branches of trees up to the sky.

"My parents paid good money for those things!" Amaranth shrieks. "We'll sue you!"

The Headmistress replies calmly, "Nonsense, my dear. It was in your forms that your parents signed. Did you not read them thoroughly?"

Amaranth cries softly, hugging her knees to her chest like a child who misplaced their favorite teddy bear, as Mistress Aster tosses her beauty supplies into the flames.

"Here at my Charm School, you will live not only in the woods but by the woods. As witches, we are intrinsically connected with Nature and within Camp Bitter Tonic you will be close to Mother Earth and her natural beauty. Do not worry, for Nature provides what you need to be your most beautiful," Headmistress Starwort says over the sounds of backpacks zippering, the fire crackling and popping as makeup is burned, and much bemoaning from her students.

Aspen dumps his bag and out rolls my crumpled coffee cup. I suck my lips between my teeth and he gives me an aggravated look that lets me know he's about had it with me today. After he's unnecessarily lectured on the benefits of herbal tea versus coffee with fancy, artificial flavorings, Mistress Aster moves on to me.

I unzip my bag. She rifles through it, separating my lip balm, deodorant, shampoo, and sunscreen.

"Wait, you are destroying my deodorant?" I ask, reaching for the item. "If I don't have that, I'm gonna smell like a forest fire. For real, though. Like, not even joking."

"The chemicals in commercial deodorant are disastrous to our environment. The earth needs us, and we need Her," Mistress Aster explains as she drops my deodorant into the fire. "It is the only way to bring you back to Nature. You need a deep infusion. We will supply you with a non-toxic deodorant. Everything you need will be available in your cabin, along with your new uniforms."

"Yeah, but mine's powder fresh," I whine, dropping my extended arm to my side.

"Uniforms?" the group squeaks in unison. Looks of exasperation are shared between students. My mint lip balm and coconut-scented shampoo are tossed into the cauldron next. The smell of burning plastic is nearly unbearable. The air witches of the group—Aspen, Fern, and Hyacinth—struggle to breathe in the smoky environment. Fern wheezes as the wind blows over us, carrying the thick, toxic smoke with it. In between breaths, she argues with Mistress Aster about her deliberate pollution of the environment. She's told the purge must be done, and we were warned not to bring these items, to begin with.

"Hypocrite," Fern mutters, lifting her top over her mouth and nose.

Headmistress Starwort addresses our question about uniforms, saying, "Yes, you have uniforms, but they are not mandatory. We encourage you to wear them because it makes laundry easier. You may still wear your own clothing, underwear, and bathing suits."

We collectively sigh in relief.

After bags are inspected and items are seized, the Headmistress strips us of our shoes. We are to remain barefoot from here on out to ground ourselves and practice something she calls *earthing*. She tosses our footwear into the fiery cauldron. I wiggle my toes, enjoying the freedom. I hated those sandals, anyways. I wish I had thought to paint my toenails, but the polish would have chipped after only a day or so in these woods.

For her final act, Headmistress Starwort tosses the parchment into the cauldron. "Clean slate, my children. I will make you as the Goddess herself intended." She makes a motion of dusting her hands. The delicate paper is quickly reduced to blackened bits. The ritual reminds me of my own, only days earlier, and it reminds me why I wanted to be here in the first place. I need this fresh start, and I have to make the best of it.

At least I have Aspen.

"Now why couldn't she have done that, to begin with? Were the theatrics necessary?" I say to Aspen.

"Were *yours,* Miss I'm-gonna-pretend-to-faint to avoid due embarrassment?" Aspen asks, turning his nose up.

Touché.

We are taken on a guided tour of the small campground by Mistress Aster. Down the trail are two dilapidated-looking cabins. The girls' cabin is slightly larger than the boys'. It's marked by the triple Goddess symbol—two crescents and a circle. It represents the three phases of the moon but is also synonymous with the maiden, mother, and crone. The boys' cabin is marked with the symbol of the Horned God, which looks much like a circle with horns. It represents virility and wilderness, but Rugosa says it represents horniness…because Rugosa is an idiot, and he will say anything for a laugh.

Before the cabins are a set of adjoined picnic tables. There's a fire pit surrounded by smooth logs and large sitting rocks. There's ample space to sleep out under the stars. Towering pines and ages-old maple trees guard the space around our little camp. Bamboo torches are scattered about, planted deeply into the ground. Between lessons, this is where we will be spending much of our time.

We approach the girls' cabin. A sharp, musty smell greets us as Mistress Aster pulls open the heavy wooden door. We complain about the odor, our noses planted firmly in the crooks of our elbows, as we file inside to drop off what's left of our things and claim our bunks. It's tight with seven of us here. The bunk beds are in a row of four, dressed with a single pillow, sheet, and stiff wool blanket on each bed.

Mistress Aster withdraws a bundle of sage from her crossover bag and lights the tip, waving it across the room, in every nook and cranny, and over the beds. Meanwhile, the boys investigate their cabin.

I unshoulder my heavy backpack onto my chosen bed, furthest from the door. In the event of a masked murderer intruding, I'll be the last to die. By the looks of things, Fern Widow-Tears will be the first, sadly. She hasn't looked at me even once since Headmistress Starwort revealed my love spell, and it hurts. I'm not sure how much more my broken heart can take.

Amaranth complains about the lack of electricity. Hyacinth reminds her that this is a Nature rehab of sorts, and it's part of the experience. Several oil lamps and flashlights are set up on a dresser, with seven complimentary baskets of toiletries, including witch hazel, beeswax, arrowroot powder, essential oils, salt, and dried herbs for hygiene and beauty.

Fern is the first to notice the closet. She throws open the doors and we crowd before it, like moths to a porch light. Hanging from wire hangers are folded collar Polo shirts in green, red, and tan, like the colors of the crest. The school emblem is sewn into each garment. There are also dresses that reach mid-thigh, in the same colors. Upon further investigation, we discover tan dress shorts and skirts. I open the dresser drawers and discover Charm School tees and soft, hemp-cotton shorts for lounging.

Mistress Aster calls us back out to finish the tour. We file out the doors and follow. Through a thicket of trees is a hidden river that empties into a small lake. A curved trail behind the cabins leads to another large cauldron outside a small building.

"Here you will find the kitchen hall, bathroom, and cold-water showers," says Mistress Aster, leading us inside the brick building. Amaranth hangs her head, depressed over the less than stellar accommodations.

On the entry door is a small doll, tied to the knob with twine. The girls, sans Amaranth who's completely miserable, marvel at the adorable kitchen witch riding a wooden spoon.

"She is more than just cute," says Mistress Aster. "She is a gift from the community. Her presence will bring good luck, inspire creativity in the cook, and help dispel kitchen disasters. Treat her with respect."

When Mistress Aster turns her back, Rugosa unhooks the doll from the door and makes a lewd gesture for his friends before quickly returning her.

Amaranth tsks. "Boys are stupid," she says to no one in particular. I nod and she adds, "So are you, Summer. You're the one who used magic to make a stupid boy fall in love with you. Don't be thinkin' we're on the same page."

Her words sting. I hang back as Amaranth, Hyacinth, and Petal giggle and walk ahead of me. I've never felt like more of a social outcast than I do right now. Fern bumps my shoulder as she passes me, not stopping to apologize.

The kitchen hall isn't much more than, well, a hall. There's electricity though and running water. Mistress Aster hits the kitchen lights; they flicker, illuminating the small galley. There's a large list of chores on a dry erase board, titled house-witchery, with space to write in our names. We are instructed to pick three a day for the duration of Charm School. I mark my name under the more desirable chores, including smudging, sweeping, and kitchen-witchery. Aspen chooses wood chopping, cauldron cleaning, and green laundry—whatever that is. I suspect he chose it to see the girls' underwear.

We browse the stocked pantry, the cabinets, fridge, and the freezer. Fellow classmates raid the freezer of popsicles, eager for a cold treat on a hot day, and we're instructed to hold on to the sticks for an arts and crafts project we'll be doing soon. Mistress Aster encourages us to take as many as we want.

"Where's the bathroom and showers?" Fern asks, her tongue and lips stained lime-green from the frozen treat.

Mistress Aster leads us back out of the kitchen into the narrow hallway, where we are shown the Headmistress's office and a spare room with bunkbeds for the volunteer camp counselors. Through an unmarked door—that I thought was a closet—is the bathroom. There are four toilet stalls and three cold water showers with little more than a vinyl curtain separating them. The Mistress informs us they automatically shut off after five minutes and most students use the river and lake to bathe in the summer season.

River waggles his eyebrows at Dahlia. I sigh, my eyes rolling back.

And so begins my nightmare…

4

The metallic scent of bloodied, raw hamburger nearly brings me to wretch. I form patties from several pounds of meat, donated from a local farm, along with kosher hotdogs, rolls, and preservative-free, all-natural condiments without high-fructose corn syrup—extremely important, per Headmistress Starwort. My mother would say they are trying to earn their social justice warrior points by donating to us charity witches. She's sorta funny, in a paranoid, crazy way. I hope things are okay back home and that she's not too mad at me for leaving without her permission. At least I don't have to worry about her coming after me and dragging me home, with her being homebound, and all.

The chore I signed up for tonight is kitchen witchery, but really, it's just glorified meal prep. After shaping the patties, I season them with a light dusting of salt and pepper. As I'm sprinkling the salt, the top pops off and I'm staring at a large pile atop one of the hamburgers.

"Holy crap…no!"

Using a knife, I scrape the salt off and shake it as best as I can. Footsteps approach behind me. My face colors as I glance shyly over my shoulder. Aspen struts toward me—because of course he would be here to witness my screw up—wearing a smirk. He's carrying a bag of Dandies marshmallows, which he tosses up on the counter.

"You signed up for kitchen witchery, too?" he asks, leaning against the counter. "What a mistake we made." He brushes his golden blond hair out of his eyes with a sweep of his hand.

"Why? It's not exactly advanced herbal magic," I say, casually sprinkling black pepper onto the patties.

"Is that why this really big salt shaker has half the amount of salt it did ten minutes ago?" Aspen smiles as he shakes the nearly-empty salt shaker before my eyes.

"Okay, so one of these is just a salt burger." I chuckle, snatching the shaker back. "I blame Rugosa. He probably angered the poor little kitchen witch."

He nods, pointing to the salt-laden burger. "I think it's this one. We'll give it to Amaranth. It's perfect for her salty self." He takes the tray of meat, parting with the comment, "And don't blame Rugosa. You're a klutz, Summer."

"Yeah, yeah," I respond dismissively. I grab a rag and some chemical-free cleaner from below the sink to disinfect the bloodied counter, liberally spritzing. It smells mostly floral, like lavender. I spray the air to freshen the room. Aspen passes me with the platter of burgers. Moments later he crashes to the ground. The tray clatters to the floor; hamburger patties and hotdogs litter the linoleum.

"Ow, my ass," he says, from the ground, his face in a tight grimace. A fine film of cleaning solution coats the flooring. My mouth gapes open like a fish.

"Five-second rule. Five-second rule!" Aspen says, eyes wide. He scrambles up painfully and peels the hamburger patties from the floor.

"I don't know. Are you sure this is the right thing to do?" I ask.

"Who's comin' to dinner, miss Kitchen Nightmares? Chef Gordon Ramsey? Besides, the fire will kill it, right?" he offers. "Have some faith in your element."

"Blame your friend, Rugosa." I cross my arms over my chest, not budging an inch.

"What? Fine! And don't just stand there, help me before someone comes!"

I crouch to the ground and peel a raw hamburger patty off the floor. "It's true. That's two kitchen disasters because he was gross with the kitchen witch," I say, picking visible specks of dirt off the meat before plopping it down on the plate. "You shouldn't encourage him by laughing at his jokes." I pick up the hotdogs next.

"I think he's funny," he says, hopping to his feet. "I'm outta here. And hey, Summer, not a word." He brings his fingers to his lips, then struts outside to the cauldron to deliver the tray to a waiting volunteer camp counselor named Oak Wormwood. There are two who have arrived for dinner. The other is Spring Widow-Tears and they have been dating for a little bit. They graduated this year and aren't much older than us. They will be staying the overnight shift to keep an eye on things.

As I'm scrubbing down the kitchen with a mixture of vodka, vinegar, and lavender oil, Aspen returns. He pokes his head through the open door. "And hey, Summer?"

"What's up?"

"Some of us are gonna get together around a campfire tonight. You know, toast those poor excuses for marshmallows, have s'mores, tell scary stories, and stuff."

"Okay." I nod. "If I'm even welcome."

"It'll be fine. They'll all get over it soon. Anyways, just letting you know." His jaw twitches before he turns and walks off.

There are three designated fire areas at Camp Bitter Tonic. One is the cauldron within the lesson space, the other is the cauldron outside the kitchen hall. The last is the fire pit, approximately twenty feet or so before the boys' and girls' cabins. It's cozy, surrounded by smooth logs and sitting stones.

I finish my dinner of a hamburger bun with all-natural organic ketchup—sans kitchen floor patty—refined sugar-free baked beans, and salad, and join the small group that has already gathered around the campfire.

The crackling and popping sound of the firewood is relaxing. The flames dance and twist beautifully. Despite the summer heat, I still enjoy the flames. I'm a fire witch, after all; it's in my blood. Rugosa, an earth witch with a strong connection to the icy north, wants nothing to do with the hot blaze.

Petal Wormwood sits beside Azalea Devil-Claw. She sets down an ice bucket full of cans of off-brand cane sugar soda. Everyone is present except River, Dahlia, and Rugosa. I leave my seat to grab a drink.

"I'm so thirsty," Amaranth complains. She opens her second can of soda. I glance at Aspen and we share a knowing look.

"That's sodium funny," he says. I bite the inside of my cheek to keep from laughing at his stupid pun.

"What's so damn funny?" she asks befuddled, subsequently taking a gulp of cola.

Aspen changes the subject. He asks the circle, "Has anyone heard about Brenna's Revenge? About a fire spirit?"

I pop the tab of my soda and take a long sip of root beer. Others remark they haven't heard of her. I sit at the edge of a smooth log beside Petal, but she leaves her seat, scooching down to the other end. I roll my eyes, wondering if I'll ever be forgiven for casting that stupid love spell. As Petal stands, I notice she's wearing her Charm School tee, but it's tied up in the back, exposing her midriff. She also rolled up her hemp-cotton shorts, which is so Petal Wormwood it hurts. She's never been shy about showing a little skin.

Aspen rubs his hands together with anticipation. "Get ready to be so scared you pee yourself. Especially you, Summer."

"Please," I mutter under my breath, taking another sip of soda.

"Okay, so, some time ago, a young, non-magical, married couple bought an old house, with the hopes to remodel and have a fresh start," says Aspen, leaning forward. "With a VA loan, they were able to buy the property—"

"What's a VA loan," Amaranth interrupts, twirling her fingers around her long, silky dark hair.

"Home loan program for Veterans. It's a non-magical person's thing and it's definitely not relevant to the story. Anyways, they thought that moving in the middle of the woods would solve all their problems. The husband, Matt, was a combat engineer or some *ish*, which has something to do with construction—I dunno, not important—and he did several tours in the Middle East in combat zones. He had some pretty intense PTSD."

"What's PTSD?" Azalea squeaks.

"Gods. We'll never make it through this story," Petal comments, throwing her head back and gazing up at the darkening sky through dreamy absinthe-colored eyes.

"Post-traumatic-stress-disorder. Again, back to my story: So, on the day they move in they detect a smoky smell they hadn't noticed before."

"Nothing smells worse than our cabin," Azalea remarks. Hyacinth and Amaranth murmur in agreement.

Aspen raises his voice, "The smell seems to get stronger as the day passes, giving Cassandra, the wife, a pretty intense headache. As Matt goes about getting their home ready, she lies down to rest and has a night terror involving fire and flames."

"Oh my Gods, this story sucks," Amaranth says with a yawn.

"You suck," Aspen says, tossing a kosher marshmallow at her. "When Cassandra wakes up, she notices the fireplace is boarded up. Confused, she asks her husband why he boarded up the hearth. He insists he didn't, but Cassandra swore she would've noticed a damn boarded-up fireplace during the home inspection process."

"Snooooooze," says Hyacinth.

Aspen continues without missing a beat, "The question remained: why would someone board up the fireplace?"

I crack chocolate squares from a chocolate bar, placing it between graham crackers, setting it on my lap. I spear a marshmallow on a stick, holding it slightly above the flames of the bonfire. I'm glad River and Dahlia aren't present—their general presence makes me feel awkward and uncomfortable—but I can't help wondering where they are, what they're doing, and if she's better than me at, well, whatever.

Aspen leans forward; the glow from the blaze highlights his blond hair. "That first night, Cassandra wasn't able to sleep. She blamed it on napping during the day and decided to take matters into her own hands regarding the fireplace. She found a hammer and a crowbar among her husband's tools. She was ready to face her opponent, you guessed it, the fireplace."

Aspen hops to his feet. "She pried away at those boards to no avail using the claw of the hammer," he says, acting the scene. "They just wouldn't budge."

He reclaims his seat, lowering his voice, "Then, she traded the hammer for a crowbar, wedging it behind the wood. But it was unforgiving... It just wouldn't move. Exhausted from her ordeal, she finally fell asleep. She dreamt of a woman with hair the color of flames, eyes of coal, and smoke pouring from every orifice—"

"Every orifice?" Amaranth asks with disgust, interrupting the story and earning a round of groans from everyone around her.

"*Every* orifice," Aspen confirms.

"Great. I'm about to pee from every orifice," Amaranth says, springing up. "All this soda. Hyacinth come with me."

"I'm far too captivated by this entrancing story," Hyacinth says with a wink.

Amaranth's absinthe gaze sweeps over the group, registering on me. "You, Summer."

"Why me?" I ask after swallowing my gooey s'more. I lick the melted milk chocolate from my fingertips.

She rolls her eyes and bounces her knee. "Just, come on," she whines. "I don't want to go alone. It's getting dark."

She walks ahead, and I reluctantly follow, wondering why she picked me out of everyone else, yet slightly thrilled I've been included in something—even this, sadly. Normally girls follow her without being asked, especially Hyacinth. Her popularity at high school doesn't seem to have extended to Charm School. Too bad. So sad.

Aspen resumes his ghost story to a less-than-captivated audience. Amaranth stops at the cabin first and I wait outside. She's shuffling around inside, searching through her things. She bumps against something and cries out in pain.

"You alright?" I peer into the dim cabin but don't step across the threshold. The air inside is heavy and smells like mildew and rot. I step aside as Amaranth hops toward me on one foot, a roll of toilet paper in one hand and a flashlight in the other

"Stubbed my pinky toe on the corner of the bed. I think I peed a little." We burst into laughter. She clicks her flashlight on and limps behind the girls' cabin. She drops to a crouch, disappearing into the darkness.

"Uh…why don't we just go to the bathroom?" I suggest. "It's just around the corner."

"Not necessary," she says in a sing-song voice.

"Alright, whatever." I balance on one leg and pull pine needles from my bare heel.

An erotic feminine moan from somewhere within the thicket of trees halts me in my tracks. I nearly lose my balance. The mystery of River and Dahlia's location is solved when a louder, more insistent masculine groan follows the first.

They are splashing around in the cold lake, with only a dense row of trees to separate us. Her cries increase until it's all anyone can hear. Back at the campfire, the group bursts into a fit of giggles.

Rugosa hoots and hollers from the boys' cabin, "Woo! Get it, my man!"

"Those idiots are gonna get a bacterial infection," Amaranth points out, rising and zipping up her shorts.

"Did you know?" I ask Amaranth, my eyes round in horror. Her lip quirks into a half-smile, giving me the answer I feared. I stumble backward, shaking my head before I spin around, retreating into the privacy of the cabin.

"Oh c'mon! It was just a little practical joke," she hollers after me.

Hyacinth darts around me, cackling as she joins her best friend. "We *so* got her!"

As I'm about to slam the door shut, Aspen calls from the circle, "We had nothing to do with that! Don't leave, Summer. Come back, please?"

I shut the door without a word, shutting myself inside the humid wooden box that is our cabin. Aspen scolds Amaranth and Hyacinth. I stomp over to my bed and plop down on my bunk, face first, burying my face into the pillow. I squeeze its plush form against my ears to drown out their noise—the cackling, arguing, and incessant moans from Dahlia and River.

My scalp prickles with fire energy and sulphur overpowers the room, leaching through my hair. My blood burns, my body convulses as I cry. Frustration mounts as I accept ownership of my mistakes. I'm the only one to blame for this heartbreak. If I hadn't forced him to love me against his will, he would have never hurt me, and my peers wouldn't despise me, nor set me up to be hurt and humiliated. If only I hadn't used bad magic, things would be different.

How do I redeem myself from this?

I'm startled by the distant sound of an animal horn, signaling an evening class. It's like a school bell, only ten times more annoying. I wearily emerge from the cabin, scrubbing my tear-stained face with my hands, and I join the others. River and Dahlia scramble out of the thicket of trees behind the cabins, their hair wet. With flashlights, we hike up the trail edged with flat stones, where we arrive at the lesson area. The cauldron is alight, and the Headmistress and Mistress are waiting. Despite the balmy summer air, goosebumps prickle my arms in nervous anticipation. Thoughts of the High Priestesses and the bathwater of the Elders dance through my head.

"Welcome, my children, and prepare for your element cleanse. Please, follow Mistress Aster," instructs Headmistress Starwort.

We're led from the common grounds, up nature trails, and through the woodland hills of Elwood by Mistress Aster and volunteer camp counselor, Oak Wormwood. The path is lit by our flashlights, torches, and the warm amber glow of the setting sun streaking through brief clearings within the forest. Pine needles and fallen leaves crunch beneath bare feet, releasing a sharp resinous scent. Imposing trees cast spooky shadows and the slightest snap of a twig has my nervous heart skipping a beat.

We come to the top of the hill, overlooking Elwood Avenue. We're greeted by High Priestess Violet of the Widow-Tears clan, an ancient woman with a face shaped like a full moon. I nudge Aspen beside me. "I told you so! We're about to be bathed in a cauldron."

"I don't think so," he says with a chuckle. "Simmer down, fiery one. Do you feel alright?"

I shrug. "I've been better."

"Things will be fine," he responds. "We'll get through this."

I roll my eyes at his easy-breezy air witch disposition. Must be nice to feel so at ease all the time.

A grouping of tealights and votive candles surrounds the High Priestess of the Widow-Tears clan. The respected air witch holds a bundle of smoldering sage to the dark sky. Earthy smoke perfumes the air as she waves her incense over us with the incantation, "With air, I cleanse you."

The smoke disperses, and we are ushered to the next cleansing station. After a bit of a wait, I'm called forth by a fire witch named Belladonna, a respected Elder of the Wormwood clan. She holds a single gray taper candle. Wax drips over her gnarled knuckles, but she doesn't appear hurt or bothered.

"As you pass your hand over the flame, visualize your problems burning up," she instructs, fire dancing in her soft green eyes.

Heat touches my palm as I timidly pass my hand a safe distance above the flame. I visualize my problems as items folded neatly in a suitcase—the messier ones, like my problems with my mother and breakup with River, packed away in zippered compartments.

"Stop being so timid!" the Elder scolds. She grasps my wrist, keeping my hand in place. As the flame caresses my palm, I imagine the metaphorical suitcase of problems ablaze.

"With fire, I cleanse you," says Belladonna, releasing my wrist. My hand stings from the slight burn as I make my way through the woods to the next cleansing station. I rub my palm against the denim of my shorts.

Priestess Winter of the Rose-Thorne clan waits beneath a majestic oak tree. Its thick branches are strung with glowing amber lanterns. Fireflies dance among the forest. The scene is beautiful, like the fancy, magical woodland wedding of my dreams.

As I approach the icy earth witch, she digs a handful of coarse sea salt and sand from within her red velvet ritual robe pocket. She asks for my hand, batting pretty icy-blue eyes. She sprinkles the salt mixture into my palm and gently rubs it onto my skin, soothing my burned hand with her magic touch. Although her fingers are icy cold on account of her extreme Northern, hyperborean blood, her gentleness warms my heart. As the salt mixture crumbles and rolls off, she says softly, "With earth, I cleanse you."

We're ushered onward. Bullfrogs drone ahead. A water cleansing ritual must be next. The path winds down large rocky hills, before finally stopping at the edge of a swampy lake. The remaining sunlight casts its fiery essence upon the murky water as it dips below the horizon.

The atmosphere is painted with amber and orange. The glow of torches and lanterns shine ocher light onto my teacher—the daughter of the High Priestess of the Devil-Claw clan—Priestess Anna. She stands at the rocky embankment. As I approach her, she encourages me to step into the bog.

I step barefooted across sharp stones painfully, sinking into the marsh. She kneels and scoops water into her hands. As she rises, she startles me by flicking her hand at my face, dousing me with dirty water as she recites, "With water, I cleanse you."

Well, wasn't that pleasant, I think, grimacing, but I say nothing.

I resist the urge to wipe my face and say something smart. As the last student is pelted with cold lake water, Mistress Aster leads us back to camp.

The campfire has been extinguished for the night. But for the lanterns, fireflies, and Luna's beautiful moon above, the forest is blanketed in gloom. We retire to our cabins and the volunteer counselors—Oak Wormwood and Spring Widow-Tears—linger nearby.

Physically exhausted, I crash into my bunk after changing, landing squarely on the shoulder I fell on in my dramatic attempt to avoid my love spell's discovery. I groan as I roll over, my muscles sore and eyelids heavy. A chorus of goodnights and flashlights clicking off are followed by the gentle sounds of crickets and cicadas.

A light evening breeze blows through the wood; trees creak and branches scrape against one another. Cicadas sing, owls hoot in threes, and Fern Widow-Tears snores like a ninety-year-old man with sleep apnea. The cool, soft cotton pillowcase against my cheek is a strange contrast to the itchy woolen blanket tucked in beneath me. As I drift off to sleep, I'm vaguely aware of a dark figure overshadowing me…

5

I awaken, but I'm unable to move—my muscles frozen, and my body immobile. The interior of the cabin transforms into a dark, evening atmosphere. A dark, robed figure stands over me. They brush their hand over my face, closing my eyes...

White knuckles clutch the green broomstick as I barrel through the night sky. A storm is brewing and I'm within the thick of it. The rain pounds against my back, soaking my thick velveteen top. My clothing hangs uncomfortably heavy on my body, and my wet hair blows around my face; it lashes my sensitive skin, each strike a painful punishment.

Dark clouds obscure my vision. I dip below, narrowly missing a bolt of lightning. I scream over the bellowing clap of thunder. The earth quakes. The wind is harsh and unforgiving, tossing me off course. I nearly lose my grip on the slippery broomstick, but I recover, squeezing the handle with my thighs for dear life.

My tongue sticks to the roof of my mouth; the taste of sour apple and cinnamon present. Acid churns in my belly, rising up my chest. Vomit threatens to erupt. My heart pounds beneath my ribs. I just want to go home, but I worry I won't make it.

The pines sway and crack beneath me. Fat drops of rain plaster my hair to my head. The turbulence is overwhelming. A wreck is imminent... I blink the rain from my eyes and collide with something large and yellow in the sky.

I awaken with a start. It hurts to breathe; there's pressure on my chest. My vision clears and my chest heaves as I try to catch my breath. Amaranth is straddling me.

"You're having a nightmare! My Goddess!" she says, slightly panicked.

"W-what are you doing?" I ask her, terrified, pushing her off me.

"Holy crap," Hyacinth Widow-Tears says, hanging her head over the bunk above.

"You were like, having a nightmare, I think…" Amaranth says, her voice trailing off. "Or a psychotic episode for all I know. It was *so* freaky. Your eyes were open, but you weren't responding. Only freakin' screaming." She sits back, crushing my hips and pelvis as she crawls off me. "You woke everyone up. I had to restrain you, so you wouldn't, like, kill yourself. You're welcome, by the way."

I sit up, finger-combing my hair. My silken tresses are a tangled mess and the neatly tucked blanket beneath me has been pulled from the corners of the mattress. The lantern between the bunks is smashed; glass and oil litter the wooden floorboards. My pillow is balled up on the floor beside the bunk. Amaranth carefully tiptoes back to her bed, mindful of the glass on the floor.

Pieces of the nightmare rush back to me in a terrifying sequence. It felt so real. I've never had a dream so vivid before. It isn't often that a Night Hag visits my sleep. I wipe the cold sweat from my brow and tie my hair up with the elastic around my wrist.

My grandmother believed that nightmares were caused by Night Hags. Some were so evil they'd sit on the dreamer's chest and suffocate the person while they slumbered. There was some variation to this, and her and my Great Aunt Ivy Wormwood would get into heated debates about whether it was suffocation by pressure on the chest or actually sucking the dreamer's breath. I suppose it is of no surprise that I slept with my lights on until I was about twelve.

The cabin door swings open, bathing the room with early morning sunlight. Volunteer camp counselor Spring Widow-Tears bursts into the small cabin with a hiccup. The air witch smells like rum and campfire smoke. A dozen or so dandelions and small wild daisies poke out of her long golden braids. I don't know her well. I only saw her for like a minute last night after dinner.

Spring is a new transplant from Tradescantia, the eastern homeland of the Widow-Tears clan. She hasn't been here long but has already made an impression because of her High Priestess Grandmother, Violet Widow-Tears, and earned herself the title of the May Queen at the last Beltane festival a couple months back.

"Everything alright?" she exclaims. Her nervous lavender gaze darts around the room, falling on the mess beside my bunk.

"We're fine. Summer had a nightmare," Amaranth says, yawning.

"That's me." I cringe, bashfully raising my hand.

Spring hiccups. "I'm relieved you're alright. I thought there was a murder. Alrighty, then," she says, making a gesture of wiping the sweat from her brow. "Who has breakfast duty?"

Azalea, Amaranth, Hyacinth, and I collectively groan.

"Great! Get dressed and report to the kitchen. We'll be making our first proper campfire breakfast." She gestures to the mess on the floor. "And, Summer, I'll grab you a broom." She steps out and the cabin door swings shut behind her.

I fall back; the coils squeak as my back hits the thin mattress. Triggered by Spring's comment about the broom, more pieces of my nightmare surface.

I lost control of my broomstick and I was headed for a wreck. Horrible dream. I have no idea why I would have had that terrible nightmare. I'm curious where it came from? I remember the urgency to go home and wonder if I had it because Charm School isn't exactly how I pictured it would be, with River and Dahlia here and all... The door swings open, disturbing my thoughts; Spring returns with a broom. As I'm sweeping, I further contemplate my nightmare.

Was a Night Hag trying to smother me in my sleep? Am I going crazy, like my mother?

Eventually, Azalea, Amaranth, Hyacinth, and I exit the cabin, leaving Fern, Dahlia, and Petal behind to snooze. We take the trail to the building carrying our personal totes and backpacks. We use the bathroom, brush our teeth with charcoal and baking soda, and change out of our Charm School shirts and hemp-cotton shorts before jumping in the showers. We scream shrilly as the frigid water pours down on our bodies, swearing off the cold-water showers for the duration of camp.

By the time we're ready to make breakfast, my head is pounding.

If depriving someone of their coffee isn't considered cruel and unusual punishment, it needs to be. My head aches from caffeine withdrawal, and my irritability is at an all-time high. My feet have scrapes and cuts from being stripped of my footwear and paraded through the rough terrain of the woods for the elemental cleanse. Each step is painful. My hair frizzes as it dries from lack of hair styling products and is in desperate need of a *real* sulfate-laden shampoo and deep conditioning treatment.

Mostly, I'm miserable.

I enter the kitchen hall with the girls and find easy-breezy, air witch Spring already inside.

"Our first campfire recipe is a Magical Blueberry Breakfast Bake," the counselor says as she tacks the recipe into the corkboard above the counter. She seems especially peppy considering we saw her merely an hour ago, hiccupping and reeking of rum.

I tie my apron behind my back and wash my hands in the large industrial sink. The cold rush of running water over my hands sends a wave of goosebumps up my arms. I can barely keep my eyes open and despite sleeping most of the night, I don't feel rested at all. My stomach growls on account of having little more than bread, ketchup, salad, a kosher marshmallow s'more, and can of soda for fuel last night.

Before we get started, Spring has us bless our kitchen tools. She sets a mixing bowl, knife, wooden spoon, and a whisk on a clean counter and lights a white candle. She asks us to join her and focus our minds on our cooking intentions.

I'm learning that everything here is a lesson. This isn't an ordinary breakfast. It's kitchen witchery.

Azalea pulls ingredients from the pantry shelves and fridge. I check the recipe and robotically pour milk into a large mixing bowl, crack eggs, and add sugar, cinnamon, and vanilla. I use a whisk to combine the ingredients. Spring tells me to stir the ingredients in a clockwise direction to build the magic within. Leftover hamburger buns from dinner last night are cut into cubes by Hyacinth. I toss the bite-sized pieces of bread into the mixture, letting it absorb the sweet-smelling liquid like a sponge.

Azalea washes the plump blueberries in the sink, then dumps them carefully into the bowl. I nab a few, tossing them into my mouth. The berries are a tad bitter but otherwise good. We spoon individual servings into carefully folded and greased aluminum foil packets. I return my apron to the coat hook in the pantry.

Spring places the packets on a tray, and we follow her outside, where she delivers them to her boyfriend, Oak Wormwood. He places the packets in a cauldron atop a grill over a campfire. Azalea disappears into the building, returning with a bag of oranges and a pitcher. She peels the rinds from the fruit; sweet citrus fragrances the air.

The morning air is chilled and damp. I stand closer to the cauldron, letting its warmth touch me. The scent of spice, fruit, and smoke is strong, intermingling with the earthy aromas of the forest. Other students are beginning to wake up. Fern passes us with her shower tote in hand. Her short hair is sticking up in every direction and she looks positively crazy. She disappears into the building without saying hello. I'm not sure if it's from pure exhaustion or if she's deliberately ignoring me. Either way, I miss her, and I wish I had someone to talk to other than Aspen. I know I screwed up by using black magic to trick River into falling in love with me, but do I really deserve this ostracization? Perhaps I do...

A *true* witch would never coerce someone against their free will. What was I thinking? I deserve the heartbreak and social banishment. By the power of the Three-fold law, or three times three, I fear what will happen next.

When ready, we carefully unfold our packets. Everyone gathers, and forks are passed around the picnic table. Other than the blueberries, nothing about this mushy slop looks even remotely edible. I'm hungry. I want to go home, much like how I felt in my nightmare.

I slide onto the bench and tuck my legs under the table. Spring leans over my shoulder, startling me, as she says in a peppy voice, "It's essentially bread pudding!"

"Mm," I say politely, barely able to hide my grimace. I take a small bite. It's okay. The blueberries are good, but I don't love the overall gooey consistency. Maple syrup could do wonders for this.

The girls look so different without heavy makeup coating their faces and products slickening their hair. The boys look the same, just smellier—their elements of water, earth, and air strong. The air witches smell like smoke, the water witches like the salty breeze that passes over an ocean, the fire witches of sulphur and soot, and Rugosa, the only earth witch, like a cold, wintry snow-capped forest. The witch hazel we were given clearly isn't cutting it for some. I swallow the lump of bread pudding and it slides down my throat slowly like sickening sludge. Petal Wormwood joins us, sitting beside me. She reeks of campfire and soot, like a dirty fire witch. I can hardly take everyone's body odor. Despite my hunger, I lose my appetite and hastily crumple the remainder of my breakfast into a misshapen aluminum foil ball, tossing it into a nearby trash can.

I return to the kitchen to clean up. Azalea is already inside sweeping. She glances up from the floor as the door swings shut and I enter the galley. Her eyes fill with disappointment upon noticing me, and she returns to her work. She was probably wishing I was someone else… It hurts.

The room is quiet. Moving around her in the small space is awkward. Minutes later, I'm relieved when the door swings open and Aspen enters. At least he has stuck by me. Good ole' dependable Aspen Widow-Tears. I probably don't deserve him.

"Fresh squeezed orange juice," he says offering me a cup.

Azalea rolls her eyes. "Thanks a lot, Aspen, for thinking of me, too."

"Chill, girl. There's an entire pitcher outside that's mostly empty," he quips. Azalea lets her broom clatter to the floor loudly; I jump, startled because it reminds me of the thunder from my nightmare. I recover, and she stomps off in a huff.

"Cheers," Aspen says, raising his cup to mine.

I snort, nearly choking on my juice.

The shrill sound of an animal horn shrieks through the forest, reminding me that while this feels and looks like a summer camp, it's definitely still school. Hyacinth, Azalea, and Amaranth rise from the picnic tables. We retrieve our backpacks before setting off. Aspen and Rugosa jog behind the boys' cabin to pee quickly. Nobody uses the bathroom, I guess. Ahead of everyone is Petal, leading the way, and puffing away on a clove cigarette. Fern passes me and catches up to her. I lag behind, waiting for Aspen to catch up.

The forest floor crunches beneath us. A layer of sap coats the bottoms of my feet and with each step, I collect pine needles and leaf debris. Twigs snap and weak branches crack along the way. The smell of smoke in the air strengthens as we near the outdoor classroom for our first lesson in Witch Etiquette.

River and Dahlia surface from the thicket of trees, adjusting their clothing. He pulls leaves from her hair and she giggles, brushing the dirt from his shoulder. My mood darkens; I swallow the lump swelling in my throat, averting my eyes as I pass them. Aspen and Rugosa catch up as they emerge.

"Whatcha playin, kids?" Rugosa asks them. "Bury the broomstick?"

Dahlia giggles as River replies, "You know it, buddy!" The guys fist bump in celebration.

I roll my eyes as we file into the clearing, holding back the urge to cry again. Will my broken heart ever mend? The ache deep behind my ribcage is constant. My stomach hurts, and I feel like I'm always fighting back tears. Why did I do this to myself? I fear I'll never be able to fall in love again. It just doesn't seem worth the imminent breakup.

We take the same seats as yesterday. Headmistress Starwort is waiting in her usual place before us, and Mistress Aster is beside the cauldron. Her eyes are closed, her back against the hot iron pot. Flames lick her back, but she is not bothered due to her strong connection with fire as a Wormwood and an accomplished witch. She rolls her shoulders, absorbing the energy and heat of the flames.

I wonder if I'll ever be as accomplished as Mistress Aster, able to withstand the heat of flames and stressful situations, and not so easily frazzled and burned. A teacher once said to me that if I put as much time into my studies and self-improvement as I do into obsessing over boys, I could be amazing. I was incredibly insulted at the time, but perhaps she was right. I need to stop obsessing over boys and that includes River. I just don't know how to let go.

Aspen and Rugosa are asked to retrieve a table and a cardboard box from the office of the Headmistress. They return with a folded banquet table and a box full of mismatched floral-patterned china. They assemble the table between the seating area and lectern where Headmistress Starwort teaches. Dahlia and Azalea—at the head of the group and therefore the first to be noticed—are asked to unpack the box. This is why I prefer to sit in the back.

The girls cram an assortment of chipped, unmatched teacups in tall stacks on the wobbly table. They pull spices, herbs, and sugar cubes from the box. Mistress Aster steps aside, revealing a large, silver kettle of water boiling above the cauldron.

"Welcome to your first lesson in Witch Etiquette," Headmistress Starwort says. "Your first lesson is how to brew a proper cup of herbal tea."

As if on cue, the tea kettle whistles.

We are given a long lecture on Tea Magic and the health benefits of different brews before we are asked to pick our herbs. I browse the small glass jars and bottles of dried herbs and flower buds and petals. The labels list each herb, its magical properties, and any health benefits. Despite being caffeine-deprived, I choose dried flower buds with sedative effects.

I pour boiling water over the dried buds of lavender and chamomile flowers, letting it steep for a bit over the cauldron in a tin. While we wait, we each receive a Book of Shadows for our quizzes.

After, we're quizzed on the chemical composition and alchemical properties of black, white, green, and oolong tea—the only true teas. I learn that herbal teas aren't really teas at all, something I find rather interesting. Headmistress Starwort asks relative questions, and we write the answers in our newly acquired Book of Shadows. Mistress Aster collects our journals and grades our quizzes.

I strain my lavender and chamomile brew into a dainty, pink floral-patterned teacup and add a spoonful of thick, natural honey. I taste my brew, enjoying the heavenly concoction. It definitely doesn't have the kick of an iced macchiato, loaded with artificial flavorings and sugar, but I can see why witches enjoy their herbal teas so much. Dare I say I even feel a bit witchy?

Aspen winks at me, chuckling.

"What's your problem?" I ask, between small sips.

"Told ya you'd be brewing tea in a cauldron," he says with a grin.

"It's actually pretty good," I remark. "Wanna try it?" I pass him my teacup.

He takes the cup, taking a tentative sip before quickly passing it back. Grimacing, he says, "Gods, it's hot honey water. What are you, nuts? That's not tea at all." He shakes his head, adding, "You're hopeless. You know that?"

"We'll just see about that," I remark, rising from my sitting rock. Happy with the brew, I bring a cup and saucer to Headmistress Starwort for evaluation. As she spits my tea out and tosses the cup over her shoulder, I learn why most of the cups are chipped and broken.

"Too weak!" she shouts, disappointed, dragging her hand over her mouth. "And completely wrong ratio. Try again, my lovely."

I retrieve the teacup—which miraculously survived the crash—rinse it off carefully with steaming water and try again. I steep it over the cauldron, avoiding Aspen's gaze. I return to my seat with my proverbial tail between my legs, Aspen snickering. "Oh, shut up," I say to him, blowing on my steaming tea.

"What?" he asks, feigning innocence. "I didn't say anything." He laughs, and I roll my eyes.

Many failed cups later, she approves my brew, and I'm the last to be dismissed.

Tucked within the thick forest is a beach alcove, separated from the rest of the lake by rocky mountain terrain and pines. When Aspen suggested we come to this particular spot during our scheduled off-time to go for a swim, he conveniently neglected to mention that the only way to get into the water is by a rope swing… hanging a good twenty feet above the lake.

"This humidity can suck it," I bemoan to Aspen, wiping the sweat from my brow.

"Quit your hesitating and just do it! Don't be such a chicken."

My sweaty palms clutch a braided, sun-bleached rope. Between my thighs is a thick angled branch, trimmed of its branches for ease of climbing, high above the body of water. The rough bark cuts into my skin as I muster up the courage to jump. It reminds me of the slippery broomstick from my nightmare; I shudder at the thought.

"I've never jumped from a rope swing before!" I shout to Aspen below. "I don't even know what I'm jumping into—"

"It's water, Summer," Aspen interrupts with a deadpan expression.

"I know that, dork." I sigh. "It's just so murky."

Aspen dips under, swimming toward the rocky edge. Sunlight ripples across his muscular back. When he emerges, his blond hair is plastered to his head. He whips his hair back, sending fat water droplets around him where it falls back into the depths of the murky water. He clambers up the rocky hill, swearing as the sharp, jagged rocks cut into his feet.

He scooches up the branch behind me like a monkey, sliding his cold, slick arm around my waist. He stretches his other arm, reaching for the rope.

"We'll do this together. Or, you can just model your dry bikini all summer."

"Stop being such a brat," I respond, squirming in his grasp. "I don't know, man. I'm not—ahhh!" He kicks off suddenly, propelling us forward. We swing over the water, our feet dangling in the air. I'm rigid in his arms but the rush is undeniable, both exhilarating and frightening at the same time.

"You alright?" he asks, chuckling in my ear.

"Uh huh," I squeak.

"Ready to let go on the count of three?" he asks, his warm cinnamon breath on my neck.

I nod, afraid to peek at the lake looming below. On three, we drop. We release the rope, momentarily airborne. I tuck my legs before falling into the water with a loud splash. Aspen plunges underwater next.

We swim to the surface and Aspen lets out a celebratory yell, echoing across the lake. I spit water and splash him. He swims away from me with a smirk on his face.

"Oh my Gods! Are you crazy?" I adjust my bathing suit top.

"C'mon, this is fun!" he says, splashing me with a wave of water as I swim to catch up with him. I dive underwater, swimming below the surface. When I reach him, I emerge and slap the back of his gold head.

"Ouch!"

"You deserved it."

"You're not enjoying yourself?" he asks.

I sink into the water, shoulder deep. "Well. Now that I'm adjusting to the temperature, it is kinda nice." I lift off, float on my back, and close my eyes.

"Good girl."

I splash him. "Oh, shut up."

He floats beside me, and we look up at the sky. Light, fluffy cotton candy clouds pass above. Birds chirp and bullfrogs drone. The water splashes every so often as turtles hop off logs into the water. A school of tiny fish swims past us, nipping at our toes.

"This little nook is kind of nice, don't you think?" Aspen asks.

"It's quiet. I can see why you like it."

"Hey, Summer?"

"Yeah?"

"Let's do it again."

I flip over from my floating position, racing him toward the rocky bank. He swims past me and cuts me off, lifting me in his arms out of the water. I shriek and he shakes his head back. A small streak of water drips off the tip of his nose and falls on my chest.

"What are you doing?" I exclaim, squirming.

"You'll hurt yourself on these rocks," he says, grimacing. He maneuvers up the bank carrying me in his arms, stumbling a bit as he goes.

"You're worried about my feet?"

He *tsks*. "I don't care about your stupid feet."

I can't help but smile.

6

"You may be wondering why we've been pushing frozen treats to stay hydrated in this muggy, hot weather and asking you to collect your popsicle sticks. Well, it's all in the name of our feathered friends. We're gonna recycle those sticks into adorable birdhouse bird feeders and hang them in Elderberry Thicket on the upcoming Sabbat," Mistress Aster tells us. "As you can see there are quite a few here, mostly left over from last summer."

"Here's another," Aspen says, pulling a grape-stained popsicle stick out of his mouth. He tosses it on the toppling pile on the picnic table.

"Gross," Dahlia says, shirking away and cuddling into River. He wraps his arm behind her, drawing her close.

Watching him touch her, only a short distance away at the adjoining picnic table, is complete and utter torture. Worse than sitting here in my bathing suit that's still wet in the crotch because I pulled my shorts on quick and didn't have time to change. Aspen and I lost track of time at the lake and had to rush back before the afternoon workshop.

"Tomorrow we'll be getting up before dawn and flying to Elderberry Thicket to celebrate the Solar holiday. So, don't stay up late tonight," advises Mistress Aster. "The four clans are meeting early tomorrow morning to have breakfast together outdoors and welcome the sun as it rises. The Widow-Tears' will be hosting the Sabbat. Now, who wants to make an adorable birdfeeder?"

"Oh, boy! Do I!" Rugosa remarks smartly, clapping his hands together in feigned elation. His insincere grin quickly falls from his face, replaced with complete disinterest.

Supplies are passed around the table and Mistress Aster guides the craft project. I line cherry, grape, orange, and lime stained sticks side by side. We use an environmentally friendly adhesive of cornstarch and water. I dip a small paintbrush into the glue mixture and drag the bristles slowly across the bottom and top of the popsicle sticks. I press two more sticks into the glue, fusing the rest together. River applies too much pressure to his and several popsicle sticks snap.

Dahlia giggles. "You're so strong. It's hot."

"It's soo hot," Aspen mimics. "Breaking a popsicle stick is such a remarkable feat of strength."

I snort. Dahlia wings a popsicle stick at Aspen; he ducks, and it whizzes over his head. River glares at him, his nostrils slightly flare. His dark blue eyes almost look black.

Mistress Aster redirects our attention. "And that's your base," she says, passing behind me, her hands clasped behind her back. I startle—still jumpy from my nightmare of last night. "Next we'll make the walls," she adds, inspecting our projects. Before long we each have quirky, multi-colored birdhouse bird feeders. I turn mine over in my hands. The rainbow colors are fun and whimsical.

I collect broken popsicle sticks, rope, scissors, and other craft supplies off the picnic tables, packing it away and returning the supplies to the office of the Headmistress. We're asked to hang the empty feeders on tree branches for the night. Tomorrow, we'll fill the bottom chamber with bird seed and hang them around the valley of Elderberry Thicket.

The birds can enjoy a special breakfast with us. It's a cute idea.

I hang my empty feeder on a low hanging branch of a birch beside the boys' cabin. Aspen approaches me. "Isn't it kinda gross that those popsicle sticks have been in someone's mouth?" He finger-combs his gold hair back, resting his hand on the nape of his neck. He smells of the lake and smoke.

"Gross. I didn't really think of it till now." I shrug, dropping my hands at my hips after adjusting my birdfeeder so it hangs straight.

"Who were you thinking about?" He stuffs his hands into the pockets of his swim trunks, pushing his shorts lower on his hips.

I lift my gaze. "Huh?"

He leans in and closes his eyes. I raise my hand, pressing my palm into his chest to push him away. His eyes snap open, his mouth tight. He exhales hard through his nose. "You're still thinking about River."

"Uh. What the hell was that? Did you just try to… kiss me?" I pull my hand back.

His saddened, lavender gaze drops to the ground.

I shake my head, stepping around him, and head for the girls' cabin to change out of my wet swimsuit and damp clothing. I yank on the old door, letting it slam behind me.

"Wow, what's with you?" Amaranth asks from her bed. She gazes into her compact as she drags a bronze-colored pressed powder down her nose with a round pad, trying desperately to cover a blemish.

"Nothing," I respond shortly, pulling my shirt over my head, then tossing it onto my bunk. I still haven't forgiven her for the little stunt she pulled with Hyacinth last night. I rifle through the closet, finding my green sundress with the tiny white daisies embroidered along the bottom hem. I throw it over my head and remove my damp bikini top, pulling it through the sleeveless arm of the dress. "Where'd you get the makeup?" I ask.

"Hidden compartment in my purse," she says, applying bronzer to her chin. "Could you lock that since Mistress Aster is nearby?" Amaranth nods at the door.

I finish changing and latch the lock. When I turn, Amaranth is staring directly at me. "What?" I ask, halting in place.

"You reek," she remarks, closing her compact with a hard snap.

I return to my bunk, stuffing my dank clothing into my laundry bag. "I know. We *all* do."

"No, it's the lake," she says, covering her nose. "River and Dahlia probably contaminated it."

"Yeah, well, I don't wanna talk about it."

She blinks, unrolling her cherry red lipstick from a silver tube. "Tell me why you stormed in all mad like a water witch."

I ignore her question. "You're not gonna be able to wear that you know." I shake my head, pointing at the lipstick. "I mean, the powder is one thing—"

"I know!" she shouts, cutting me off. "I just wanted to look at it. So. Pretty." She pouts and caps it, tossing it back into the zippered compartment of her backpack.

"I was mad because Aspen lost his damn mind and tried to kiss me, then blamed my rejection on me still thinking about River."

She zips her bag, tosses it off the bed, and swings her legs out. Her feet hit the ground and we're sitting facing one another. "He likes you," she says.

"Huh? No, he doesn't." I shake my head. "He likes Dahlia."

"No!" Amaranth closes her eyes momentarily. "Not River, weirdo. Aspen!" She slaps the bed beside her with impatience. "You both link up and go off together for hours at a time. Trust me, any boy you can spend hours on end with is your boyfriend whether or not you want to admit it."

I dismiss her with a wave of my hand. "It's not like that. He's like my brother, not my boyfriend."

"C'mon girl... You'd see what's real if you weren't always watching River like a serial killer. This entire time, you haven't taken your eyes off him. And Aspen's always watching you. And I'm watching *all* of you." She turns her head, adding, "Gods, I need a life."

My cheeks color with embarrassment. I open my mouth to speak, but I'm stunned speechless.

"Aspen's jealous of him," she says with a smirk.

"You're seriously crazy."

"Girl." She tilts her head. "What'd you think about that crack Aspen made at River today?"

I snort. "That was actually pretty funny. I thought they were gonna go at it, though."

"Ha! Yeah," she says, laughing with me. "You'd like that."

"Me?" I blink. "Nah, I really wouldn't..." The mood lightened, I ask, "Can I just ask you, why did you set me up like that last night?"

She shrugs, her gaze falling to the floor. "Just thought it'd be funny. You need to get over him."

"And you thought *that* would help?" I exclaim.

"I dunno. Maybe? It's just a fling, Summer. Don't worry so much about them and what they're doing."

"I just can't believe he dumped me for *Dahlia*..."

"You're so hot," we say together. Amaranth tosses a pillow at me, giggling. Footsteps outside approach the cabin, followed by someone frantically tugging on the locked door. As Amaranth kicks her book bag under her bed, I leave my bunk and unlock the door. It swings open; Dahlia is on the other side. She storms past me into the cabin, collecting her belongings and muttering under her breath.

Her eyes are bloodshot from crying. Black mascara streaks down her face. Apparently, she has a secret makeup stash too. She looks awful, the polar opposite of the happy-go-lucky girl we saw this morning with the leaves in her hair from a roll around in the dirt with her boyfriend.

Outside, Hyacinth, Petal, and Rugosa are delivering platters of food to the table from the kitchen hall. As Rugosa calls everyone to gather for dinner, my stomach grumbles.

"Yeah, so… I'm gonna grab dinner," I say, scratching my head.

"Eff off!" Dahlia spits out with fury. She yanks her clothing off hangers; they clatter to the floor. "I'm so absolutely sick of you today!"

"What did I do?" I ask, flabbergasted.

"Oh my Gods. She's insane," Amaranth mutters from her bunk. "Whatever you're having is good, Summer. Just make me up a plate."

"Uh, okay," I respond, unsure how I became her errand girl. I step outside. Everyone is gathered at the adjoining picnic tables eating dinner. Everyone except River, that is.

Grilled kosher hotdogs and homemade potato salad are set up on a table beside the grill. I pick up two paper plates and grab a couple of hotdog buns. Oak Wormwood places a hotdog in each bun using tongs.

River emerges from a trail at the edge of the woods. He stumbles out, hands in his jean pockets, then kicks a maple tree out of frustration. I round the table, spooning two hearty portions of potato salad onto each plate.

"Trouble in paradise?" I remark over my shoulder with a smirk. He curls his lip in anger.

Aspen approaches me. "Hey, Summer. We should talk."

"Look, don't worry about it," I reply easily, shaking my head.

"No, it's just… I don't know what I was thinking." His skin flushes. "I'm so sorry—"

"I've already forgotten about it." I squirt mustard on my hotdog. "Hey, do you know what Amaranth has on her hotdog?"

"Uh, the blood of her enemies? Why?" he asks. "Is that who the other plate is for?"

"Uh huh." I squirt a line of mustard on the other hotdog.

"What? You hate her. She was a see-you-next-Tuesday to you."

I set the mustard down with more force than intended and it spatters on my arm. "That's real cute, Aspen." He grins at his cleverness. "I don't *hate* her," I say, dabbing my arm with a napkin.

"So, now *you're* her servant? Can't Hyacinth run her Majesty a hotdog?"

I grab utensils and a pile of napkins before returning to the girls' cabin, leaving Aspen staring after me, a look of bewilderment on his face. I balance the plates on each other and pull open the door. I nearly drop everything from the shock of what I see inside but recover in time.

Amaranth whispers "Help" from across the room, her eyes round, wearing a smirk on her face.

I pause for a moment, surprised. The room is completely pulled apart. Dahlia's bunk is stripped. I step over the wire hangers that litter the floor and nearly trip over Dahlia's legs sticking out of the closet. I deliver Amaranth's plate to her. "Uh. Hope mustard is okay?"

"I'm starving, it's great."

"Aspen sends his regards," I add with a smirk.

"Um, okay." She nods toward the closet. I close my eyes and shake my head.

"Dahlia?" I ask, plopping down in my bunk with my plate. I take a large bite of the potato salad.

"What do you want?" she snaps.

"*What?*" I exclaim. I pick up my hotdog and take a bite. "What do you think?" I ask around a mouthful of food.

She exhales heavily and scoots herself out of the closet.

"River dump you?" Amaranth asks with zero tact.

"Of course not!" Dahlia's eyebrows cinch together as she rises from the braided rug covering the hardwood floor. "I'm just so sick and tired of hearing about *her*!" She gestures to me before storming toward the door. Red carpet fibers cover her short black shorts and white tank top. My shoulders tense as the door slams, reminding me of the clap of thunder from my nightmare.

He talks about me?

"Well that was a lovely visit from Hurricane Dahlia," Amaranth says.

"Hurricane Dahlia?" I ask.

Before I have a moment to process Dahlia's nickname, and that my ex is talking about me, the cabin door swings open. Mistress Aster steps inside. I drop my plastic fork in my lap. She has Dahlia by the elbow and is followed by Fern, Petal, Azalea, and Hyacinth. Some are still chewing, interrupted mid-meal.

"Everyone sit," Mistress Aster demands. She peers around the room, exclaiming, "Did a tornado tear through here?"

I share a confused look with Amaranth.

"We haven't spent two nights together and already couples are fighting." She directs her attention to Dahlia and furrows her brow. Her gaze drifts to me before she says, "And running off together in the woods alone… Your heart is still in a delicate state after your recent breakup, so why are you going off in the woods alone *already* with a boy?"

I straighten my back. "How do you know that and who are you to ask, my mother?"

"Like your mom would care," Dahlia mutters. I whip a pillow at her and she raises her arm, blocking it.

"Boarding schoolmistress, camp mother," Mistress Aster says, raising her voice over Dahlia. She shrugs her shoulders. "Same thing, right?"

Amaranth shakes her head. "No, not really."

"You don't know my mother," I spit back to Dahlia.

"No," she replies with a mean-spirited chuckle. "But she knows all the men—"

"Enough!" Mistress Aster shouts. She directs her attention to Amaranth, while I seethe from my bunk. "And you, my dear. You've spent all your time in this cabin alone acting secretive. Ladies, we should all be outside, enjoying and pulling our oxytocin from Nature, not boys."

"Oxy what? Like pills?" Fern asks.

Petal and Azalea burst into laughter. They bury their heads in their pillows to stifle their giggles.

"Oxytocin, not Oxycontin. For the love of the Gods… It's what you feel when you fall in love, but you can also achieve it in less self-destructive ways," the mistress explains.

"Self-destructive?" Dahlia asks, sniffling.

"Sex," Mistress Aster says with a sigh.

"Sex isn't self-destructive." Fern *tsks* from her bunk. "At least not for me and Rugosa."

We all collectively gasp. The room is riotous with questions. Pillows are tossed across the room at Fern. In a chorus of, *when did this happen*, and *oh em gee how was it*, Mistress Aster brings our attention back to her.

"We all agree we like that feeling, right? The oxytocin, I mean, not the other… thing. It's called the cuddle hormone. It's what drives us biologically to reproduce, but while there is protection from STDs using barrier devices, there is absolutely nothing to protect your tender hearts and feelings. Weakening your hearts is only going to hamper the progress we are making with preventing Nature Deficit Disorder. We only have two weeks and we need to make it count.

"Let's discuss some other ways to introduce oxytocin into our lives. One is to get outside under the sunshine. Have a mini adventure. You have an entire summer of adventures awaiting you here. Focus on Nature and all she has to offer you. Nature will never disappoint you. Nature won't make you feel jealous. Nature doesn't leave mascara running down your face."

"Unless it's raining," Petal quips.

"Yes, Petal." Mistress Aster smiles. "Lovelies, I'm advising you to make better choices. Can we please try to make the best of this experience and have fun this summer? Don't get caught up in drama with those boys. Also, try to get some rest early tonight. Remember, tomorrow is the Solar Solstice. Be good, girls." She places her hand on the knob of the cabin door, pausing, then spins around, peering at Dahlia. "Your eyes…" she says, holding out her palm.

Dahlia lets out a heavy sigh and digs the mascara out of her back pocket, placing it into Mistress Aster's palm. She opens the door and exits.

"Rugosa Rose-Thorne?" Hyacinth exclaims.

The room bursts into a fit of giggles followed by a series of embarrassing questions.

7

As the sun begins to set, the familiar piercing shriek of the animal horn cuts through the otherwise peaceful forest. We smother the campfire with a pail of lake water and head to the lesson area for our evening class.

When we arrive, the Headmistress is behind a table, grinding berries into a thick fuchsia paste with a mortar and pestle. She looks up from her craft and greets us, asking us to have a seat. I take mine on a smooth log up front. Fern Widow-Tears plops down beside me. Her short hair is missing its usual texture without pomade. It has a fluffy appearance, like the feathers of a young bird. She ruffles it in an attempt to give it some body, but it flops over the moment her fingers leave her hair.

"Today's lesson is on natural beauty—"

Headmistress Starwort is cut off with a chorus of, "Thank the Goddess," said by nearly everyone, except the boys, who don't seem to mind being gross.

She clears her throat. "As I was saying, today's lesson is on natural beauty and products of Nature that can aid you. You've all become familiar with witch hazel."

"Yeah, it ain't workin' for the guys," Fern says, hooking her thumb over her shoulder. Behind her, Rugosa hops off his rock and puts her in a headlock, her nose in the crook of his underarm. She pushes him off and punches him in the arm.

"We really don't need to see your guys' version of foreplay," Amaranth says from a rock furthest back, prompting laughter.

Rugosa's icy-blue eyes sparkle with excitement. "What? Is she bragging that she hit it? That's pretty cool."

Behind us, Aspen pats him on the back, chuckling.

"Ugh, regretting it already," Fern says under her breath.

"Wait, you knew and didn't tell me? Aspen! I'm shocked," I say, my hand to my heart.

"What? I don't tell you *everything*," he says to me, grinning.

"Since when?" I exclaim.

The shrill sound of the animal horn puts an end to the group chatter and joking around. Headmistress Starwort looks furious; her lips are pursed, her eyes are intensely green, and her brow is furrowed.

"Mistress Aster informed me of the talk she had with you girls, and I must say, I am quite disappointed in *all* of you. You're all walking a fine line for expulsion, I will tell you that right now. If you don't straighten up as a group, you won't like the consequences."

Dahlia giggles. Headmistress Starwort's gaze narrows behind me. I look over my shoulder and River is nuzzling Dahlia's neck.

"You two split up right now. Dahlia, I want you to switch places with Fern, immediately," the Headmistress commands.

"I don't wanna sit next to Summer," Dahlia responds, not budging an inch. "I'll sit literally anywhere else."

"Good. Have a seat in the flaming cauldron. I don't want you next to me anyways," I retort with a shake of my head.

Headmistress Starwort tears past me; her long blue dress drags in the dirt. She stops before Dahlia and leans down, so they are nose to nose. "Stand up and take your seat beside Summer."

"Yes, Headmistress Starwort," Dahlia responds meekly. She trades places with Fern. I roll my eyes, catching the frightening glare of the Headmistress.

"Summer, I'm assigning you to help Dahlia with her potluck dish for the Solar Solstice party. I don't know what the issue is between you two, but tonight, you'll be partners in kitchen magic. Is that a problem for you ladies? Because if it is, you could always come back here next summer, while your peers are graduating and accepting their diplomas."

"Nope. Not a problem at all," I respond, wishing my rude comments and signature eye roll didn't get me into so much trouble all the time. I really need to retire that move. I also need to remember to stick to my rule of only sitting in the back of the class, so if I do practice my signature move, it isn't noticed as easily. This outdoor lesson area is throwing me off.

"Not a problem," Dahlia echoes.

"Fantastic. Now let's get back to our natural beauty lessons before it's black as pitch out here." Headmistress Starwort weaves around the logs and sitting rocks, finding her place behind the table. She resumes her lesson, picking up a bottle of witch hazel. "This bottle contains a topical astringent made from the bark and leaves of the witch hazel shrub. It's an herbal remedy used to treat skin irritations, but it can also be used as an astringent for pimples, facial cleanser, and toner—what is it, Petal?" she asks tiredly.

I look over my shoulder, Petal is chomping at the bit. Her hand is raised, and her knee is bouncing.

The Headmistress sighs, repeating, "Yes, Petal?"

Petal drops her hand, bringing it to her face. "My skin feels amazing from the witch hazel. It's like I have no pores!" she squeaks.

"Yes, my dear. It strips the oil from your skin and that will shrink down pores. I'm glad you have found good use of it. It also fades the discoloration of bruises and other blemishes," the Headmistress adds, eyeing Dahlia's neck.

Dahlia self-consciously brings her hand to her neck, making motions of massaging her muscles. It takes everything within me not to roll my eyes…and/or strangle her.

"And other skin discoloration, razor burn, and eye puffiness from exhaustion, or even crying," her absinthe-colored gaze falls on me. "So, it's a multi-use product for your skin, but it also has other uses," Headmistress Starwort tells us. "One use is for swimmer's ear. We've provided you with an eyedropper in your toiletry basket for this purpose. If you experience swimmer's ear after swimming in the lake, drop a few drops of witch hazel into each ear. It will dry up pus and break away any wax, oil, or debris that may be in your ear canal. Then lay down on your side and let it drain. Clean gently with a cotton pad and you'll be as good as new again.

"If you experience a sunburn this summer, mix your witch hazel with Aloe Vera. We've provided both cabins with Aloe Vera plants in the windows. Mix the sap from plants with the astringent. The sap will feel soothing and the astringent will aid your skin in healing.

"If you encounter poison ivy, poison oak, or poison sumac, witch hazel can counter the effects of the sap oil because of its drying and anti-itch properties. For the same reasons, it works wonders on bug bites and stings.

"You're already using witch hazel as a deodorant. The reason we took away your commercial deodorants is because of the aluminum and harmful chemicals that are linked to a host of maladies, including cancer, developmental disorders, and allergies. I realize most of you are blending in with the non-magical community, but I must stick to my guns on this. If you choose to use commercial deodorant once this experience is over, that is your decision. I'm hoping you will take on a more natural approach… Yes, Hyacinth?"

"It wouldn't be so bad if it helped with the sweating. I've been dabbing essential oils under my arms to smell fresh, but I'm sweating really bad. It's embarrassing," Hyacinth says, her face flushing.

"Ah, you like the aluminum. The aluminum in commercial antiperspirants interferes with the important bodily function of regulating your body temperature and excreting toxins. Sweating is as natural as breathing. Would you use a product that stopped you from exhaling, just because your breath smelled bad?"

"Well, no…" Hyacinth answers, with a troubled look.

"Of course not! We need to get past this *sweating is bad* mentality. I apply witch hazel several times a day to make good use of its properties. It's moisture wicking and should help dry out your underarms. Of course, proper hygiene needs to be followed first. We don't use commercial soap here and have provided you all with complimentary bottles of homemade body wash with honey, Castile soap, and coconut oil in the showers. You may also take it with you into the lake, but please use sparingly as to not upset the delicate balance of the water."

"It's lovely," Amaranth chimes in, smelling her skin.

"It is in fact. I use it every day, on my hair too," the Headmistress says, stroking her long silver braids. "You may also use mud to scrub yourself clean—"

"Ew! Won't that make it worse?" Amaranth interrupts.

"No, darling. If you ever find yourself without water, and I certainly hope you don't, mud can be used on your hair and skin. For oily hair and scalp, simply work mud thoroughly through your hair, and allow to sit until it's caked and dry. Then comb it out. You can also give yourself a dirt bath like a bird. Cover yourself in dry, clean dust to absorb any oils and allow it to sit on your skin for a bit. Then dust yourself off and you'll be as good as new."

We stare at the Headmistress in horror. Her gaze darts to each of us before she says, "Okay, I can see you aren't fans of the dirt bath. Let's move on to something the girls will like." She picks up the mortar and pestle and walks to the pulpit. "In this mortar, I have a tasty, natural raspberry lip balm."

The girls *ooh* and *ahh*. Aspen's eyes glaze over and Rugosa looks like he's about to fall asleep. And River, well I'm not paying attention to him. I refuse to look at him. If he would have kept his paws off Dahlia, I wouldn't have gotten in trouble for rolling my eyes. Now I have to make a potluck dish with her and it's going to be awkward…as…hell.

"It's simple to make, with only berries, coconut oil, beeswax, and coffee grounds."

"Did she say coffee grounds?" I whisper to Dahlia, my head throbbing from caffeine withdrawal. She scoots away from me on the log.

Like I was just thinking, awkward.

Headmistress Starwort passes the mortar and pestle to me to examine and pass on to the next person. Sure enough, the little gritty bits are coffee grounds. I can't believe coffee grounds have been on the premises and I haven't even discovered them.

I'm gonna get buzzed on coffee tonight.

"Summer, what are you doing?" Dahlia asks with a sigh. She taps her foot impatiently on the linoleum.

I slam the cabinet door and open the next, removing unbleached flour, cane sugar, and baking soda. I feel around the dusty shelf, trying to connect with anything that isn't visible to me. "An old container of chocolate powdered milk and a stupid salt shaker," I say, more to myself than to Dahlia. I set the ingredients back and slam the cabinet door. "Either you're with me, or you're against me here."

"I'm against you, but tonight I'm being forced to work with you on this stupid dish so let's just get it over with."

I open the next cabinet. "I want my caffeine fix. Headmistress Wart has coffee hidden somewhere around here."

Dahlia slaps her hand down on the counter impatiently. I ignore her and continue my search, pulling a bag of rice and a large box of macaroni from the shelf. As I swipe the all-natural peanut butter, Dahlia taps me on the shoulder.

I whirl around, a gigantic jar of peanut butter in my hand. "It's probably in the tea drawer," she says with a straight face.

"There's a tea drawer?"

She nods. "Uh huh, follow me."

We cross the galley kitchen and she comes to an abrupt stop next to the sink. She yanks open a deep drawer, revealing an assortment of teas and herbs stacked and piled inside. We sift through tea bags until Dahlia finds a small jar. She lifts it to the light. "Oh, it's instant."

I squeak, "Dahlia I could just hug you!"

"Gods, please don't," she tosses me the jar. I accept it and put on a kettle to boil some water. "Make me a cup too. I'm gonna need it to get through this," she says with a sigh. I pull two mugs from a shelf and dance around the tea kettle as I wait for the water to heat. "Gods, stop dancing… So, what do you want to make?" she asks, fidgeting with her curly hair. She examines her frizzing split ends, cursing.

"Let's make a dessert. Something chocolate," I suggest, tapping my chin.

Dahlia's eyes sparkle. "Cookies?"

"Sure. I have a great recipe for Cocoa Bombs. They're easy peasy, no-bake, and sure to be a hit." As the tea kettle whistles, I break into a tap dance.

"Like you need caffeine."

"I do, actually." I retrieve the kettle and pour the steaming water into the mugs, then I measure the instant coffee granules and give each cup a good stir. I hand Dahlia her mug. "Cheers."

"Cheers," she replies, clinking mugs.

"We should probably save some of these for tomorrow," Dahlia says around a Cocoa Bomb cookie, spitting crumbs as she speaks. Her teeth are covered in chocolate and her apron is covered in peanut butter fingerprints and cocoa dust.

"So, stop eating them," I say with a laugh. I pop the last tray of cookies in the freezer to firm up and set, and I rinse my gooey hands in the sink. Dahlia finishes stacking the layers of cookies in a large Tupperware container. She uses wax paper to separate each layer to keep the cookies from congealing into a gigantic Cocoa Bomb. When left with one too many, she asks me if I want it.

"I know you want it, so you can have it," I say, but before I finish my sentence, she pops it into her mouth and closes the Tupperware container. Dahlia strolls to the refrigerator hugging the plastic container to her chest, with the chocolatey, peanut butter oatmeal cookie between her teeth. As she finds a spot in the fridge for the dessert, I finish off my third cup of coffee.

She chews the cookie thoughtfully, then asks, "What are we doing with the last batch?"

"Well, we could save them. I could keep a few and maybe give a couple to Aspen."

"Yeah, I want to give some to River… are they ready yet?" She whirls around and peeks in the freezer, testing their firmness with her finger. My mood instantly darkens; It's the first time River has been brought up and I was hoping he wouldn't be. She closes the freezer and hoists herself onto the counter, reaching for her coffee mug beside her. She's on her fourth refill and between that, the sugar, and the chocolate, Dahlia won't be sleeping for at least another week.

Her brow furrows as she swallows her coffee. "What's wrong with you?"

"Dahlia, if River wants cookies, he can have them tomorrow at the Solstice party," I say bitterly, wiping down the counter with a damp rag.

"So can your boyfriend Aspen," she bites back.

She scoots off the counter and dumps her coffee in the sink. Her motions are frenzied and caffeinated. She jerks the arm back on the tap, hurriedly rinsing her coffee mug. Her fingers tremble slightly, and her inky blue eyes have a wild look.

"You know he isn't my boyfriend. He's my brother."

"For like a month. C'mon." She brushes a stray lock of cinnamon-colored hair from her eye with her finger, then points at me. "You're not trickin' anyone with that. Staying with someone in temporary placement doesn't make you blood-related. You're not even *bloodline* related."

"Why does everyone keep saying that?" Molten indigo blood crawls up my neck, coloring my cheeks.

"Why are you the last to discover what's so obvious to everyone else about *your* life?" Dahlia retorts.

"I don't feel that way about him. He's just my friend," I say, tossing my rag into the sink. "Like my older brother." I feel the familiar prickling sensation across my scalp creeping up, my fire energy burning within as I'm put on the spot.

Dahlia props her hand atop her hip and stares me down. Her large blue eyes remind me of the deep dark ocean, and

I can't help but wonder why she lines her eyes with so much black crud when she has such natural beauty.

"What now?" I ask, feeling uncomfortable within her deep gaze. I feel like she can see right through me.

"He sure doesn't look at ya like you're his baby sister," Dahlia replies, lifting an eyebrow. "And I don't think you *really* think of him as your older brother."

Without the wet rag to ball up and wring, my hands hang uselessly at my sides with nothing to occupy my fingers. I open my mouth and close it, then push errant strands of greasy hair behind my ears that has escaped my braids. I suspect my quick-onset tan is actually dirt, and my deep color will rinse away once a *real* bar of soap—with parabens, synthetic colors, and fragrance—touches my skin.

"Thinking about that one?" Dahlia asks, interrupting my thoughts. Her eyelids narrow, and she fixes me in another penetrating stare. I'm not sure how River can stand it, with all the lies he tells, but he's so narcissistic he probably likes the challenge.

"I wasn't actually, but I think we're all done here." I stroll past her and retrieve the kitchen broom, sweeping up cocoa dust, oats, granules of sugar, and ground coffee from the floor in a feverish rush.

"Have you stopped to think why Headmistress Starwort, or Wart, as you so charmingly called her, forced us to work together tonight?"

"Because you annoyed her during the lesson and I rolled my eyes at the worst time possible," I answer with a *tsk*.

"I don't think so," she says over the roar of the water, rinsing and wringing the soiled rag in the sink. She slaps it down on the counter and washes the same surface I did minutes ago. "I mean, yeah, but don't you feel a little closer now?" She bites her lip and blinks, a look of nervous anticipation on her face.

"I suppose I don't hate you as much as I thought I did," I say, realizing my heart does feel a little lighter. "And it was kinda cool making cookies and drinking coffee." I shrug.

"And I don't see you as such a jealous, manipulative psychopath, who places love spells on victims because she's not likable."

"Is that what he's telling you?" I ask, offended.

"Among other things." She tilts her head, adding, "As are others, but I draw my own conclusions. I have the gift of clarity. When things get chaotic, I have to take a moment to meditate to clear the murkiness."

"Oh, you mean metaphorically?"

"No, literally. I'm a water witch, you nutty." She laughs. "I can see things in the water."

"I thought you meant people, too."

"People are fifty to sixty-five percent water—"

My eyes widen, and she pauses. I feel the color drain from my face.

"What?" she asks, befuddled. "Don't look so scared. I don't see anything bad in you. After spending some time with you, I'm kinda surprised you'd use black magic. You don't really fit the profile."

"Yeah well, that's my mom's gig. She sells those charms, you know. Kinda got the idea from that, but whatever. So, can all water witches see through people?" I ask, scratching my chin.

"Not really," she answers, walking away with purpose. She pulls a bowl from the cupboard and fills it with water. "It's a skill I've honed over the years. I'm gonna show you something."

"If you can see through people, or read them, or whatever it is that you do, what on earth do you see in River?"

She giggles, then sets the bowl on the counter; water sloshes over the side. "It's more of a surface attraction," she admits.

I laugh, completely understanding. "That's pretty much why I liked him too. The artsy thing helped. Makes him *seem* deep." I hold back the urge to say that in actuality, he's as shallow as a puddle.

"Yeah, his artistic side is pretty cool." She shrugs. "He's just someone cute to hook up with for the summer. As a bonus, his bad attitude annoys my parents, so that's kinda fun." Dahlia rifles through drawers, a look of steely determination in her eyes.

I chuckle, then ask, "What are you looking for? I know the entire layout of this kitchen and everything in it after searching for the coffee."

"White and black candles, and something to light it with," she says.

"Bottom drawer, all the way at the end. Do you need that for the clarity?"

"Nah, not really, but it helps set the mood." She smiles.

As she digs out the candlesticks, I have a quiet moment of reflection. It's almost freaky that hours ago we hated each other and after making cookies and having coffee, a casual observer might think we're good friends. I feel more self-aware, and maybe that's Dahlia's gift of clarity rubbing off on me, or maybe it's because we've connected, and I don't see her as the girl who stole my boyfriend. She's just *Dahlia* and I've been wrong to think badly of her. It's crazy how jealousy can pollute the mind, clouding it up with smoke so that one can't see straight.

She drags a match across the matchbook and the scent of sulphur overpowers the space. I wrinkle my nose, all too familiar with that terrible smell. She lights the candlesticks and waves the match, extinguishing it before discarding it. Then, she flees to the end of the galley and hits the light, bathing the room in gloom. When she returns, her eyes are wild and joyful in the glow of the candle flames.

"It needs to be dark," she tells me, rolling her shoulders. "My bodily eyes need to take a back seat to let my psychic vision flourish."

I blink. "Bodily eyes? I have no idea what any of that means."

As she gazes deeply into the water, I find myself growing fond of her energy and spirit. The light of the candlesticks dances across her face. The corners of the room are darker than the deepest shade of black. Tall, spooky shadows fall against walls. A loud tap against the window brings us to scream. I drop to the ground, pressing my hand against my beating heart. In a panic, Dahlia's arm sweeps across the counter, connecting with a candlestick and the bowl of water. It collides with the other candle on its way to the floor, extinguishing the light until a flashlight shines through the window and a familiar, yet muffled voice calls through the glass.

"You two kill each other?"

"Aspen," we say in unison between our teeth.

The building door opens with a groan and the thuds of footsteps can be heard outside the kitchen, coming down the hallway. Light spills through the crack under the door; it swings open, and Aspen steps inside, followed by River. He shines his flashlight on us before turning the light switch on. Dahlia squeals, running to her boyfriend. As they embrace, I step over the puddle on the floor and retrieve the last pan of Cocoa Bombs from the freezer, dumping them into a container to busy myself.

I don't think it will ever not bother me to see Dahlia and River together. I'm not sure if Dahlia and I could ever truly be friends because of him, and that really sucks; I was just starting to like her. Part friend, part enemy—she's now my frenemy.

"Hey, who peed?" Aspen asks, pointing at the spilled water on the floor.

Hopped up on caffeine and chocolate, I'm not nearly ready for bed yet. We bring a batch of cookies back to the cabins to share. Amaranth and Rugosa are still awake, sitting together at the campfire. He sweats icicles. River joins them. He sits on a log and pulls Dahlia toward him; she crashes into his lap and giggles before he shoves his tongue down her throat.

"You taste like coffee," he tells her. She repositions herself to straddle him, cupping his face in her hands.

I've seen enough tongue for the day. *Do they ever actually talk to one another? Wait, did River and I ever talk? Not really, now that I think of it—Gods, did Dahlia just moan?* I shake my head.

I trade Rugosa a few cookies for a marshmallow sphered stick and pass the rest to Amaranth and Aspen. I hold the stick above the fire, letting the flames lick the marshmallow until it's blackened.

"You've always liked your marshmallows burnt," Aspen says after polishing off a chocolate cookie.

"They're good this way," I reply, my gaze never leaving River and Dahlia. His hands rest on her backside. I shove the hot marshmallow into my mouth and yelp when the searing confection burns my tongue.

"Easy, girl," Aspen says with a chuckle.

"Ah, that freakin hurt," I complain.

"I think it was still flaming, Summer." He leans in, whispering into my ear, "Wanna get back at River?"

My mouth puckers in pain. "How?"

He slides his arm around me. I shrug it off. He smells. Everyone smells.

He glances down at the ground sullenly, drawing figures into the dirt with his toe.

"Don't start *that* again." I set the stick down, bringing my hand to my mouth. "Oh my Gods, why did I eat a flaming marshmallow? Am I new to life?"

Aspen chuckles.

"What's so funny?" I respond irritably.

"Oh, nothing. Just reminds me of that summer night us kids set up a tent outside and made a fire pit for some marshmallows and hotdogs. You did something similar, like ten years ago. Shows you never learn." He slaps a mosquito that lands on his arm and shakes his head. "Say, you wanna get outta here? I know it's late but you wanna go for a walk? We can hike up that hill." He points to a trail beside the boys' cabin. "The sky is clear, we can see the stars better up there."

I ponder this for a moment.

He gestures to Dahlia and River and lowers his voice, saying, "Or you can watch the free porno—"

"You're not gonna try to put your arm around me again, are you?" I ask, abruptly cutting him off before he finishes his sentence.

He hangs his head and laughs. "No, I can only handle so much rejection."

Aspen leaps up, jogs, and disappears into the boys' cabin. He returns moments later with his backpack and blanket, bundled in his arms. I snatch the cookies away from Rugosa, and Aspen and I set up together up the hill. The light of his flashlight bounces across the trees and illuminates the trail ahead.

Pine needles and crispy fallen leaves crunch under our bare feet. Aspen leads, holding back branches for me. I almost expect it to be a trick, that he's going to let one of the branches go like he would have when we were kids, and it's gonna *thwap* right against my face, and perhaps I'd deserve it. But he doesn't. He seems different, and I'm not sure why.

Twice he's tried to make a pass at me. I hope he doesn't think that since River and I are over, that he has a chance. He most certainly does not.

I can't lose him to the wreckage of my romantic history. He's my best friend and right now, my *only* friend.

We reach the top. The humidity is thick and the air smells like pine and campfire smoke. I inhale deeply, dropping my backpack and Tupperware of cookies at my feet. It's dim, but for the light of the moon and the flashlight.

Aspen spreads a checkered red and black flannel blanket on the ground. He lays down and pats the coverlet beside him.

I blink. "You're not gonna try anything are you?"

"I give you my word." He crosses his heart with his finger.

I crash down beside him and hug my knees to my chest, wiggling my toes. "Is this from your bed?" I ask, patting the nubby blanket.

He chuckles, gazing at the stars as he responds, "Nope. From Rugosa's." We laugh together.

In the distance, someone plays drums. The tribal beat thumps softly through the forest. Nature responds with a tune from a late-night mockingbird and the chirps of a cricket. I nod along to the woodland band. My head feels clear and I can breathe freely.

"Do your allergies feel better?" I ask Aspen.

"Haven't really thought about it, but yeah, I think so. I mean, we're pretty much laying in a pile of dirt." He pats the ground beside him. "And I'm not sneezing." He rubs his nose. "Not congested either."

"That's what I mean," I reply. "And it's only been a couple of days."

"I guess this Nature infusion is working," he says.

"Mm hm."

"I sometimes wonder if throwing us into a school system with non-magicals that try to be all-inclusive and diverse was a bad thing, for us witches, anyways. Like, their ways are rubbing off on us. That's what probably led to this Nature detraction disorder."

"Deficit," I correct him. "Meadow calls them social justice warriors." I snicker. "You should've heard her goin' when I got the letter for Charm School. Holy wow." I shake my head.

"Oh my Gods, I can't imagine. She must've gone nuts with that one. Did she think they were trying to take you away?"

"If she did, she didn't say it. Didn't have a lot of time to before Ash came out of her bedroom."

Aspen rises to a seated position. His back straightens, his brow furrowed. "That ass clown is back?"

"A-yup. She slapped me for talking back to the pig."

Silence falls between us. Aspen hangs his head. A warm summer breeze, carrying the scents of pine and campfire smoke, blows over us, stirring his golden hair.

"It was worth it though," I say with a smile. "Feels good to just say things sometimes, you know what I mean?"

"You don't deserve that, Summer," he says, his eyes downcast.

"Wasn't the first time I've been hit." I shrug. "No big. I can handle it."

I redirect my attention, focusing on the night sky. The stars gleam like diamonds set against black velvet. It's beautiful. I feel connected with Nature and Mother Earth. The ground below my body and the smoke in the air fuels me with magical energy. I sigh contently, soaking up my Nature infusion.

We sit together quietly, enjoying one another's company. I love that about Aspen—he doesn't feel the need to fill the silence with needless conversation. We're comfortable together; it's never awkward. This is why he's my best friend.

"Where did you learn to make these?" Aspen asks, cracking open the Tupperware. He takes a large bite of a cookie and falls back onto the blanket. "They're amazing."

"Ugh." I hug my knees to my chest. "Remember when I was placed in that terrible non-magical foster home outside of witch territory?"

"Those losers who punished you for being a witch?" he asks.

"Yep, them. *Don't speak of magic. Don't feel magic. And never, ever be magical.* They thought they could beat the witch out of me. Like that's a thing." I roll my eyes. "I am what I am."

"Yet it stayed with you." He dusts his hands on his clothing; cookie crumbs roll off his shirt.

I frown. "I suppose it has. It's hard to break out of that conforming mold when you fear something bad will happen if you do."

"Like being beaten."

"Exactly. Then I do that stupid spell on River, and now everyone hates me." I peer back at him, offering a slight smile. "Except you... You know, I was with that family the shortest amount of time, out of my other placement homes, but their mark on my life seems to have affected me the most."

"You know, I only tease you about the coffee and stuff, right? You're a witch warrior, Summer."

I grin. "Don't get sappy on me."

He rubs his sap-covered feet on my legs. "Oh, what, like this?"

"Stop!" I laugh, shoving him and scooching away on the nubby blanket. "Anyways, I learned how to make no-bake cookies from one of the older, non-magical girls in the house. She was nice, at least. The rest of them can suck it, though."

"Indeed. Sorry, Summer."

A meteor streaks across the sky. Aspen sits up. In unison, we both say, "You see that?" My mouth hangs open.

"That was pretty cool," he agrees.

"Will we see another?" I ask, sitting up.

"I dunno. We could hang out for a bit. I'm in no rush." He shrugs his shoulders and lays back down. "Unless you're in a hurry to get back to watching River and Dahlia."

I fall back beside him, combing my hair with my fingers. "Not really," I respond. I drop my hand beside me, and it falls near Aspen's. Our gaze meets. I weave my fingers within his, platonically. He smiles and looks up at the night sky.

"Thanks for taking me away from there." I squeeze his hand; it's covered in cookie crumbs and sticky chocolate.

"Anytime, Summer." He grins and gets a dopey look in his eyes. I shift away from him. "Hey, what's wrong? What're you doing?" he asks.

"Maybe we should head back down. We didn't tell anyone we left." I reply. Something feels off about this moment—like he's my lover, not my former foster brother. I know we aren't related by blood, but he's too familiar. If something were to happen, as it inevitably always does, I'd lose the great friendship we share. It feels odd to lay beside him like this. I love Aspen, and yes, I do find him ridiculously cute, but he's my closest friend. I don't want to give him the wrong idea that we could be anything more. I need to nip this in the bud. I shouldn't even so much as hold his hand.

I hop to my feet.

"Okay, whatever you want, weird girl."

We fold the blanket together. He stuffs it into his backpack, smacks his dying flashlight a few times, and leads the way back to camp. It's a quiet, almost awkward walk, beside the crickets and the snapping of branches as we pass.

"We should tell some scary stories again. I have tons of great campfire ghost stories. I'll keep you entertaaaain—" Aspen slips on a patch of loose earth and stones, skidding to the bottom of the hill on his butt. He rolls once, recovers, and jumps up waving his arms. He's covered in dirt and pine needles. "I'm okay!"

I laugh hysterically, dropping the container of cookies to clutch my ribs. I pick it back up and catch up with him. "Yeah, you do keep me entertained."

I'm paralyzed—unable to move. The wooden walls of the cabin gradually transform into the night sky. A robed figure approaches my bed. They brush their wet hand over my eyes.

I'm flying. Thunder crashes, causing me to momentarily lose grip of my broomstick handle. I right myself as my broom dips, ascending the sky through dark gray clouds. When did it start raining, I wonder, *as I glance down at my sopping wet clothing. My black velvet robe is ruined, and my mother is going to disown me. She advised me to use a water-proofing spell, but I've been too busy to bother. So much schoolwork...*

The rain pours over me as I make my way home, obscuring my vision. Branches of trees sway, bending with the whipping winds. I push my wet hair from my face as a bolt of lightning strikes beside me, bringing me to scream.

My broomstick picks up speed with the wind; I'm traveling dangerously fast. I've been in the skies for what feels like forever. Where is my home? I steer to the best of my ability, but I fear being thrown off my broomstick or crashing into a nearby tree.

With a hard thwack, *I'm thrown off course.*

"Really, Summer? Every morning?" a disembodied voice asks with a groan.

I glance around, confused by my surroundings. My heart pounds in my chest and beads of cold sweat dot my body. I run my hand down my face and blink my blurry eyes several times. Early morning amber light streams through the windows. A cardinal chirps outdoors.

I'm wedged between the bunks, my body angled unnaturally. I release my pillow, its corner balled up in my fist. I let out a deep breath and right myself, crawling back up on my bed and falling back against the stiff mattress. Finger-combing my hair, I respond softly to Amaranth who glares at me, "I keep having the same stupid nightmare."

"What on earth about?" Hyacinth asks. Her head hangs over the bunk above, her lavender eyes piercing me. Soft golden hair falls around her face. She looks like an angel.

I blink, hesitating before I respond. My other bunkmates snore softly, filling the silence. "It's about a broomstick accident in a bad rainstorm," I finally admit.

"*That's* what has you screaming and rolling out of bed?" Amaranth asks, incredulous. "You need to get it together." She rolls over, fluffing the pillow beneath her head and adding, "You woke me and Hyacinth up, and the Solar Solstice party begins soon. We already have to be up ridiculously early."

"I know. I'm sorry." I close my eyes. "It sounds wicked stupid, but it's really scary when it happens. It just feels so real, not like a dream at all." I respond, embarrassed. I scrub my face with my hands, wishing I could wipe away the shame that colors my cheeks. Cold sweat drips down my chest. The bed above squeaks as Hyacinth rolls over and gets comfortable.

Why am I having these nightmares? I wonder. Is this part of my punishment for the love spell I cast?

8

Litha, The Solar Solstice

"There's nothing more emasculating than carrying birdhouse birdfeeders on the whip," Aspen grumbles the next morning as he slides the rope hangers of ten popsicle stick birdfeeders onto his riding broom.

I straddle a borrowed broomstick, chuckling. "Just be happy you got your precious whip back for the day."

"I *am* happy," he says smugly, his nose turned up in the air. He zooms past me in a puff of sage smoke, ascending in the sky. An ember glows from the bundle of herbs tied carefully to a section of stiff broom fibers. The popsicle stick feeders clatter and smash together on the yellow-handled broomstick.

"Why can't I get this stupid thing to start?" I exclaim, slapping my broom angrily.

"It's the lack of light," Amaranth says, struggling to start hers beside me. "Or it's that dumb dream you keep having."

I groan, wondering if she's right.

"But, hey, look, it's not's raining! Just think of something you're passionate about. Might be enough to stoke your inner fire magic," she says, surprisingly helpful.

"Well, how'd they get up there so fast?" I ask, gesturing to the Wormwood witches above us.

"I dunno. Reserves?" Amaranth soars into the sky, her bare feet dangling. "Weeee!" she squeals, on her way to the Sabbat party.

My frustration is enough to stoke my inner flames. I'm the last to rise in the air. I catch up to the group and together we fly to Elderberry Thicket to celebrate the Solar Holiday.

"Nice tiara," Rugosa says with a curled lip, sarcasm practically dripping from his tongue. He zips past me before I can supply a witty comeback.

"Where'd you get it?" Aspen asks, flying beside me. His lavender eyes sparkle in the amber morning light. Petal zooms in between us.

I pat my headband, wincing as sharp jewel appliques scratch my palm. "Spring gave it to me," I tell him, shouting over Petal between us.

"Cool," he replies without asking me *why* she gave me the gift. I narrow my eyes at him and he speeds ahead, sage smoking from his broom. I'm not sure why the smoke of sage is tolerable to air witches or what the difference is. They even seem to enjoy it.

My headband is green, adorned with jewels and handpicked summer-blooming flowers. Spring crafted it for my birthday. Her gift reminds me of a crown. It makes me feel like a Priestess despite my Charm School uniform that lacks style and individuality. We were asked this morning to wear them to the party to look like a united group. I don't think anyone will care, either way.

We approach Elderberry Thicket, passing over an old yellow Victorian that was once a mortuary. The house has always given me the creeps. Counselor Spring Widow-Tears lives here with her grandparents—the High Priest and High Priestess of the Widow-Tear clan. I adjust my headpiece as we float down into the green valley.

Witches of all four clans are gathered together for the Sabbat. There are several banquet tables with a potluck style feast set up. A multitude of breakfast dishes, including scrambled eggs, waffles, and cheesy breakfast bakes makes my mouth water and my stomach growl.

After parking our broomsticks within a thicket of elderberry along the edge of the valley, we greet our hostess, High Priestess Violet Widow-Tears. She wears a golden ritual robe of crushed velvet. It sweeps across the green grass of the valley as she approaches us. Behind her, Sunna's glorious sun rises in the sky.

Headmistress Starwort wraps her arm around the elderly woman and we're all formally introduced. High Priestess Violet hugs us all, wrapping each of us up in her soft golden robe. Her velvet garment carries the scents of lemon, savory herbs, and cauldron smoke.

"Let me get a good look at you kids," she says, stepping back and clasping her wrinkled, paper-thin hands together. "Well, aren't you all just adorable, in your matching Charm School shirts and khaki shorts!"

Headmistress Starwort looks on with pride. I feign a smile, sharing a look with Aspen. His expression mirrors mine. He twitches his eye purposefully, and I struggle not to laugh.

"Oh, where's High Priest Hazel?" Headmistress Starwort asks, peering around the valley.

The smile falls from High Priestess Violet's face. "He's not feeling so well," she says, with a frown and quick shrug of her shoulders. "He's just gonna rest and take it easy today."

"Of course," Mistress Aster says, joining the conversation. "Please give him our best regards."

"Will do," High Priestess Violet says, smiling sweetly.

"That's so unfortunate! Why, wasn't he absent from Beltane too?" Headmistress Starwort asks, scratching her chin. Her gaze sweeps to the old Victorian atop the hill, overlooking the valley.

"Yes, I believe he was," the High Priestess says through her teeth. She shares an odd look with her granddaughter, Spring, who then walks away. Oak follows her, his puzzlement matching my own.

I peer back at the yellow house atop the hill. *Weird.* Why would a High Priest miss not one, but *two* Sabbats?

Within the field, a row of hanging iron cauldrons hover above smoking fire pits. The scents of apples, cinnamon, and cloves rise from a large pot of mulled cider. A group is gathered around one of the cauldrons, each taking turns to ladle their drinks into glittering colored-glass goblets.

High Priestess Violet takes Rugosa, Hyacinth, and River up the hill to a dilapidated shed, where they retrieve a bushel of bird seed. Aspen, Fern, Amaranth, and Petal hang the bird feeders on low hanging branches along the woodland edge of the valley. Headmistress Starwort and Mistress Aster split, and Dahlia skips off to the banquet tables, where she squeezes in our Cocoa Bombs between other dishes.

I scan the vast crowd for my younger sister, finding her close by with a gaggle of her friends. She graduated from the eighth grade and will be a high schooler with me next fall. We haven't shared a school since elementary. It's almost surreal. I cup my hand around my mouth, shouting, "Wisteria!"

Her dark head twists in both directions, her long ponytail slapping her in the neck. Her eyes round as she spots me. "Summer!" she shouts, pushing through her friends. She jogs toward me, throwing out her skinny arms for a hug.

I wrap my arms around her back and squeeze her tight. She smells like my pineapple body spray, coconut shampoo, and mango lip gloss. I hold her at an arm's reach, looking her over. Sure enough, a slathering of lip gloss across her mouth and the telltale glitter of the pineapple spray marks her arms.

"Are you using my stuff?" I exclaim, brow furrowed.

"Is your hair in braids?" she asks simultaneously. She pulls on the tails, a perplexed look on her face. "I can't remember the last time I've seen you without iron-straight hair. When's the last time you've bathed? You're not depressed, are you? Aww, over River?" She tilts her head, her eyes full of pity.

"I'm fine, but seriously, stop using my stuff. What else are you using of mine?"

She shoves me, pouting, her brow furrowed. "Knock it off. You're mean."

"No, it looks good," I tell her, chuckling, shoving her back. "I just want to return and have some left. Yesterday I learned how to make raspberry lip stain. I'll show you sometime."

She smiles genuinely and fidgets with her purse.

"How's Meadow?" I ask, afraid of the answer.

"Ash has been around, a *lot*," she tells me, twisting her ponytail around her finger.

I nod and change the subject. "So, do you have a birthday present for me, or what?" I grin and gesture to her handbag.

"Maybe!" Wisteria says in a sing-song voice. She pulls a small plastic bag from her purse.

"Here." She passes me the gift in a small Winter's Cures and Curses bag. "I didn't have time to wrap it."

"You've never wrapped a gift," I reply, laughing.

Inside the bag is a beautiful silver ring with engraved hearts and a large aquamarine stone. I pull it out, sliding it onto my finger. I hold my hand out to admire my jewelry. It glitters under the sunlight. "Aww, Wisteria!"

"It's to attract love. Plus, it's hella pretty," she tells me, batting her eyelashes.

"Oh," I say. "I'm not really looking to get with anyone right now." I twist the ring around my finger. "But, I love it. Thank you, sis."

"You're welcome! Happy birthday!" She throws her arms around my neck before bouncing off to return to her friends. I watch her as she goes, happy to see that she's doing well and isn't miserable without me.

"We draw the Summer sun into our souls!" High Priestess Violet Widow-Tears says, facing the horizon. Her arms are stretched, her hands reaching for the sky. She wiggles her pale, wrinkled fingers. Large chunky rings sparkle under the sunlight, the crystals glittering with her movements.

I'm standing within a large crowd behind the High Priestess, mirroring her actions and the ones of others because I'm not really sure what to do with myself. The faint smell of an earthy perfume catches my nose. I have no idea where it's coming from, but it seems to be from Aspen. As he moves the scent strengthens.

River's nearby separated from me only by Petal. His hands are stuffed in his pockets and he's wearing a grimace on his face. He looks miserable and for once, I don't feel the urge to make things better. I don't feel the desire to bend over backward for the off chance that he might appreciate my effort and possibly be interested in me again. It isn't my job to make him feel happy.

I glance at Dahlia. She's chatting quietly with Hyacinth, paying no attention to her miserable boyfriend. And why should she? She's not entertaining his weird manipulation attempt to get attention. I realize now that's all it is because the longer she ignores him and enjoys herself with Hyacinth, the poutier he gets. I wish I had done the same, but instead, I canceled plans with friends when he asked me to. I canceled a *lot*. Eventually, my friends stopped inviting me over and who can blame them? The only person who ever sticks around is Aspen.

However, it's not *all* River's fault. I can't put all the blame on him. I've never been good with relationships in general, apart from Aspen, but he's not like most people.

I make a friend and things are cool until I get involved in a new relationship with whatever boy I'm crazy in love with at the time. I forget to keep in touch. I don't return phone calls and sleepovers become less frequent, if at all. Then, the relationship ends with whatever boy, as it always does, and my former friend has moved on from me with a new bestie.

That's what happened between me and Petal Wormwood after River asked me to be his girlfriend at her Esbat. Now she'll barely look at me.

Petal's black hair has a shiny blue cast under the rising sun. She bumps hips with Azalea, giggling as they make fun of whoever. They point and laugh at someone in the crowd. Azalea throws her head back laughing. Her naturally wavy hair—now weighed down by oil and dirt—doesn't have its usual bounce this morning.

Petal was my best friend before I met River. We did everything together. I replaced Petal with River. We hardly speak now. And then there's Fern, I miss her too. I hate this feeling—of being a social outcast, but I brought it upon myself with that terrible love spell. Now everyone thinks badly of me. I'm not even sure why Amaranth talks to me, other than the fact that our bunks are only feet from each other. I sigh, refocusing my attention on the High Priestess of the Widow-Tears clan.

"Sunna, shine your golden rays upon us, bathing us in light and love. Your warmth fills us with comfort and hope. On this longest day of the year, we celebrate!"

High Priestess Widow-Tears swirls around, facing us. Her ritual robe billows at her feet. "And I don't know a better way to celebrate than to eat! Go." She gestures to the tables with a wave of her hand. "Dig in!"

Witches bump elbows with one another as they crowd around the banquet tables. I help myself to an assortment of delicious-looking breakfast dishes. Pancakes are piled high in stacks beside several bottles of dark maple syrup and packets of butter and homemade jam. Plates of breakfast sausage, crispy bacon, and ham are between breakfast casserole bakes, pastries, and oversized muffins. I scoop warm scrambled eggs and a portion of peach cobbler with fresh whipped cream onto my plate. I butter up a blueberry waffle, excited to eat *real* food. Next, I pour myself a cup of fruity herbal tea, grab some plastic cutlery, and find a place to eat away from most of the crowd. I plop down onto the ground, leaning against a tree. I set my cup of tea into the grass and hold my brimming plate over my lap.

As I'm tearing into my waffle, Aspen approaches and sits down beside me. He shoves a rosemary garlic biscuit into his mouth, biting off half of it. After swallowing, he says, "No offense, but your breakfast lacked originality and creativit—"

I shove him.

"Ow! I was kidding!"

"For that, you're losing your biscuit." I take it from his hand and break off a piece, tossing it into my mouth. "And there's only so much I can do with eggs, leftover hamburger buns, and wild blueberries."

"That blueberry breakfast was terrible," he remarks, shoving a spoonful of eggs into his mouth.

"What's terrible is you not wishing me a happy birthday," I say around a mouthful of food, spraying him with biscuit crumbs.

He wipes the side of his face with a grimace and digs into his pocket. "Actually, I've been working on your gift since yesterday…" He pulls his enclosed fist out of his pocket. "Fully charged it in the sunlight. Happy birthday." He grins, dropping something sharp into my hand.

A beautiful glittering crystal rests in the palm of my hand. My jaw drops. "Oh my Gods. Aspen, I was teasing you. I didn't *really* expect you to get me anything. Where'd you charge this?" I carefully slide my plate into the grass beside me.

He reaches over me, steals a sliced peach from my plate, and pops it into his mouth. "Up on the mountain where we watched the shooting star."

"That's dangerous. You charged a crystal, in summer, in the forest? What if the woods caught fire?" I scratch my chin.

He shrugs. "I wanted to give you a crystal at its fullest potential. What's the point otherwise? It's like giving someone a battery-operated gift without batteries. Stupid, really."

"So, you risked burning down Camp Bitter Tonic?" I snort.

"Well, when you put it that way it sounds a little, uh, ill-advised," he says with a laugh.

"Just a tiny bit." I smile. "Thank you, Aspen. This is really sweet."

He blushes and averts his eyes. "Besides, I'm not sure that could really happen—the forest burning down from a charged crystal, I mean."

"My mother says otherwise," I retort, setting the crystal in my lap and taking a sip of warm herbal tea."

"Your paranoid mother says a lot of crazy things… Is that tea?" he shrieks dramatically, his hand poised over his heart.

I laugh, nearly choking on my drink. "It's not too bad. I appreciate it more after Wart's lesson."

He nods, impressed. "Don't forget, that's not *really* tea, though."

"Oh, I remember." I smile. "Maybe that's why I like it?"

He shrugs.

I nestle my tea in the grass beside my plate and clutch the sharp stone in my palm, turning my chin up to the sun and closing my eyes. What feels like small electrical shocks buzz against my skin from the crystal. Sunna's energy courses through me. I feel connected to the sun, her light, and my Wiccan faith. When I open my eyes, I feel invigorated and slightly powerful, as if the Solar Goddess herself infused me. I blink several times. Glowing amber orbs drip from my fingers then float around me, popping like bubbles in the air, soon dissipating entirely. Aspen doesn't appear to notice as he yanks the top off his corn muffin and tosses the stump behind him to a gathering flock of feisty sparrows.

"There's magic in this stone," I remark, tucking the crystal carefully into my stuffed pocket. "I just saw these things," I say, uncertain.

"Oh yeah?" he asks skeptically.

"I'm not sure? It was these, like glowing blobs. I don't know if it was real, or just my vision going wonky from squeezing my eyelids so tight, but I can't doubt the way it felt in my hand."

He puffs his chest, proudly. "Cool. It's for restful dreams. Just place it under your pillow."

I snap my head toward him. "How'd you know about my nightmares?"

"Everyone knows."

"Are you freakin serious?"

"Summer, our cabins are only so far from each other. We heard you screaming and peeked in the windows."

"This morning?"

He nods. "And the morning before."

I fall back in the grass, folding my hands over my stomach and sighing heavily. Several sparrows flutter their wings, taking off in flight.

"What's wrong?" he asks, his brow furrowed.

"Don't be creepin' on me."

"I'm not." He takes a bite of muffin, chewing it slowly. "Just checking on you. Making sure everything was okay. I hope the crystal will help."

I smile. "Me too."

"So, what's your nightmare about, anyways?"

I rise to a sitting position, the wind stirring my hair and rippling the grass around us. "It's honestly really stupid. I'm flying on a broomstick in a rainstorm, scared out of my mind, and just as I crash, I wake up. What's scary about it is how *real* it feels."

"I hate dreams like that. You have the same one both times?" he asks, popping a berry into his mouth. "You done with your plate?" He reaches across my lap for the plate beside me.

"No!" I slap his hand away and pick up my plate, setting it back into my lap. "The first time I thought I was hallucinating, or something. Like, I saw this robed figure come into our cabin. They put their hand over my eyes and just like that, I was flying."

"*They* did?"

"I don't know if they were male or female," I admit, pulling apart my waffle with my fingers. "And my bunkmates have little to no sympathy. It's really not helping me feel any better about myself. Just alienating me further from everyone." I drag the bite-sized piece through syrup and pop it into my mouth, licking the corner of my lip.

He pulls a pouch of herbs out of his other pocket and tosses it at me; it falls in the grass, hitting the side of my thigh, narrowly missing my syrup covered plate. I'm struck with the odd scent I smelled earlier, during High Priestess Violet's lengthy ode to the Sun Goddess. I bring the small bag to my nose, inhaling the scents of dried lavender, chamomile, sage, and valerian.

"Maybe that will help with your nightmares. You can toss 'em in your pillow."

"Did you learn that from the Tea Magic lesson?" I ask grinning. I throw my arm around his shoulders, squeezing him. Syrup drips from my plate onto my lap.

"Yup," he says, with a goofy smile on his face.

I tuck the herbs into my pocket and we finish up our food, chatting amicably and people-watching.

After breakfast, my sister Wisteria drags me into a Spiral Dance, introduced by Priestess Winter of the northern Rose-Thorne clan. Winter's long scarlet hair cascades down her back in beautiful, bouncy waves as she dances like no one is watching. Literally, it's like she isn't self-aware at all. She moves her nimble frame on time with the music in her head... maybe. Even though she isn't the best dancer on earth, her confidence is enviable. Turmeric Wormwood—the man she tied the handfasting knot with last Beltane—plays a drum as the women spin around and dance to the tribal beat before joining hands.

The grass scratches against my calves. I sway my hips to the beat, unwind my braids, and run my hands through my hair, feeling uninhibited under the sun. I wish I could have worn a long skirt, like I see the other ladies wearing, instead of these ugly khaki shorts with the grass-stained bottom. Wisteria takes my hand and we join the formation.

Priestess Winter leads us. We follow in a counter-clockwise motion. As she comes to close the circle, she whirls around in a clockwise motion, using what she refers to as a grapevine step. She teaches us her "moves" and we raise energy through the art of dance. The northern Priestess moves clockwise, facing the dancing witches who mirror her movements when it becomes their turn in line. Eventually, all the dancers face one another and are expected to kiss one another on the cheek. I'm standing across from, of all people, frenemy Dahlia Devil-Claw.

I take a deep breath and peck her on the side of the cheek. She smells like River; she wears his patchouli. From the sidelines, my ex-boyfriend River says smugly, "I've had them both."

I take a deep breath to center myself, ignoring him. She flashes him a stormy look of anger.

The beat ceases and we clap hands, hugging one another. The atmosphere is joyous, even a little romantic. Flowers are passed around as gifts between witches. I receive a daisy from a young Widow-Tears child. Her violet eyes are alight under the sun. I pat her on the top of her golden head and she buzzes off like a little bumblebee, plucking a daisy from her bouquet for Spring Widow-Tears.

I twist the ring around my finger, remembering what Wisteria said about attracting love. The funny thing is, I truly don't even care to do that anymore. I haven't even been checking boys out today…

"Hey, Summer!" Aspen calls out, interrupting my thoughts.

I grin and wave him over.

I'm glad I'm here, I realize, gazing around at the community celebrating the Solar holiday. I may not always feel like I belong, but it feels amazing to be a part of this.

9

The celebration continues late into the evening. A bonfire is alight; its flames reach for the sky like the branches of the elderberry trees at the valley's edge where we earlier parked our brooms. Sage bundles and campfire smoke fragrance the air. It's any wonder the air witches can breathe.

"Darkening atmosphere above, cool soil below. We light this fire as our families did years ago…" The High Priestess of the Widow-Tears clan pauses before instructing, "Please join around the bonfire and hold hands." She feeds the flames of the bonfire with dry wood.

Aspen approaches me and weaves his fingers within mine. He leans in, whispering into my ear, "Don't worry. Nothing creepy." His touch is reassuring. He gives himself to me so freely, even when I reject him. I'm just the opposite. If I feel slighted, I'm done.

My arm is tugged, snapping me out of my thoughts. River grabs my hand, squeezes my palm possessively, and glares at Dahlia. He's using me to make her jealous. Playing his games as usual. I'm sandwiched between him and Aspen. He cranes his neck and glowers at River. Dahlia's dark eyes are stormy; she glares at us from within the crowd, Azalea beside her. She crosses her arms over her chest.

I take a sharp breath, inadvertently inhaling a gnat. I burst into a coughing fit, doubling over. River releases my limp hand and storms off, grumbling. Dahlia follows, calling after her boyfriend. They disappear into the sea of witches.

"Did you fake that?" Aspen asks, releasing my hand and slapping me on the back.

"Nope," I reply, recovering from choking to death. I clear my throat. "Swallowed a fly."

"He died of a noble cause," Aspen says with a simper, grasping my palm.

"The Wheel of the Year has turned once more," the eastern High Priestess says, her rounded chin tilted upward toward the darkening sky above. "The light has grown for half a year and today it's met its capacity. Litha is a time for festivity. We celebrate because tomorrow the light will dwindle. The Wheel of the Year turns endlessly!"

We raise our enclosed hands to the pink and orange streaked sky. A strong fire blazes before us. Its heat is almost unbearable, combined with the stifling summer air. I absorb it into my chest, utilizing its energy and recharging my inner fire.

"What are you doing?" Aspen asks, distracting me.

"Refueling," I respond easily, rolling my shoulders.

"Since when do you do that?"

"Starting now," I answer, haughtily, turning my nose up.

"We honor you!" High Priestess Widow-Tears concludes to Sunna's sun dipping below the horizon. We release hands and applaud.

"Who's ready to eat?" a deep male voice shouts from somewhere in the crowd behind me.

The circle disperses but for a few witches who volunteer to remain behind to watch over the campfire.

"Why does someone have to watch it? Can't it just be put out?" I ask Aspen as we walk to the banquet tables. I slap a mosquito on my leg.

"I always forget that you don't normally come to these things… It's just practice allowing it to burn out on its own during the Litha Sabbat," he responds with a shrug. "Once it does, they'll spread it and do a firewalk."

Excited commotion startles us both. Aspen and I weave our way around others to get a look at what's ahead.

Solar lights flicker like fireflies, hung between the trees over the banquet tables. The tables are dressed up for the solar holiday, covered with several burnt orange tablecloths to represent the burning summer sun. A fiery red table runner runs down the center, accented with small acrylic mirrors that reflect the fire of lit yellow candles. Tall vases of coneflowers, fern, and other summer blooming wildflowers are on each dining table. A collection of acorns is scattered across table runners.

"Was this set up all while our backs were turned?" I ask, scratching my head.

"Yeah, but there was like, a bunch of people behind us. Why would we've noticed it?" Aspen asks.

"I guess, but still." I shrug.

A potluck barbeque is set up on the banquet table. I get a paper plate and heap it high with potato salad, a summer fruit and fennel salad with a light mustard vinaigrette dressing, and grilled veggies. A plate of hotdogs on buns are snatched up quickly. Aspen grabs two before the platter is empty but for breadcrumbs.

"Savages," he says, passing me a hotdog.

I squirt a line of mustard down the hotdog and take a proper seat, this time, at the beautiful table. A bottle of mead is passed around. We all take a sip of the alcoholic beverage to celebrate our Midsummer feast. We have no such rules as the silly non-magicals do regarding alcohol. Down the table, our high school instructor, Priestess Anna, falls face first into her plate. Her drink is spilled onto the lap of her mother beside her. High Priestess Ruth Devil-Claw scrambles up, waving her pungent clove cigarette around as she scolds her drunk daughter.

After dinner and more dancing—led by Priestess Winter Rose-Thorne, who desperately needs dance lessons—I snack on candied ginger while a firewalk is prepared. Other Wormwood clan members—associated with the south and the fire element—carry dry bundles of wood across the valley. It's lain in piles, several feet from the bonfire.

I watch them from afar, feeling terribly cut off from my clan. I should be helping out, too, but I barely know any of them, and I'd feel awkward just jumping in. When I was separated from my mother, I bounced around from house to house, none of which were Wormwoods. Us kids were bunched together, regardless of clan. My sister and I were torn apart. And for the short period of time that I stayed with a non-magical family—horrible experience, that was— they did everything within their power to strip my magic. Disposed of my trinkets, my grandmother's pentagram necklace, and anything and everything associated with magic and my Wiccan faith. I wasn't allowed to play with fire, and I was punished for emitting sulphur—something that comes as naturally to me as breathing. I was taunted and beaten regularly as a nine-year-old. Perhaps Aspen is right—that's why I don't feel as witchy as I'd like to. That experience, albeit eight years ago, still haunts me to this day. I want that to change, though. The only good thing that ever came out of foster care was my friendship with Aspen.

Aspen joins me on a bench with two burgundy jeweled goblets. "Holy friggin sunset," he says, handing me a chalice of dandelion mead. He sits, and we clink glasses. "Happy birthday, Summer."

I smile, raising my glass. "Cheers."

"Cheers." He sips and leans back, resting his arm behind me. We gaze at the beautiful skyline.

I take small sips from my chalice. The mead tastes earthy, with a healthy kick of flowers, sweetened by honey and not bitter at all, like some dandelion mead I've had the displeasure of tasting. I can't imagine the time nor patience of the person who crafted this, removing all the leaves and stems from the blossoms, and scraping the petals of thousands of dandelion flowers. I gaze around the valley; not a dandelion is in sight.

"I wonder if the dandelions were plucked from the valley of Elderberry Thicket?" I marvel out loud.

"Oh, what—you mean for the mead?"

"Duh."

"High Priestess Violet enlists the help of the young Widow-Tears children to pick them. I can remember doing so when I was little."

"Oh, neat." I take another small sip. "Does she make it herself? It's really strong."

"I assume so. Dunno." He shrugs.

Aspen smells nice, like witch hazel, smoke, and the forest. It's almost unreal that those things would appeal to me. Nature has infused me deeply in only a matter of days. It may still take me a minute or two to start a broom, but I'll get there. I sincerely hope I'll reach my full, inborn potential. Accepting and coming to awareness of my witchiness is a beautiful thing.

I pass him some candied ginger and he tosses it up, narrowly missing his mouth.

"I'm digging these Sabbats," I say in turn. "I wish my mom could be here."

Aspen flinches. "I'm kinda surprised to hear you say that... Maybe someday," he responds, squeezing my shoulder. "You know, I've always liked Meadow."

"Of course. I do too. She's my mother, and I love her. She just has her problems."

Aspen sighs. "Don't we all?"

We gaze forward, sitting quietly together while the festivities continue around us. Sunna's sun looks almost tangerine in the sky as it sets. Streaks of pink and magenta color the night's atmosphere. Dandelion mead warms my belly and chest. I relax into the moment, sinking into the crook of Aspen's arm that rests behind my shoulders.

His lavender gaze shifts from the skyline to me. My heart flutters in my chest as I lick my lip—the taste of honey at the tip of my tongue.

Aspen blinks.

I pull him close to me by his Charm School shirt and kiss him.

10

Boy did I misread that one…

"You're not kissing back," I say against his dead mouth. I withdraw, releasing his wrinkled shirt from my fist.

"Oh, Summer." He sets his drink into the grass and runs his warm hands down my arms, holding me.

I swing my arms out of his grip. Mead splashes over us, soaking my shorts. I leap from the bench, storming off. He calls me back and I stop in place, placing my hands on my hips. I don't turn to look at him. I'm too ashamed, and now to add to my embarrassment, it looks like I've freakin' peed myself. My scalp prickles and sulphur leaches from the tips of my hair, perfuming the air around me with the sickly scent of rotten eggs.

"Please, come back. Talk to me," Aspen shouts.

I reluctantly turn, because I know my butt is covered in grass stains, and I probably look ridiculous. "Yeah? What is it?" I swallow against the lump in my throat. He pats the bench beside him and I huff before returning. I reluctantly take a seat, crossing my arms over my chest and slouching.

He takes a deep breath, grimacing as he says, "I can't say I'm not flattered."

"Ugh. I don't care if you're flattered or not. That's such a cop-out, Aspen."

"No, it's not." He pivots his legs to me, sliding his hands up into my hair from my neck. His fingertips barely touch my scalp, sending shivers down my spine. His thumbs and forefingers hook around my ears. "I like you, Summer. And because of that, I don't want to be your rebound."

"You're not," I say, my voice cracking with emotion.

He nods. "Yes, I am. You might not realize it, but that's exactly what you're doing. You're trying to escape the pain of your breakup with River by hooking up with me. You've never liked me before. Hell, you pushed me away from you just yesterday," he exclaims. "So, I don't know if it's the mead or your heart is messed up." He hangs his head.

"You just don't understand, Aspen." I close my eyes, sniffling. I'm startled when he blows lightly on my eyelids, drying my tears with the power of his element. It's so much better than the pads of thumbs wiping away tears, like in the romance novels I read and love. My eyes snap open. My cheeks are dry. He slides his hands out of my hair and folds them in his lap.

"And I have to admit I kind of feel like you're settling a bit." He scratches his chin and chuckles. I laugh through my tears. "For real, though. I thought you thought I was annoying."

"I *still* think you're annoying."

"Fair enough. But I think once your heart is mended from this whole, *I put a love spell on River Devil-Claw thing*, you won't feel the same about me."

I glare at him, shooting metaphorical fireballs with my eyes.

"I know you, Summer. You've never changed on this. I should know; I've only been trying to get your attention forever. Your head's just confused, and I think you've had a little too much to drink."

I want to tell him the reason for me being so standoffish in the past is because of my fear of losing him and our great friendship, but our conversation is interrupted when the firewalk is announced. He turns his head toward the speaker, Elder Belladonna Wormwood, and he tells me how he's always wanted to firewalk, but he's been too afraid and chickens out at the last minute.

Like him, I lose my courage.

"...Those who wish to firewalk later are asked to take a log from the stack at the woodland edge and gather together at the cauldron."

"I'm doing it," I state matter-of-factly.

"No, you're not," he says, rolling his eyes.

"Watch me." I bolt from the bench, a bit wobbly at first—perhaps I have had a little too much to drink—and make a beeline toward the crowd.

Aspen catches up to me as I retrieve my piece of firewood. "C'mon, Summer. You don't have to do this to prove your point. I get it, okay. You're just like the seasons, you change. Now, just stop being so stubborn. I *really* think you've had too much to drink."

I whirl around, the tips of our noses touching. His eyes widen with surprise as my face contorts with anger. "I'm not doing this to prove a point to you. It's not always about you, Aspen. Back off. I'm doing this."

He steps back, putting up his hands in mock surrender. "Okay, if this is what you want. I just don't want you to feel like you have to do this to prove a point."

"Will you just shut up?" I scream back, cutting between witches to get away from him. He's so infuriating. I thought he liked me. Why did he reject my kiss? I join the front of the crowd with Headmistress Starwort and my Charm School classmates, clutching my firewood to my chest. Amaranth, Petal, Dahlia, and Azalea are here too, holding their logs.

"First, let's focus on your goals," Belladonna tells the group gathered before her. "I want you to step forward, placing your firewood in the cauldron, while telling the flames your intentions. Remember to speak up."

I hang back and wait my turn as other witches eagerly step forward, feeding the flames with their logs. They confidently state their intentions.

I don't know what I want. I thought I wanted Aspen, but then he rejected me, and now I just want to shake him and shout in his face. I consider the horrible nightmares, knowing what I have to ask for.

The Charm School students are called forward next. The cauldron fire grows as Azalea asks for weight loss, Petal asks for modesty, Dahlia asks for artist-grade, hot-pressed watercolor paper with four deckle edges—whatever that is—and Amaranth asks for clear skin. My knee bounces in anticipation as Elder Belladonna nods me over. It's my turn to feed the fire and ask the flames for what I wish.

"I ask for restful sleep," I say, releasing the log into the fiery cauldron.

"We *all* do, Summer," Amaranth says as I rejoin my classmates in the crowd.

"I'm surprised she didn't ask for love," Dahlia remarks snidely, surprising me, but then again, her boyfriend did grab my hand tonight to make her feel bad.

My classmates disperse to dance, eat, and enjoy each other's company, but I remain with the crowd. Despite being surrounded by witches, I feel alone, like the outcast that I am.

And now I've burned my last bridge, with Aspen. My pride too much to swallow.

I watch Headmistress Starwort deliver her firewood into the bonfire, asking for her students to graduate on time. More clan members step up, feeding the flames. Some weep openly as they deliver their firewood. They embrace one another, joyous. Smoke churns from the pot, reaching for the sky. The wood cracks, startling me with each loud pop.

As darkness blankets the sky, the bonfire set before dinner is reduced to embers. The cauldron of firewood is smothered by Elder Belladonna Wormwood, and we're asked to take a handful and deliver it to the remains of the bonfire. I reach into the black pot, scooping the ashes and chunks of charred wood into my palm; the dark soot begrimes my hand.

We cross the valley and deposit our cauldron ashes. Several Wormwood clan members spread the fiery remains of the bonfire and it's time for the firewalk. The Charm School members are called forward.

"Who's first?" Belladonna asks as we rejoin.

"Me," I holler, clenching my fists.

Amaranth looks incredulous beside me. Her eyes round in alarm, then she purses her lips and raises her arm. Not to be outdone, ever, she shouts, "And then me!"

I straighten my shoulders as I approach the fiery trail. The embers are red hot. Maybe Aspen was right. I can't change. There's a certain comfort in routine…

The crystal he gave me digs into my thigh. I adjust it in my pocket. Maybe I'm doing this to prove something, but it isn't to Aspen, it's to myself.

I'm a fire witch, I tell myself, *and I can do this*. I just need to take the first step. If only someone would give me a little shove…

"You're more powerful than your fear," Headmistress Starwort says in encouragement, stepping out from the sidelines. "Walk quickly, at an even stride."

It's just the shove I need to move forward, except it's verbal, not physical.

I step onto the searing trail, walking briskly across the hot embers. I make it to the end and let out a celebratory yell. I step into a bucket of water and close my eyes, letting its coolness soothe my burning feet. The crowd cheers for me as I rejoin them.

Aspen cuts through the mob. "You did awesomely! How did it feel?" Rugosa stumbles behind him, his eyelids barely open and an empty goblet in hand.

"Fine," I say, shrugging his hand off.

"Okay," he says, unconvinced. "Can we talk for a bit, then?"

"I don't wanna talk, Aspen. I'm exhausted. It's been an insanely long day." I pat my pocket. "Maybe with this new crystal, I won't have to worry about being visited by the Night Hag."

"The Night Hag?" Aspen asks, his face twisted in confusion. "You mean your nightmares?"

"Yes, she's responsible for nightmares. Haven't you heard? She'll sit on your chest and pin you down, suck out your breath—"

"What in the Sigmund-Freud-undigested-potato-nonsense are you goin' on about?" Rugosa interrupts. Aspen raises his hand to his face, stifling a laugh. "Ut!" Rugosa loses his balance and drunkenly crashes into Aspen, pushing him into me. The collision sends us all to the ground.

"Or your spirit guides are delivering a warning," an elderly woman rasps above us.

11

Rugosa and Aspen burst into a laughing fit, fueled by mead, friendship, and good times. I untangle myself from the jumble of arms and legs, pushing Rugosa's stupid drunk face away from me for good measure.

We pick ourselves off the ground. Out of breath from laughter, Rugosa bends at the waist. His hands on his knees, he loses his balance and falls forward doing a complete somersault. I step over him, brushing myself of dirt and debris. I approach the elderly Rose-Thorne witch, who remarkably, hasn't been scared off by us rowdy teens.

The strange woman wears a gauzy dark pine-green dress that almost looks black. A fuzzy gray shawl is wrapped around her pale shoulders, covered in black animal fur. Her inquisitive eyes are icy blue, and her shoulder-length hair resembles the coloring of dirty gray dishwater. She holds a skinny, sleeping black cat in the crook of her elbow.

"Were you speaking to me?" I ask hesitantly, glancing around.

"C'mon, Summer. She doesn't know what she's talking about. Let's just get outta here," Aspen says behind me. He chuckles as he peels his best friend from the ground. Further back, a splash of water is followed by Amaranth's squeal of triumph. The crowd applauds.

"You said something about a warning?" I ask the mysterious woman. "And spirit guides?"

"Hey, I gotta bring him back," Aspen says in a strained voice as he hoists Rugosa up. He drags him through the grass, his heels digging into the dirt. "Be back after—"

I snap my head in Aspen's direction, fixing him within a glare of death. "You really don't need to tell me your every move, you know!"

Rugosa bursts into another bout of laughter, bringing Aspen to lose his patience. I whirl around, reaching for the retreating witch. A thud behind me is followed by Rugosa's groans from the ground and Aspen stomping off, grumbling to himself. I get a fistful of the Rose-Thorne witch's gray shawl.

As the woman spins around, the little black cat awakens. Wide emerald cat eyes look at me briefly. She stretches in her owner's arms and yawns, exposing a mouth with a missing canine tooth. She closes her little green eyes and snuggles into her mother.

Anger flashes in the witch's eyes like lightning bolts. I immediately regret my action, and rewrap her shawl, straightening and smoothing the wool around her shoulders as I apologize. She purses her lips and breathes icy breath through her nose. She clutches her cat to her chest, bouncing her like an infant.

"What is your name?" she asks, her cool stare drawn to the top of my head, where my unclean, braided tresses are undoubtedly frizzy beneath my headpiece. Her gaze slowly drops to my bare feet, earth-brown from embedded dirt and scraped from twigs and sharp rocks.

"Summer," I respond in a nervous breath. "My name is Summer Wormwood."

Aspen returns with his broomstick. As I look over my shoulder, he rolls Rugosa from the ground onto his yellow riding broom, telling him to hold on for dear life. As they lift off, errant wisps of hair that has slipped from my braids blow with the wind. Above, Rugosa lays limp across the broom. Aspen sits behind him with a fistful of Rugosa's shirt to steady him. Before leaving, he shouts down insolently, "Bye everyone, except Summer who doesn't need to know my every move."

As I roll my eyes, I catch Aspen winking at me. He buzzes back to Elwood, disappearing into the night sky.

"The nerve of that boy," I mutter as the color-streaked clouds swallow them in the dark sky. It looks like rain is coming. The air cools.

The Rose-Thorne witch raises a gnarled finger. "I know you," she says, a glittering spark in her eye. "I never forget a face. I know your parents too."

I shake my head and sigh, feeling let down. Aspen was right. This woman doesn't know anything.

"You're mistaken," I respond, stepping away.

Icy, bony fingers circle my wrist. An Arctic chill snakes its way up my arm and neck. I stiffen from fright. I glance at the crowd, realizing how far away they are. Aspen will be in no rush to return after I was so rude. My anxiety spirals as I grasp the gravity of the situation.

"Your mother is Meadow and your father is—" she releases my arm and taps her head. When she mentions my mother's name, my defenses drop. "Oh, it's... It's that terrible man," she says, her brow furrowed, struggling to remember. Her gaze lifts suddenly, connecting with mine. "No offense, dearie."

"None took. I'm not a huge fan of him either."

"Chicory!" she shouts, startling me. I stumble backward. Her cat awakens and lets out a low mewl.

"But, how? This is my first Sabbat. Meadow doesn't come either. And her, uh, sperm donor?"

"That's no way to speak of your parents. You call your mother by her first name? That is shameful!" She tsks, shaking her head.

"Look, lady... I'll call my mother whatever I want. I was separated from her for the better part of my life. You don't know my situation." I flip my braids over my shoulder and cross my arms over my chest.

"Fiery. I like that." She cranes her neck and narrows her eyes. "You have no idea who I am, do you?"

I peer at her carefully. By her fancy dress, I assume she is someone important. A psychic witch, perhaps? *She knows things*, I reason with myself.

I respond guiltily, "I'm sorry I don't." A wide smile spreads across her face. My answer seems to please her, and I'm not certain why.

"Are you leaving right this second?" I ask. "Do you have a little time to talk to me about the spirit guides? I'm really interested in dream interpretation."

The witch yawns. "I'm on my way home, dearie. I have to put the baby to bed." She lovingly glances at her cat. "Of course, you could come back with me." She shrugs, then walks away, calling in a hoarse voice over her shoulder, "Come, if you must. I need to get my broomstick, first."

I stand perfectly still, my feet firmly planted in the grass of the valley. My practical side screams *not* to do it. My inquisitive side asks, what could *possibly* go wrong?

She's ancient, possibly crazy. She can't physically overpower me. I really don't want to stick around after I made an ass out of myself with Aspen. With age comes wisdom; maybe she can help me? She knows my family. She mentioned them by name. How bad could she possibly be?

"Wait!" I shout to the elderly woman. "Could you tell me how you know my parents, first?" I fidget with my hands. "I just don't feel comfortable leaving with a stranger."

The old lady halts in place then spins around to face me. "Why you're not a stranger to me at all, my dear." She takes slow steps toward me, stopping feet away.

I blink. "I'm not?"

"No. I've been here for you since the beginning, my lovely. I was there when you were born in a field of flowers on Litha, seventeen years ago during a Midsummer Sun Ritual. Your mother, heavily pregnant, was led by your father, a Green Man, and several Wormwood Elders, to take a walk to ease her labor pains. It was within minutes that her water broke, and after hours of agonizing labor, you found your way into the world, surrounded by Wormwood witches with torches and fistfuls of summer blooming wildflowers. And at that moment, a photo was taken. Your mother's face over-joyous and your father's proud. You, my lovely, were a screaming, wriggly, bloody mess. I was the one who snapped that photo. I still have it. At home in a trunk."

"You have a picture of my parents and me?" I ask, surprised. "I don't even have a picture of my parents and me. If you don't mind me asking...if it was a celebration of the Wormwoods, why were you there?"

"Hm, yes. I was showing support for your grandfather, Rowan Wormwood." She nervously adjusts her shawl.

"Oh, the murderer of High Priestess Clover Wormwood… Another winner. Why were you showing *him* support?"

"Yes well, that's a long story. You may have the photo if you'd like. I have no need for it." The black cat mewls in her arms. "I really must get home now."

"Sorry, one more thing. It's just, did you mean my nightmares could be warnings from like, ghosts?" I squeak the last word.

She rolls her eyes, then walks away without responding.

"Wait! I'll come with you. It's just... I have to check if it's okay with Headmistress Starwort. I'm with the Charm School." I point to my shirt.

She spins around. Her Arctic stare is probing, almost eager. Her knee bounces beneath her dress. "I'll tell you what. I'll speak with Starwort. Then, we'll fly."

"Well, okay. I guess," I respond unsurely. "If she says it's alright."

She strolls toward the firewalking ceremony, her cat snuggled in the crook of her arm. I study the elderly woman carefully as she approaches the edge of the crowd, pulling Headmistress Starwort aside.

She says something and the Headmistress nods. The witch raises her arm, pointing at me. In reaction, Headmistress Starwort shrugs her shoulders and rejoins the ceremony.

Minutes later, I'm on the back of the Rose-Thorne witch's broom, wind in my braids, my arms wrapped loosely around the icy witch's waist. Her black cat sits at the head of the broomstick, and I'm not certain, but I *think* she may be steering.

This has broom wreck written all over it.

I'm not sure what makes me more nervous—an elderly, possibly narcoleptic, cat driving the broomstick or accepting an invitation from a stranger to go back to their house *alone*. Memories of my nightmares about broom crashes flit through my mind as we navigate through the midnight sky. Drops of rain begin to fall. I take a deep breath, reminding myself that it was *just* a dream.

We reach Forest Park, the territory of the Rose-Thorne witches. The broomstick dips, heading for a large gray colored house. The home is hugged by sprawling rhododendron bushes that crawl up the windows. The yard is dirt, completely devoid of grass, and guarded by a thicket of thorny red shrubs. Large branches and twigs are piled along the woodland edge beside a copse of blackened, charred trees.

We land next to a large iron cauldron. Dust clouds rise in the air as our feet hit the dirt. Amazingly, I don't burst into a coughing fit. Charm School is working; it's actually making a difference! I think. The Rose-Thorne witch smiles at me slyly as we hop off the broom. The cat trots up the steps, her tail up and curled at the tip. A glint of moonlight peeking from between the dark clouds illuminates the silver placard on the entry door.

"The Stitch Witch," I read aloud. Why does that sound so familiar? My exhausted brain ponders this for a moment.

Realization blazes through me like a forest fire... I'm at seamstress Iris Rose-Thorne's house, the disgraced High Priestess who was exposed on the Winter Solstice for using black magic on her own granddaughter, Priestess Winter Rose-Thorne. The same High Priestess who was caught having an inter-clan affair with my grandfather, Rowan. *That's* why she was at a celebration with Wormwoods.

Oh. My. Gods. This was a huge mistake...

I let out a bloodcurdling scream that could wake the dead.

12

"My goodness, child. What is your problem?" Iris asks, pressing her hand against her ear, cringing. Shame colors my cheeks. Behind her, the cat's fur stands on end as she arches her back. "Get it together, my darling." The old woman clutches her broomstick handle, shaking her head as she shuffles through her dirt yard. When she reaches the top of the stairs, she hollers over her shoulder, "I'll make you some tea, my lovely. You're gonna need it to soothe your throat after that spine-tingling scream." She removes a key from her bra and unlocks her door. The cat sprints into the dark house, disappearing into the gloom. Iris follows, slapping on the foyer light. "Teenagers," she mutters under her breath. "Spooked by every little thing."

Amber light shines from the interior of the house onto the front steps. Moths hover at the entry, twirling and flapping their paper-thin wings.

I don't know whether to be embarrassed for screaming or terrified of this controversial woman. *I came here willingly*, I remind myself. She didn't kidnap me. Headmistress Starwort knows I'm here... I can leave at any time.

I creep up to the house, hesitating before I step inside. I'm greeted by the cozy scents of sandalwood and lemon. A pentacle wreath of thorny branches and dried rosebuds hangs in the foyer. I close the door behind me as Iris descends the stairs, sans cat.

"She's sleeping," she says, bringing a wrinkly finger to her lips. "Follow me to the kitchen, my dearest, and we'll talk about what ails you."

"You mentioned spirit guides?" I remind her, fidgeting with my hands impatiently. My heart pounds against my ribcage. I know better than to be here, but I stay anyways, my curiosity getting the better of me. In the kitchen, a ceiling fan spins above an oak table. The wind flutters the edges of a stack of napkins on the counter. She stoops down to pick several off the floor, then restrains them in place with a large salt shaker. The plaster walls are painted a cheery yellow.

I drag a chair from the table, plopping down. Under the artificial lighting, I realize how dirty my skin is. I thought I was getting really tan, but I think it's just dirt. Gross.

"Before I sit, would you like a cup of tea? A bar of soap, perhaps?"

I laugh. "No thank you. We're not allowed to use commercial soap for the duration of boarding school."

She sits across from me and steeples her fingers. "That's a shame, really. You smell like a wildfire, dearie." She wrinkles her nose, digs into her bra, and pulls out a blue lighter. "Deodorant?" she asks.

I shake my head. I've never felt so awkwardly uncomfortable in my life.

She pulls a stick of cranberry scented incense from a slim cardboard pack on the table, lights the tip with her lighter, and blows it out with icy cold breath. She sticks the incense into a decorative bottle dirtied with incense ash. It smokes between us, twirling from the mouth of the bottle. The fan above disperses it around the room.

"Oh!" she exclaims, her hands to her face. "I've almost forgotten! Your picture!"

She scurries off, leaving me behind in the empty, quiet kitchen. Her footsteps thunder up the stairs as she makes the ascent, then thump across the floor above my head. The ceiling light above the kitchen table shakes and flickers.

She's rummaging around upstairs. A box unlatches, and items are tossed on the floor in quick succession. Curses are followed by a hushed celebratory yell.

Her footsteps thud back across the floor, shaking the ceiling light, then down the stairs. She rushes through the foyer, returning to the kitchen. She smacks a glossy photograph down on the table.

I pick it up slowly. I almost can't believe my eyes. As she said, my father looks proud. He holds me up to the sun, my mother beside him, wearing a pretty floral dress, stained by indigo blood. Tears stream down her grinning face. My face looks smushed, and I'm covered in blood and amniotic fluid. Wormwood witches surround us with torches and bouquets of wildflowers. A dark sac lays at my mother's feet, partially obscured by the grass.

"What is that?" I tap the picture.

Iris takes her seat and leans across the table. She chuckles, covering her mouth with her wrinkled hand. "Oh my goodness, yes. That was your placenta, my lovely. In celebration, we brewed it in the cauldron with lady's mantle, cramp bark, and red raspberry leaf. It was a wonderful afterbirth tea."

I lift my head, my gaze slowly rolling from the photograph to her. "Are you freakin kidding me?" I ask, my face screwed up in disgust.

"Why would I kid you? It was lovely. It helped your mother with her cramping," she says, a look of fondness in her blue eyes.

I shake my head. "Gross." I pick up the photo to get a better look. "My mother looks so…happy."

"Well she ought to have been," Iris replies, folding her hands.

"Why?" I ask, setting the picture down.

"Do you not know your birth story at all?" the old woman questions. When I shake my head, she rolls her eyes. "Chicory, your Green Man father, was honored for his fertility, and your mother was named a Goddess, simply for birthing you on the Wiccan Sabbat. They were revered, honored, cherished even. A Greenwood throne was created in your father's honor—"

"Only for him to abandon all of us several years later," I interrupt, upon recollecting that stupid throne. "I remember that damn chair. In a fit of rage, my mom pushed it down the cellar stairs. She changed after he left. She spoke in riddles, developed a raging anxiety disorder, and couldn't cope without him. She began to have panic attacks and eventually became homebound. Lack of sunlight rendered her depressed. When she went to a Shaman for help, he sectioned her, and me and my little sister were pulled out of our home and tossed into the foster-care system. It's no wonder she's now reluctant to keep her appointments."

"I'm sorry, my dear. They put her in a mental ward because of her depression?" Iris asks.

My leg bounces beneath the table. "There were other things."

Iris offers a sympathetic smile. "Yes, dear."

"It doesn't matter. Truthfully, I don't remember a whole lot about my father. However, the moment the greenwood throne crashed and the wood split and splintered is permanently embedded in my mind... You know what, I don't even want this picture." I slide it across the table.

"I'll hold on to it in case you change your mind. Let's change the subject. You mentioned a nightmare?" she asks, turning the photograph over on the table.

"Yes, thank you." I sigh with relief, feeling some of the tension leave my shoulders from speaking about my father. "I appreciate you taking the time to interpret my dreams. I keep having this dream about a broom wreck in a bad storm.

As the broom crashes, I wake up. I scream wicked loud in my sleep and wake up my cabinmates. I'm still shaken by it; every little bang makes me jump. It's different from other nightmares. It feels real, and it's *so* embarrassing to me. This never happens at home. I don't know why it's happening at Charm School."

"It's happened more than once?" She narrows her eyes at the window. Rain pelts against the glass, picking up its intensity.

"On my first night of Charm School and again last night. And this is weird, but on the first night, I feel like I woke up to it, like *before* the nightmare began. This robed figure came into the room. My grandmother and aunt spoke of Night Hags that crush you and steal your breath. That's the first thing that came to mind."

Iris sits back in her chair, her lips in a thin line and expression grim. "Oh dearie, you don't need dream interpretation." Lightning flashes followed by a clap of thunder.

I scream, instinctively bringing my hands to my ears. "Gods!"

Iris scooches forward in her seat and rests her hand on my shoulder. "It's okay, Summer," she says, releasing me.

"Sorry. See what I mean?" She nods. I sit on my trembling hands to still them. "What were you saying?"

"I don't think you need dream interpretation. It sounds to me like a Mare is trying to deliver you an urgent message."

"A Mare? Is that a Night Hag?"

She nods. "It may be a cursed woman issuing a warning."

"Really?" I squeak, my leg bouncing to the racing beat of my heart. "Do you think it *could* be a warning? How can we tell the differences between an urgent message and a bad dream that is just a nightmare and nothing more?"

"I believe that all dreams are messages. Some are warnings from spiritual guides. I believe that Mares are cursed witches, whose bodies are carried in their sleep without them knowing. If you have another nightmare with the same theme, I'd be led to believe there is some urgency to it. Otherwise, it could be nothing, I suppose." She shrugs, then leans over the incense and inhales the scent, closing her eyes. The wind outside picks up, rattling the old glass of the kitchen windows.

"I'm so glad you believe me. Even my best friend thought it was stupid. Well, he didn't say that, but he didn't *not* say it, either." I dig into my pocket and drop the pouch of herbs and the crystal on the table. "He gave me these, though."

"I'm afraid if it's a Mare, those won't help. Lovely gifts, though."

"So, what can I do?" I whine, tucking the items back into my pocket.

She taps her chin. "I have an old recipe for a tea that might help. It has a bit of a hypnotic effect that will allow you to dreamwalk. It will help you go deeper into a dream state to uncover any veiled messages. We'll burn tobacco, mugwort, and lavender to encourage the Night Hag to come to us." Her sly gaze rolls to me. "Are you interested?"

"There's no placenta in it, right?"

She blinks and sighs. "No, dear."

I take a deep breath. "I'm interested."

13

I tuck myself into bed in an empty guest room on the third floor of the house. A late-night summer breeze blows through the windows, carrying a rainy mist that soaks the sheer, pale-blue curtains. A wicked storm is brewing outside. Every so often, thunder crashes and lightning strikes. The tea kettle whistles downstairs. Moments later, the elderly woman stomps up the flight of stairs, the china of the teacup clanging against the saucer with each step.

Beneath a sheet, I'm in an old nightgown. My Charm School t-shirt and shorts are spinning in the wash. My floral headpiece is wrapped around a bedpost. A salt lamp in the corner illuminates the room. The walls are stark and as bare as my bedroom walls after a breakup. Cones of lavender, mugwort, and tobacco incense burn in a small iron pot, on a table beside the bed. Beside it, my crystal and pouch of herbs. The fragrant smoke swirls, ascending in the air and blanketing the room in a dreamy haze.

The wooden door whines as the old woman pushes her way through, shaky teacup and saucer in hand. With a heavy sigh, she perches at the edge of the bed and passes me the drink. The liquid is creamy and indigo-speckled.

I accept the steaming tea, bringing it to my nose; it's sweet smelling. Iris looks at me carefully, her eyes sparkling with interest. I raise an eyebrow, asking, "What's in it?"

"Oh a bit of everything, dear. A splash of milk, a spoonful of honey, a little sprinkle of nutmeg, and a pinch of cardamom—"

"What's the blue stuff?" I interrupt, taking a small sip.

"Poppy flower seeds."

I spit the drink, spraying the sheet atop me and her bare arm. "Why didn't you tell me you were drugging me with opium?" I drag my hand across my mouth.

She wipes her arm, shaking her head. "My goodness, my child. That is no way to thank a person for preparing you a lovely drink. No wonder you need Charm School. If you are so concerned, I will drink it." She snatches the teacup from me, taking a gulp.

"Okay! I'm sorry. I want it," I exclaim, reaching for the cup. Tea dribbles down her chin and onto her dress as I pull it back. "Just… why do you want to help me? I'm confused."

She wipes her chin, her eyes downcast. "Because I screwed up, royally, with my granddaughter, Winter. When I overheard you talking, I saw it as an opportunity to do good. Upon realizing who you were, I knew it was fate we had met. You're Rowan's granddaughter and were it not for the Segregation Curse of Old, you may have been my own."

She lifts her head and her eyes meet mine. She nods, her gaze darting to the teacup in my hand, and then back to me.

"But, what will we do if she comes to us?"

"We'll destroy her," she responds coolly, her expression grim.

I take a deep breath and nod before I throw it back in two gulps. It's nutty, sweet as honey, and earthy. A wave of drowsiness spills over me with the last drop. I lay my head back against the slim pillow.

The teacup falls from my hand. The last thing I remember is the sound of the china cup crashing against the wooden floor, and Iris's Arctic colored eyes as she draws close, chanting:

"Sleep and dream of things to come.
Do not awaken before the rising sun.
Oh, lovely lady of the night,
bless Summer's soul within your lunar light.
Silver dust and visions of Mars,
Let her wander in your realm of stars…"

I'm on a broomstick, barreling through the sky, barely able to hang onto the slick wooden handle. Rain showers me and clouds obscure my vision, making it dangerous to navigate. Ribbons colored in shades of a setting sun twirl in the air from below, slapping my feet. They coil around my legs, pulling me down as I desperately try to hang on. An icy breath whispers into my ear, "We did it."

I fall from the sky, my arms and legs spinning like a pinwheel. I land within a dark, twisted forest. The ribbons unfurl from my legs. As the dust clears I pick my aching body from the ground and brush myself off.

Above me is a canopy of gnarled branches, like an old witch's fingers, just waiting to pluck me up into the sky. A pastel green, humid morning mist spreads out low across the ground. I wade through it, awestruck. Iris Rose-Thorne falls from the sky, landing on her feet.

"Is this real?" I ask, pinching myself.

"You're dreamwalking, my darling," she replies matter-of-fact, dusting off her red ritual robe. "Woo, it's been a long time since I've worn this!"

"What?" I exclaim.

"Oh my goodness. Have you never heard of astral projection?" Iris asks. "What kind of witch are you?"

I roll my eyes. "But why are you here too?"

"Because I drank the potion!"

Behind her, the colored ribbons evaporate into the mist, giving way to large trees bursting from the ground with great thunder. I scream as roots emerge from compacted dirt. Baby ferns sprout, popping up around my feet. The trees crack as the branches expand and wind around one another. I gasp, my throat tightening with fear. Iris, on the other hand, doesn't appear bothered. She smiles at the changes around her, embracing the frightening forest run amok.

As the mist spreads, an ancient wood settles around us. Nature has run wild. The cheerful songs of birds become sinister. Squirrels scurry up trees; their claws scratch and scrape up the rough bark. Darkness falls upon us. The air tastes of sulphur. The morning mist is my only illumination, casting a creepy green glow upon the forest. Bright red poppy flowers burst from the ground. Iris picks a bunch and hands them to me.

The broomstick falls from the sky next, clattering to the ground. It disappears into the mist and is sucked into the void with a rumble. I shudder in terror. Iris Rose-Thorne cackles. My heart pounds against my ribs and my throat is tight. "Where am I? What is happening? How will this give me answers?"

I never receive a response. Something cracks above my head. I gaze up as a strange animal swings from a vine and lands on a thick branch. He scratches his underarms and stares at me peculiarly. Red hot coals drop from his eyes, leaving him with barren eye sockets. The coals disappear into the mist. There are several more of these odd creatures in the trees above, each with the same coal eyes. They flick their tongues and sparks roll from their mouths. I scream in terror, dropping the bundle of poppy flowers. I run directionless, deeper into the forest.

Iris calls me back, "Stop being such a baby!"

The atmosphere lightens considerably. The sickly green coloring transforms into a golden yellow from the sun's rays. With each step, something squishes beneath my feet. The smell of fungus replaces the sulphur. The scary forest creatures are absent, but something still isn't right. The scene is familiar, but I can't quite place it. Feeling sick, I brace myself against a tree with my hand. I lean over and throw up. A puddle of indigo-colored cream pools at the base of an oak tree. Sweat pours from my head in droplets as I wipe my mouth with the back of my hand.

The golden mist clears, revealing groupings of wild mushrooms. My head swirls. I slowly sit, perching on an erupted root of a large pine. *Was I poisoned by the poppy flowers?* I wonder as I hug my knees to my chest. I want to wake up. A soft melodic giggle stirs my attention.

"Dahlia?" I gaze around, searching for her.

It isn't Dahlia, instead, it's a blue lady, perched on a stump. That's when I recognize the scene—I'm within one of River's watercolor paintings.

I attempt to stand, but the ground feels unsteady below my feet. My eyes cross. My ears ring sharply. I stumble forward, reaching for the trees to guide me. Small mushroom caps are smashed below my feet. They squish between my toes and ooze slime onto my skin. Desperate for release from this terrible place, I cry in frustration. I'm trapped within his technicolor world—the world I once wished to be part of, but definitely not like this. I bawl my eyes out, falling into a pile of soft mushrooms.

"Summer?"

I sit up promptly, sniffling. "What did you do to me?" I ask Iris, blinking back my tears.

"We are dreamwalking, lovely... Our astral bodies have left our physical bodies," she explains. "Why are you crying?" Iris crouches to the ground before me, offering me her hand. I take it and she lifts me up. The crushed stems and caps of mushrooms fall from me. A glittering golden residue colors my skin, smelling of fungus and rot.

"Oh, Gods," I complain. "That smell."

"Let's explore, dear. You won't find your answers lying in a pile of mushrooms." She shakes her head, adding, "It's a good thing I'm here."

I follow her through the strange gold-tinted forest, passing over large collections of mushrooms that burst and crumble beneath our feet. We approach a massive oak tree with a large knothole. She stops before it. I shoot her a perplexed look.

"What are you doing?" I ask. "Why have we stopped?"

"Follow me," she says, easily climbing into the knothole. I gasp, as the oak tree shakes its branches, sending an avalanche of acorns onto me. They pelt my head and my arms. I scream as I'm showered by hard-shelled nuts. "Come!" she calls from somewhere within the tree.

Cautiously, I peer into the tree. With a strong tug of my arm by Iris, I fall into the open cavity of the oak.

It's surprisingly spacious; large enough to fit us both with a little wiggle room. An affectionate baby squirrel scurries over my leg and crawls onto my shoulder, nuzzling my neck. My stomach does somersaults. I dig my nails into layers of decomposing bark and leaves. I gaze above. The fiery eyes of mysterious creatures lurking in the shadows stare down upon us. I recognize the scene as another painting of River's.

Nope. I can't.

"I can't breathe in here," I pant. "There's not enough air. I need to wake up." I pull my upper body out from the tree when Iris's hands tug on my nightgown. She pulls me back inside by my hips. I fall against her.

"It's a dream," the elderly woman says in my ear. "Just relax. I'm here. It's okay." She nibbles her fingernail and peers out the knothole.

My head rolls back as I slip into darkness. Iris clutches my shoulders, digging her nails into my collarbones. I startle awake.

"Oh my Gods. I just had the strangest dream." I straighten my back, rubbing my eyes as I scoot backward. My spine slams into a hard, impenetrable surface. I peer over my shoulder; It's the inner wall of the tree.

I close my eyes in disbelief as clarity comes. "I'm still inside this damn tree. This is really happening."

Iris releases my shoulders. She chuckles, her icy-colored eyes sparkle with amusement. "Come," she says, scooting aside. She brushes aside several inches of rotten leaves and dirt, revealing a trap door in the ground. She lifts the door by the vine of a creeping plant and steps down onto a braided vine ladder. "Follow me," she calls from the void.

I stare in stunned silence before scrambling down myself.

The braided vine ladder leads to another extraordinary land. The ground is blanketed with crisp oak leaves. The air smells of wood and spice.

A torchlight ahead illuminates an acorn home, the size of one of our cabins. My eyes round at the sight, impressed, yet cautious. I tiptoe across white round mushrooms that spring back with each step. The arched entryway door is stained burgundy. The windows are complete with window-boxes of teeming mushrooms. Iris turns the doorknob, but it doesn't budge.

"Does someone live here?" I peer into a window.

"How should I know, dear?" She adjusts her red ritual robe and uses more force opening the door. It pops open.

"Then why are we here?" I ask, following her inside. I stop short.

Aspen is asleep, inside the hollowed cavity of an oak tree. Lobed leaves stitched together with scaly bark, like a forest patchwork quilt, covers him. He's tucked inside the hollowed tree. His arms are crossed over his chest, and he appears peaceful.

"What is this?" I whisper.

"Is this the young man you were with earlier?" she asks, tapping her chin.

I nod, swallowing hard. "Why is he here?"

"I don't know, my dearest. He may be a symbol of something. Sometimes the people we see in our dreams are merely symbolic. What does he represent to you?"

"Security," I answer. "He's my best friend."

"Hmm, interesting that your security symbol is sleeping. Perhaps you need to take action and stop being so ignorant of an important matter related to either your physical, emotional, or spiritual security."

I pace the cabin, passing my sleeping friend in his oak tree coffin. A wispy string of smoke connected to my body like an umbilical cord trails out the window. I pass my hand through the smoke. "What's this?"

"The link between your physical and astral body." Iris gestures above me.

My chin to my shoulder, I spin around. "Why have I only noticed it now?"

"Oh wow, you just made your cord spin." She claps, cackling.

"Where's yours?" As I ask, it materializes before me. "Wait… what's that smell?" Dark smoke seeps through a crack in the window; it smells of mugwort, lavender, and tobacco.

"She's here." Her eyes widen in alarm.

Smoke fills the cabin. We elbow each other as we topple out the arched door, falling down the rickety steps. A shadow falls over us. I roll over; terror engulfs me. The Night Hag stands over me, her black dress soaked and tattered and cinnamon-brown hair windblown. Her face is blurred like an out-of-focus photograph. She holds a battered broomstick.

I pinch my arm. This can't be real. The Night Hag that haunts my dreams stands before me. An imposing figure of my nightmares, I can hardly believe my eyes. A gray smoky fog churns around her feet. She throws her head back and laughs a wicked cackle.

"Finally, we meet," she says coolly.

I crawl backward, across springy mushrooms. Fungus gets under my long fingernails. Slime covers my palms. With the witch's attention on me, Iris uses the opportunity to escape. She runs across the mushrooms. So much for destroying the Night Hag. I've never felt so betrayed before in my life. I swallow against the fear in my throat.

Moments later, Iris returns, rounding the acorn home with a large stick. She holds it like a baseball bat, creeping up behind the Night Hag. As she approaches, a mushroom gives under her foot with a loud pop. The witch whirls around. Iris swings the stick, but it's too late. I scream.

The cursed witch digs her hand into a pocket of her tattered dress and says, "This is not the place for you. Be out of my sight." She tosses a handful of black sea salt at her.

Iris Rose-Thorne is reduced to a pile of ash. Her stick falls beside her. I scream.

The witch returns her attention to me. She makes motions of dusting her hands. I throw up my palms in surrender. "Please, just leave me alone. I'm sorry I summoned you."

She shrinks back, her hand to her heart. Tears drip from her blurry face. "My whole life, I've worked for you kids. I love you kids. Everything I do, I do for you kids…"

I blink. "Huh?"

"Your friend is in trouble," she replies, her voice cracking with emotion.

"Yeah, I see that," I say, angrily gesturing to the pile of ash.

The witch waves her hand. "Oh, she's fine. She isn't the one in trouble."

I pinch myself as hard as I can. My nails cut into my forearm. Blue blood seeps from my cut skin. "This is all just a nightmare," I tell myself. "Astral projection isn't real and old ladies with weird tea are never to be trusted."

The woman dissipates into a smoky haze, leaving me with more questions than answers. Moments later, I wake up in a strange bed, the sun shining in my face. A doorbell rings urgently.

14

"Ow, ouch," I complain, as Spring Widow-Tears drags me out of Iris's house by my ear.

"What were you thinking?" she exclaims as we reach the bottom of the steps. She releases me, throwing up her hands in vexation as she stomps toward the edge of the woods.

Sweat rolls down my back and chest. My head aches and my mouth is dry, but at least I'm wearing freshly laundered clothes. I clear my throat, calling ahead, "I had permission. You didn't have to *save* me." I weave around charred trees, stepping over pine saplings. "Where's your broom?" I rasp, rubbing the base of my throat.

Spring spins around. "You had approval from who?" She furrows her brow and props her hand on her hip.

"Headmistress Starwort," I croak out.

She rolls her eyes and walks ahead. "C'mon, I'm not stupid," she says. "I don't have a broom. We're walking. Now, hurry. No one knows we're gone." She moves quickly around thorny rugosa bushes and steps over an old stone wall, entering the dense forest.

Iris calls from behind us, "Goodbye, my dear and good luck!"

I spin around. "Will you please tell my camp counselor that I had permission to leave?"

Iris lowers her eyes, guiltily. She steps forward. "I may have made that up," she says with a grimace.

"What?" I exclaim. "But I saw you!"

"I didn't ask for her permission. I simply informed her that I'd be happy to sew uniforms for her students, but she wasn't interested in my services."

My jaw drops. "But... she looked at me. I saw her look at me!"

"Only because I mentioned how poorly constructed yours was."

"C'mon," Spring says, pulling me along.

Iris hollers behind me, "I was only trying to help!"

Tears prick the back of my eyes, threatening to fall. We walk for some distance in silence.

"Your buddy Rugosa told me you were last with Iris," she says eventually. "Ran into him looking for food in the kitchen."

"Rat," I respond, half-jokingly. I step over the rotting wood of a fallen branch; its crevices are teeming with pale, soft-bodied insects. My stomach turns.

"Can I just ask you something?" she asks cautiously.

"Mh hm," I respond, swallowing the acid welling in my throat.

"Why'd you leave with a crazy old bat like Iris?"

I clear my throat. "Long story, but she said she knew my parents and even had a picture from the day I was born. She got my attention because she mentioned something about messages in dreams and spirit guides—" I touch my head, realizing that my headpiece is missing. Spinning around, I say, "Oh no! Your gift! I have to go back." As I retrace our path, a hand clamps down on my arm.

"No! Are you crazy? There are so many reasons why you should *not* do that. You could risk not graduating on time for starters," Spring says, releasing her grip as I reluctantly turn back.

"I thought I *had* permission," I reiterate, frustrated. I dig into my pocket, confirming my crystal and pouch of herbs are on me.

"Don't worry about the flowered headpiece. I can make you another. We need to get you back." She marches off ahead of me, stomping through the forest easily with thick-soled leather boots.

I'm too tired to argue back.

Spring ushers me into the kitchen hall, only minutes late for breakfast prep. The artificial light is particularly blinding this morning; I squint as I open the door where we part company. Fern and Azalea are already inside prepping for breakfast.

"I'm not sure how this contributes to our survival skills," huffs Fern as she passes through the kitchen. "I don't think I'll ever be in the middle of the woods with a random carton of eggs, a package of bacon, and a paper freakin' bag." She wings a package of brown bags on the countertop, sending it skittering toward the sink.

Azalea snorts as she laughs. "But, if you are, now you'll know." She startles, shrieking, as the door closes behind me, echoing throughout the room. Azalea spins in my direction, her dark blue eyes stormy with anger. "Where were you?" she asks, raising an inquisitive brow. "Drunk in a bush somewhere?"

"More like stoned on weird tea in a strange bed," I respond tiredly, retrieving a dingy-looking apron from a hook on the wall. I tie it around my back. "Can we like, not yell today?" I ask, grimacing in pain.

"You're so weird," Fern says, her angular face twisted with confusion. She gestures to the recipe tacked up on the wall. "Campfire eggs in a bag this morning."

I wash my hands and crane my neck to read the instructions. I dry my hands on my apron and cut greasy strips of bacon, lining the bottoms of the brown paper bags. Together, we work on an assembly line. I pass each bacon-lined paper sack to Azalea, who cracks two eggs into each bacon nest, then sets it on a tray.

"So. Tired," Fern says. "I feel like I'm missing a huge chunk of my evening. Like, right around the firewalk. I don't remember much after that. I totally blacked out last night and woke up in the wrong bunk. Drank way too much... What's wrong?" she asks me, her brow furrowed.

"Nothing," I squeak, shaking my head, unwilling to tell her about my night. Fern is the most energetic person I know. She reminds me of the reincarnation of Tinkerbell. I'm surprised to learn she's hungover. I didn't know she drank, but I haven't been paying much attention.

"Wanna whistle while we work?" Azalea asks in a sarcastic tone. She cracks an egg into the next bacon-lined bag. "Like a chain gang song," she adds with a snort.

"Otherworld no. I'm off to find stupid sticks for everyone," Fern announces to the room. She exits the kitchen hall.

"What is she doing?" I ask.

Azalea snaps her head to the side, her gaze on Fern's retreating back. "She's gettin' sticks for the campfire eggs. We gotta puncture holes through the tops to hold the bags over the campfire."

"Oh." I run the tap to wash my greasy hands. Azalea has quite a few bags left to complete. She cracks an egg, cursing when an eggshell falls in.

"You need help cracking eggs?" I ask, scratching my chin.

"Um, no." She scoffs, dumping the egg liquid off the bacon into the sink. She cracks another egg against the counter and splits it carefully over the bag.

"Azalea, can I ask you something?" The brown paper rustles as I fold the tops of the finished bags.

"Depends." She raises an eyebrow as she folds the top of her last paper bag and sets it on the large meal tray.

"Do you believe in dreamwalking?"

"Huh?" She tosses her cinnamon colored hair back.

"Like, astral dreams."

"I dunno. I guess," Azalea says flippantly with a shrug. She retrieves the kitchen broom, sweeping up broken eggshells and debris from the corners of the room.

"But do you think we can travel in our dreams? Or that our dreams are messages?"

"Is this about you screaming in your sleep? Don't you have someone else you can talk to about this? Like a counselor? You sound like a crazy chick." Azalea leans the broom against the wall, bumping her shoulder into mine as she passes. "Grab the meal tray. I hear Fern outside." She steps ahead and holds the door.

I blink, taken back momentarily. "Did you just do that on purpose?" I rub my upper arm.

"Do what?" she asks with a deceptive smile.

"You bumped me. Why is everyone being so damn rude to me? Can't you all just get over it?" I exclaim.

"Why don't you cast another spell to manipulate our feelings? Hmm? Because that's what you do, right?" Azalea spins around, heading for the door.

Hurt, I do my best to shake it off and gather the tray in my arms. We exit the kitchen and find Fern outside, sharpening the ends of sticks with a hunting knife.

Azalea and I puncture the tops of the bags with the sharp sticks. We pass them out to everyone as they emerge from their cabins and line up for their breakfasts. With Oak Wormwood overlooking, we hold our bags several inches above the flames of the campfire, careful not to burn the paper bottoms.

The bacon sizzles and pops. The greasy layer acts as a skillet for the eggs. I impatiently check my sack, until finally, my breakfast is ready. Azalea passes out utensils and we eat directly out of our paper bags. It's much better than the Blueberry Bake, even with the occasional eggshell.

"Oh my Gods. Is there glass in this?" Petal asks to my amusement.

Dahlia hand-feeds River a slice of bacon further down the table. It isn't enough to turn me off from my food, but it's close. Amaranth sits alone, barely touching her eggs. Her thick black hair covers her face like a velvet curtain. She pushes her breakfast around inside the bag with her fork but doesn't raise her utensil to her mouth. When the wind blows, her hair lifts, exposing a fresh cropping of acne across her cheek and chin. She rests her head on the table.

Fern snaps back to life once she begins to eat. After a few forkfuls, she has the energy of a triple espresso. She's animated, swinging her arms around as she talks about what she remembers from last night. Her voice strengthens and she's practically shouting at Petal, who looks exhausted.

"Does someone have a lithium for this chick?" Petal asks, her eyes hooded and heavy.

Rugosa stumbles out of the cabin, his clothing in disarray. He plods toward me, snatching a paper sack from the table. He sits beside me with a loud *oof* and looks at me through a squinted eye. "Never drinking again."

"You say that literally every time," I respond. "I thought you already ate?"

"That was my pre-breakfast," he responds, opening the bag.

"Is Aspen still asleep?"

"Um, no." He stabs his eggs with a fork, shoveling them into his mouth at mock speed. "Wasn't he with you last night? When he dumped me in my bunk, he said he was goin' back to talk to you. Haven't seen him since—hey!"

I take his fork from him, demanding, "What'd you just say?"

15

After searching the grounds, I knock on the volunteers' dorm room, my fist thumping against the door urgently. Rugosa rests his icy palm over my fist, complaining about the loud sound and his piercing headache. I argue that my head feels worse, and we spar in a verbal debate over what's worse, poppyseed flower tea hangover or alcohol. The door swings open mid-argument.

"What on earth are you two carrying on about?" Spring asks with a yawn, rubbing her eyes and squinting against the light in the hallway. She steps into the hall, closing the door softly behind her. Her golden hair is in disarray, and she's wearing a sleeveless pink top with unicorn patterned pajama bottoms. She must have fallen back asleep after we parted this morning.

Before I can alert our camp counselor to our missing friend, Rugosa blurts out, "This dumbass drank tea from that fallen High Priestess. She's lucky if she ain't infertile or worse."

I shift my gaze on him, narrowing my eyes. The roots of my hair spark with small jolts of electricity, and I feel the familiar prickling across my scalp as my agitation grows.

"Why would you bring that up?" I shriek. The rotten scent of sulphur fragrances the narrow hallway.

"Wait…" Spring interrupts, holding up a palm. "You drank *tea* from *Iris*, Summer?"

I blink, swallowing hard as I nod.

Spring's posture straightens and her eyes round with alertness. "Why would you do that? Especially after what happened with her own granddaughter?" She presses her palm against my forehead. "Do you feel alright?"

"I feel fine," I snap, my impatience brewing like lava from a volcano. "It's Aspen. He's missing."

"Oh… Gods, him too? I'm sure he's fine," Spring says, gently laying her hand on my shoulder. "You all drank a little bit, right? I'm sure he's around, sleeping it off. But we better go find him before Headmistress Starwort arrives." She releases me from her grip, adding, "I'm more concerned about you. Are you *sure* you're feeling okay?"

"I'm only worried about my friend. I don't want him to get in trouble… I promise I'm fine." I blink, wondering if I *was* poisoned. My head hurts and my memory is scattered. The dream I had was out of this world—of enchanted forests, an acorn home, and tethers that suspend you between the astral and physical realms. "Iris isn't that bad," I insist, more to myself than her.

"Even though she lied to you about having permission to leave?" Her golden eyebrows draw together as she shakes her head. "I'm a little concerned about your judgement, Summer."

"Same," Rugosa adds smartly. I roll my eyes and push him; he barely nudges an inch.

Spring retreats into her room, returning moments later wearing boots. She closes the door behind her and walks ahead of us, calling behind her, "You comin', or what?"

Rugosa and I share a look, then follow her.

We walk the trails again, combing the campground for Aspen, calling his name with only our echoes responding. Rugosa—an earth witch with ties to the terrestrial north pole—sweats ice. He isn't fully acclimated to Springfield, having only been here for a year. He perspires in frozen droplets. With each step down the narrow trail, an icicle falls from his body, crashing to the forest floor. Behind him, I step over the frozen shards, mindful of my blistered and callousing feet.

The forest feels like a steam bath from last night's rain; the heat and humidity oppressive and thick. A throbbing behind my eyes adds to my misery, but the urgency to find my friend drives me forward. I need to drag him out of whatever bush he fell asleep in, back to his cabin before the headmistress arrives and expels him.

Rugosa stops abruptly, and I slam into his frozen solid back, much like I did on the last day of school. "I'm ready to call it quits," he says, sweeping frozen drops of sweat from his scalp to ground with the back of his hand. The tiny ice fragments melt as they hit the earth.

I frown when Spring agrees. "I'm gonna keep looking for him—" I say, before a voice from behind startles me.

"You're going to keep looking for who?" Headmistress Starwort asks. We simultaneously turn to face her, gasping in unison. She leans against her broomstick, her silver hair tousled and windblown from her recent flight. Her lips are set in a thin line, eyes narrow.

"Nobody," I squeak, panic-stricken.

"It's okay, Summer," Spring says, stepping around us on the trail, closing the distance between herself and Headmistress Starwort. She shields us from the angry woman, her small shoulders squared, and her boots firmly planted into the forest floor. Her nature is protective, like that of a mother hen. She isn't much older than us, but she safeguards us like we are her own—even Rugosa, who towers over her by a good foot. My teeth chatter nervously in my mouth.

"Good morning Headmistress Starwort. I'm surprised to see you here so early," Spring remarks. "We're looking for Aspen."

"Aspen's not here?" Headmistress Starwort asks Spring. She hardens her stare. Her angry, absinthe-colored gaze sweeps over the three of us.

"I'm sure he's here, around the woods somewhere. But he wasn't in his bunk this morning. They came to my room concerned."

She scoffs, incredulous. "And I am being made aware of this only now, because?"

"Because we didn't want to alarm you, and I hadn't realized you already flew in. Most of the kids drank at the Solar Solstice. Again, I assume he's around, somewhere," Spring replies, gesturing to the woods.

"Yes, well this is rather unfortunate. I'd like to speak to you alone, Counselor Spring." Headmistress Starwort directs her attention beyond Spring, to Rugosa and me, fixing us within her stern glare. "Run along now." Her voice deepens, "We'll handle this."

We don't need to be told twice. We scatter off, like frightened pigeons.

"I'm sure he's fine," Rugosa says, on our way back to the cabins. "Probably sleeping it off somewhere."

"Uh, he won't be fine when he's expelled from Charm School and is unable to graduate on time," I retort.

Rugosa shrugs, walking ahead of me. Over his shoulder, he remarks, "Well maybe you should've kept your mouth shut."

I grimace, fighting the urge to cry and realizing the enormity of our mistake. I only wanted to find my best friend. I never considered we could be discovered by Headmistress Starwort in the process. Between that and the way I treated him last night, I hope I haven't lost his friendship for good. Without him, I will feel truly alone.

Later that morning after a lesson on herbalism and green magic—which included a heated debate on whether or not plants have souls and are capable of feeling pain, using a depressing case study about a barley plant that screamed when its roots were plunged in hot water—the humidity breaks as a rainstorm rolls through Elwood.

Water runs off branches, dripping off the tips of vibrant green maple leaves. Rain pelts the cabin rooftop and water trickles from the ceiling, collecting in a tin bucket in the middle of the floor. A fine spray blows through the bug-screen windows.

Without Sunna's sun, the Wormwoods are left feeling down. I'm hungry for the light. My reserves are low, and I'm feeling the familiar darkness that drags me down. It's no wonder my mother uses herbs to deal with being stuck inside all the time.

The Devil-Claw water witches use the stormy weather to their advantage. Dahlia and Azalea strip off their clothing and throw on their bathing suits before dashing outside, where they dance under stormy clouds and are soaked quickly by the rain. I watch them from the window as they spin around in circles, praising Tefnut, the Goddess of rain and dew. It gives me an idea; I need to get out of this dark cabin before I'm completely miserable.

I change and sprint outside in my bikini, rounding the cabin for the lake behind the thicket of trees. I'm carrying a bottle of Nature-friendly liquid soap, made with Castile, coconut oil, and honey. Soft, muddy earth squishes beneath my calloused feet and between my toes. I toss my belongings at the edge of the wet, sandy shore beside a discarded tin pail. Stepping cautiously into the lake, I wade through the water.

I have so much to tell Aspen about last night—my crazy dreamwalking episode that included him, the poppy flower tea, and the picture Iris had of me and my parents. Most of all, I hope he's okay. He was hitting the mead a little hard last night. I hope he returns soon.

I bend my knees, sinking down until the lake water is at shoulder level. I unwind my braids, running my fingers through my hair to release the tension. The cool water invigorates me, pulling me from my groggy, post-poppyseed tea mental state, despite the clouds above threatening to darken my mood.

I dip under the greenish-colored water, pulling handfuls of grit from the sandy floor. I emerge and drag the sand across my filthy skin, exfoliating layers of surface dirt before I use the body wash.

Once I'm scrubbed, I step out of the water and retrieve the tin pail someone left behind. I dip it into the lake, filling it to the brim. I'm careful not to let any water slosh from the bucket as I tiptoe behind a copse of wiry trees with my bodywash. I keep a careful eye out, ensuring nobody is about to pop out around the corner.

I set the bucket down and quickly strip out of my bathing suit, hanging my bikini over a wet branch. The rain washes over me as I pour the bodywash into my hand, lathering up my hair and body with the silky, sudsy mixture. As I pour the bucket of lake water over my head, the familiar shriek of an animal horn screeches through the forest. I groan and slip back into my bikini.

I return to the girls' cabin, freshly scrubbed by earth and washed by rain. Azalea and Hyacinth are playing tug-of-war with the last available umbrella. I move about the room, digging a clean towel and clothing from the shared dresser. The girls bicker and argue over the umbrella.

"Azalea, you're a Devil-Claw. Why does a water witch need an umbrella?" I ask, pulling clean grass-stained khaki shorts up over my hips.

"Look at my hair," she sputters, releasing the umbrella. "I just fixed it. Do you have any idea what weather does to my waves? They poof out!"

Hyacinth tucks the umbrella under her arm, bolting out the door. Azalea pursues her, cursing up a storm. As Hyacinth opens the umbrella it slips from her hands, snapping backward and thwapping Azalea in the face.

"Ouch," I say from inside the room, overseeing it.

I'm running out of time to get to the afternoon lesson. We have about fifteen minutes to be in our seats once the animal horn sounds. I hang my towel to dry over the bed frame and rifle through the dresser drawer for a tub of coconut oil for my hair.

After locating it, I dip my fingers into the pot. The oil is more liquid than solid on account of the heat. I rub my hands together before applying it. On my way to the lesson area, I braid my hair. It feels so good to be clean again. I inhale the relaxing scents of Castile and wet earth. All the while, I'm hoping—and expecting—to see Aspen in the afternoon class.

I'm disappointed when I come around the bend of the trail; the sitting rock beside Rugosa is empty and Aspen is nowhere in sight.

"Any news?" I whisper to Rugosa, taking the rain-soaked stone beside him. I drop my book bag on the muddy ground.

Headmistress Starwort begins her lesson on witch etiquette. She opens with the importance of making a good first impression.

"They think he left," he says from behind his hand, his gaze trained on the Headmistress. "Wart said, and I quote, 'he's probably lying on a beach somewhere, drinking a green witch herbal tea.'"

"Bull-ogna," I say, cleaning up my crude language when I catch the attention of the schoolmistress. Her green eyes darken as they narrow on Rugosa and me.

"Summer are you volunteering?" Mistress Aster asks from the edge of the group. She lifts a spellbook from the table and calls me forward.

I rise, stepping forward. "I'm sorry. I wasn't paying attention," I admit bowing my head, accepting the heavy spellbook.

"Return to your seat, balancing the book on your head," Headmistress Starwort instructs sternly.

My head snaps up and I stare at her, speechless a moment. "Are you punishing me for not paying attention?" I ask aghast, my mouth gaping open.

She rolls her eyes, asking the Goddess for patience. "*If* you were paying attention, my dear, you would know you aren't being reprimanded at all. We are only asking you to demonstrate your straight back. First impressions are crucial, and one mustn't slouch. Now, go on. Walk for us."

"Oh," I grumble, my face as hot as fire. I place the book on my head, looking to Rugosa to share a look, only he's absorbed in himself, picking at his nails. Aspen would have fully appreciated this. With him, I can communicate through only a glance and he gets it. Words aren't always necessary. We've shared unspoken, private moments through our eyes over the years across classrooms and within a crowded gathering. I'm missing my best friend terribly, and I feel awful for the way I treated him last night.

I should have asked for humility when I delivered the firewood into that cauldron, instead of restful sleep.

Where are you, Aspen? I wonder, for the millionth time.

I frown as I take cautious steps forward, weaving through students perched on rocks. I balance the rocking spellbook on my head.

Maybe he is on a beach somewhere, enjoying a green witch herbal tea. I didn't handle his rejection well. I was so rude to him. On top of that, he had to babysit drunkity-drunk Rugosa. He probably got on his beloved broom, had a little taste of freedom and split.

I really did burn my last bridge. As I come to this depressing realization, the leather-bound spellbook clatters to the forest floor.

Later that evening, the girls' cabin door swings open suddenly, disturbing me from my read. Amaranth Wormwood skips into the cabin. She's wearing a red Charm School uniform. A cherry popsicle in her mouth stains her lips clown-red. Her face is covered in some kind of white paste that is several shades lighter than her caramel-colored complexion. She slides into her bunk beside mine and pulls the popsicle out of her mouth with a loud pop. "Why so blue, bugaboo?" she asks with a peppiness that I'm not in the mood for.

I mark the page in my book and set it aside, grumbling, "What's the look you're trying to accomplish, here, Amaranth? Bozo the witch?"

She hisses playfully, pawing the air. Her popsicle drips red juice on her knee. "Wow. You're a feisty one today. What's crawled up your butt?"

I reach across, touching her chalky face. She swats me away. "*What* is this?" I ask, rubbing my fingers together. I brush the remnants off on my shorts.

"Flour and water," she replies, her nose in the air. I shake my head.

Fern Widow-Tears steps into the cabin and yanks her blanket off her bed with a strong tug. She bundles it into her arms, asking, "Are you two sleeping outside tonight? A bunch of us are." She crouches down beside her bunk, her violet eyes aglow from lanterns inside the cabin. She opens the drawer of the end table, rifling through it with determination. "Dammit. Do either of you have any herbal bug spray? Bugs are brutal."

"No, to sleeping outside tonight. Yes, to bug spray," I say, digging through my backpack and tossing her the bottle once I find it.

She thanks me and directs her attention on Amaranth. "What about you?" Her forehead furrows.

"Nah, I'm staying here," Amaranth says after pulling the popsicle out of her mouth.

"Suit yourselves, then," Fern says, spraying herself liberally with a concoction of steeped basil in water, lavender and lemongrass oil, witch hazel, and vodka. "Think fast!" She tosses it back to me and I duck; it lands on the floor and rolls into the closet. She giggles as she exits, slamming the door behind her.

"Rude," I say with a scowl. I retrieve the bug spray and tuck it back into my backpack. "You don't have to stay, Amaranth. I was just going to read."

"Oh, don't do that!" she whines. "That's so boring," she adds with a pout.

"Not if you're reading the right book." I return to my bed in the corner of the room and lean against the wall. Amaranth tosses her popsicle stick in the trash.

I read all of two sentences before Amaranth interrupts me.

"What's that one about?"

"It's a friends-to-lovers romance," I respond tightly. "The tagline is cute—love is friendship, caught on fire. This girl was searching for love in all the wrong places. Turns out, he was beside her all along. It's sweet don't you—"

I'm interrupted by Amaranth pretending to snore. I lift my gaze from the page to glare at her.

"Maybe that's your problem," she says, raising her head from her pillow. "You read these kissing books and expect too much."

I roll my eyes and scoot out of my bunk. "Do not."

"You're too thirsty."

"Amaranth, could you just stop? I'm not thirsty. Why don't you want to sleep outside with the rest of everyone?"

"I'm not sleeping with the bugs," she responds, her face twisted with revulsion.

"There's just as many in here," I point out, slapping a mosquito on my arm. Amaranth is quiet for a moment. I finish the paragraph of the book I'm reading when she disturbs me again.

"Why don't *you* want to sleep outside? Don't tell me because of smoochy-face River and duckface Dahlia." She puckers her lips, making kissy sounds. "Are you gonna press your nose in a book *all* summer and be dull?"

I sigh, placing the bookmark. I click off the flashlight. The lantern between our beds glows. "I just can't deal with it tonight is all."

"What's so different about tonight?"

"I made an ass out of myself at the Solar Solstice party."

"What happened?" she sits up and tucks her legs beneath her.

"I kissed a guy...and he didn't kiss me back."

"Damn." A muscle in her jaw twitches.

"I know! And now he's gone. Nobody knows where he went. So, what do I do now?" I hide my face in my hands, grateful for the dim lighting when I emerge flushed.

"Wait." She giggles, bringing her hand to her face. "Are you talking about...*Aspen*?" she exclaims, tossing her pillow at me.

"Just shut up."

"Oh! My! Gods!" Amaranth leaps from her bunk, diving on mine. She perches herself at the edge of my bed. "Why doesn't someone call his parents?" she asks.

"His guardian is an eighty-year-old bitty who has seven other kids in her home. The woman is senile and doesn't know him from her others. He's just a paycheck."

"Oh. So, you really kissed him?" Her eyes sparkle with amusement.

"I think it was the mead. I dunno. He gave me this beautiful gift. Hold on..." I leap off the bed and crouch to the floor, reaching under the bunk. Something sharp grazes my hand. I pull the crystal out, showing Amaranth.

"Why you got that dusty thing under your bed?" She wrinkles her nose.

I sigh, losing my patience. "It's for nightmares. The visits from the Night Hag really shook me up." I shake my head and slide it back under my bunk. I rise and plop down onto the thin mattress, grabbing my pillow. I open the case. "He gave me these herbs too... So, what do you think? Do you think he left because I kissed him? I assumed he was drunk somewhere, but now I'm genuinely worried he's left."

Amaranth peers into the pillowcase, closes her jaw and blinks. "I've never had that problem. I'd even bet boys would pay to kiss me. One time—"

"Ugh, whatever." I fluff the pillow and set it behind me, turning to the wall. "Goodnight," I snap. She yammers on about an incident at a Samhain party.

I don't even know why I bother with her sometimes.

I blink rain out of my eyes as I stir awake, sore and stiff. Thick bark scrapes my leg as I struggle to move. Warm fluid trickles down my calf. I'm stuck in the crook of two branches.

Bullfrogs drone from below. A weak tree limb snaps, landing several seconds later with a splash. I crane my neck, confirming that I am, indeed, really freakin' high up.

Dandelion mead churns in the pit of my belly, threatening to erupt. Stunned, I try to make sense of where I am and how I got here, to begin with...

"Wake up! Wake up!" Amaranth pulls me by my wrists, dragging me out of the dark closet. I slide across the unforgiving hardwood floor on my butt, the edges of uniforms brushing across my face. "Are you alright?" she asks, releasing my wrists and pushing the tin pail of collected rain water out of the way. She crouches on the floor, her hands on her hips.

I gaze around the dim room, swiping my unruly hair from my eyes. Small feathers float in the air. Pillows are strewn about. My bedding is rolled up, pushed to the wall. The small trash can is overturned; tissues and popsicle sticks litter the ground. A clean uniform is in a heap in my lap. Something is in my hand; I release the wire hanger from my clammy grip and it clatters to the wooden floor.

"I can't live like this," I say, pulling my fingers through my tangled hair. "These nightmares have to stop. It must be this place. I think I need to go home."

"I can't live like this either," Amaranth says, speaking over me. "I thought you said those crystals and herbs warded off the Night Hag? Where'd he get 'em? The dollar store?"

"You actually believe in the Night Hag?" I ask, feeling a small glimmer of hope.

"Yeah," she replies, shrugging her shoulders. "You're definitely hag-ridden. Some wanna call it sleep paralysis, but we know what's really up." Amaranth taps her foot, her eyes darting around the room. "You know you're gonna be cleaning this all up, right?"

I glare at her. Leave it to her to have little sensitivity and even less tact. I have no idea why Amaranth is so popular other than her pretty face—although it's not looking so great caked in flour.

I tidy the cabin, dump the rain bucket outside, pick up sticky popsicle sticks, and straighten the bedding. Amaranth complains about everyone while she thumbs through a beauty magazine.

"And don't get me started on Petal," Amaranth says, pausing only to take a breath before rattling off the top ten things she dislikes about one of her closest friends. "One, she doesn't always shower." She pinches her nose. "Two, she thinks she's like, so pretty. I mean, she's got a great body, but that face… Eh. Three, her fire magic is crap. Four, she always talks about herself! Like, nobody is *that* interesting. Five, she could probably win a gold medal in the Olympics for complaining—"

"You could take the silver," I grumble under my breath.

"What?"

"Nothing. Forget it," I reply, over it.

"Six, her nails are always chipped. Seven, her eyebrows are weird. Eight, she eats like an elephant yet gains no weight.

I bet she has an eating disorder; like bulimia, or whatever. Nine, she can't keep a secret. Ten, she's always in love with random celebrities—"

"Oh my Gods, Amaranth! If you dislike Petal and everyone else so much, why do you hang out with them?" I ask, exhausted, as I slide into my bunk.

She crosses her arms, her cherry popsicle stained lips pressed in a thin line. For once she has nothing to say, but I never expected an answer.

"Goodnight, Amaranth." I roll over, soon falling back to sleep.

When I awaken, I'm alone in the cabin. The scent of campfire smoke wafts through the bug screen windows. A conversation between Petal and Azalea outside is followed by giggles. I quickly change into a Charm School tee-shirt and shorts and dash out to use the bathroom.

The showers roar inside the bathroom. I step into a stall, locking the door behind me. As I'm spooling toilet paper from the roll, my name is mentioned.

"—Summer is so lame. First, she puts a love spell on *my* boyfriend, and then she's making out with Aspen! That's disgusting. What kind of *freak* kisses their brother?" Dahlia asks over the roar of the water.

My cheeks flame. My heart drops into my stomach. I shouldn't have trusted Amaranth! If she talks badly about her closest friends, of course, she's gonna speak about me too. What on earth was I thinking?

"I was biting my lip, girl," Amaranth shouts back with a cackle. "When she told me, I just about died."

Hyacinth joins the conversation, adding, "Yeah, but guys c'mon. Like, it's her foster brother, or *was*. Not blood or anything."

The girls dismiss Hyacinth as I finish up and duck out of the stall quietly. I quickly soap my hands at the sink. As water trickles from the faucet, tears fall down my cheeks.

"Someone should look into his disappearance. I'd bet my bejeweled magenta broomstick that his rejection stirred a violent response from her," Dahlia says.

"I'll take that bet!" Amaranth responds eagerly.

"I'm out," Hyacinth replies. "That's so stupid."

I dry my hands on my shorts as I step out of the bathroom unnoticed. Once outside, I nearly pass Rugosa on the trail. He gets my attention by snapping his fingers inches before my face.

I wipe my eyes and blink back my tears. "Any news on Aspen?"

Rugosa scowls. He's wearing a gray heathered shirt and cartoon pajama bottoms. His hair has grown in a bit; it's spiky and slept on. "Wassup, to you too."

I sigh. Sadly, without Aspen, Rugosa is my closest friend here now. I've seen firsthand I can't trust Amaranth. I like Fern, but like Petal, our relationship changed when I was with a boy I liked. Since the Headmistress revealed my love spell on River, our conversations are brief and awkward. If I blow it with Rugosa, I'll have no one.

"Sorry. It's just weird that he hasn't been around. If he was drunk, he would've stumbled back by now," I reply, sadly. "He seemed like he liked it here. I mean, we've been through much worse. This place is like Disney World compared to some of the places we've been."

He nods, yawning while he stretches. "Yeah, yeah. I've heard it all before. Your tragic upbringings." He waves me off and I frown. "He's done this before, anyways," Rugosa adds with a shrug.

I step back, genuinely surprised. "What? He's disappeared like this before? When?"

"What'd you know about it? You're only around when it's convenient for *you*." Rugosa says, pressing his finger gently into my forehead. I scowl, swiping his hand away. "I barely even knew you existed until Charm School, other than what I heard from him. For a while, I thought you were made up." He chuckles. "Don't worry so much. He probably just went back home, or he's off pretending he's Mr. Survivor-Man like he did last summer."

"He did?" I ask, scratching my chin.

"Yeah. He left for the summer and came back mid-autumn when it got too cold to live outdoors. He was all skinny from surviving on berries and roadkill. His foster home was a nightmare. They threw him in with non-magicals because of the influx of refugee teen witches from their respective homelands and had nowhere better to put him. The older kids would organize fight clubs and the adults collected children for paychecks."

"That's horrible!" I say, remembering my own experience in a non-magical foster home.

"Again, if you were around more, you'd know this… We met around that time and despite his problems, he went out of his way to befriend me. I thought that was pretty cool of him, although I wonder if part of the reason was because of my size. Like he needed protection or something... Anyways, sometimes he just needs time alone. Like I do, now." He smirks and steps around me.

I frown, knowing that although his approach was harsh, Rugosa speaks the truth. I've been a terrible friend to not only Petal, Fern, and countless other girls, but to Aspen too.

"Wait!" I call to him. He turns, and I catch up. "So, I had this weird dream where Aspen was in a tree coffin—"

"And?" he asks, chuckling.

"Remember how Iris mentioned it could be a message from a spirit guide?"

He blinks. "You're kidding, right? Summer, she gave you some weird hypnotic tea that made you trip balls. It doesn't mean anything if that's what you're worried about."

"Yeah, you're probably right."

He walks ahead, chuckling and muttering, "Tree coffin. So stupid."

I watch Rugosa until he disappears around the bend of the trail. The crunch of leaves beneath his feet quiets, leaving me alone with the dark, nagging voice in my head.

What if Aspen really was saying "goodbye" the night he vanished? His choice of words bother me; my anxiety spirals to a dark place as I wonder if I made my best friend upset enough to leave. It was never my intention. I just needed some alone time. What if I destroyed a friendship that meant the world to me?

Maybe he did leave on his own.

I step off the trail and shuffle along through the woods with my hands stuffed in my pockets. As I'm walking through the forest, I ponder my strange dream, with Iris, Aspen, and the strange out-of-focus witch. Why was he in that weird tree coffin, covered by a quilt of leaves? If it was symbolic of me neglecting to act to protect my sense of security, is it referring to Aspen's disappearance? Should I be doing more to find him? If so, why would my nightmares have begun before he vanished? Upon my return to the cabins, breakfast has finally begun.

I pour myself a cup of fresh squeezed orange juice and find an empty space at the picnic table. Breakfast is served late this morning by Azalea and River, which means Azalea did everything while River watched and complained.

I rub my tired eyes. I don't understand for the life of me why my nightmares are continuing despite stuffing my pillowcase with herbs and placing the charged crystal under my bed. But Iris did say it would be ineffective against a Night Hag—if a disgraced High Priestess who lied to get me there and wasn't fully forthcoming about the effect of the tea can even be trusted.

Further down the table, Azalea giggles. I meet her gaze and she grows quiet, stifling her laugh by biting her lip. I sigh, realizing she's probably laughing about Aspen rejecting me. She tosses back her cinnamon-colored tresses, striking a memory about my dream—the out-of-focus witch with hair color that resembled the chestnut tresses of the Devil-Claw witches.

Could the cursed woman be a Devil-Claw?

If the Night Hag is a cursed witch, why would they have chosen me to be their victim, out of everyone else in the cabin? More giggles interrupt my thoughts. I leave the table and head for the cabin, carrying my bowl of lumpy oatmeal and a cup of juice.

I don't know what to do anymore. I miss Aspen. I've never felt so alone. I just want to leave this place. It takes everything within me not to cry.

Above, gnarled branches crack, scraping against one another as the wind blows. *Aspen, where are you?* I wonder, looking to the sky for answers.

16

During a grueling morning lesson led by Mistress Aster on table etiquette and various cauldron stew recipes, I brainstorm ideas to find Aspen and bring him back. I need my best friend.

My plan happens to include breaking and entering, vehicle theft and could greatly jeopardize my future. But Aspen is worth the risk, even if he does tell annoying hipster coffee jokes that make me want to punch him a hundred times in the face.

When no one is looking and is otherwise distracted after class, I dip under a hemlock. Tiny pinecones crunch under my calloused feet as I wind from the lesson area through the woods off-trail. I brush tiny pine needles from my hair and shoulders, nearly colliding with a shed as I come around the corner.

"Oh, thank the Goddess," I say aloud. I'd found the magical broom shed and a dirt trail.

It's a dusty blue color; the paint is heavy, layered and chipped. The roof is partially sunken in, covered by a frayed black tarp that's held down by two crumbling bricks. Flakes of blue paint dot the forest ground. There's a large flat stone covered in brown leaves before the entry and a fading yellow star painted on the door. As promised by Mistress Aster, the shed is secured by a padlock.

I step up on hard-skinned tiptoes and peer into the small barred window beside the door. The wood of the shed smells like mildew and rot. I rub my nose. Inside the dim space are rows of dusty broomsticks leaning against the walls. I recognize Dahlia's bejeweled magenta broom and the corn husk and feathers of Fern's. Spellbooks are organized on a high shelf and there are canvas totes on the ground holding art supplies. What I don't see is Aspen's yellow broom.

A hurricane of anxious, troubling thoughts rushes through my head. *What if he's mad at me? What if he got into trouble? What if he was hurt or targeted?* I remember my dream—the tree coffin and the billowing smoke when the Night Hag arrived, further endangering him. *What does it all mean? Was it a product of the tea? Or dream symbols for me to further explore?* The questions haunt and frustrate me. It's all I can think about.

I pull on the entry, testing the padlock, but it doesn't give. Frustrated, I kick the door. The soft rotten wood at the bottom gives with my foot, cracking and splintering against my toes. As I'm extracting my foot from the mushy rubble, a lightbulb in my brain turns on.

I step down from the rock, rounding the shed, carefully testing the wooden boards with my feet. I find a soft, pliable spot at the base, still wet from our last big rain.

I don't think I've ever been this grateful for the rain. Dreary weather and the witches of my clan pair about as well as pouring water over fire. In our case, we're extinguished. We garner our energy from the sun. Without it, we are depleted of magic, even depressed. It's almost funny that I'm finding such joy from our last rain. It reminds me of a slogan printed in Latin. Aspen and I passed it all the time and one day, we looked up its meaning. It hasn't made sense until today…

Post tenebras lux—the motto of a Springfield college that Aspen and I fly over on our way to and from the Coffee

Cuties—loosely translates to: "life is about finding the light from the darkness".

I glance around the forest and listen for a moment, ensuring nobody is around. A wren sings her song from somewhere within the woods. The wind blows, stirring the leaves of trees.

I suck my lips between my teeth and kick the bottom of the shed as hard as I can. My foot goes right through, sending things clattering to the floor inside the hut. I kick and push and kick some more, working myself up into a sweat. I look over my shoulder frequently, ensuring nobody has heard me or is approaching. I pry back a piece of splintered wood, creating a gap that's big enough for me to squeeze my hand through.

The wood scrapes me as I reach through the gap. Dark blue witch blood streaks down my arm. I bite my lip, looking away. I try to ignore the sharp pain and the warm gory mess atop my arm. I almost give up until my hand finally connects with the handle of a broomstick.

I yank it out and laugh. Oh, the irony—it's Dahlia's. I seem to always covet what she has. With a final tug, it's free from the shed. Blood runs down my arm, dripping on to the magenta handle as I straddle the broomstick. Expecting it to lift, I'm disappointed when it doesn't start.

"Damn rain," I mutter to myself, scowling. I close my eyes and concentrate on my inner fire. I know it's there; it manifests several times a day when I think of Dahlia. I become inflamed with jealousy. She incites my envy, insecurity, and the general sense I have of feeling left-out. It burns me up, reducing my self-esteem to ashes…

The broom lifts, and like a phoenix, I rise. My eyes snap open as the soles of my bare feet leave the ground. "It worked!" I shout, grinning in celebration. I soar through a clearing between the trees, into the open sky above the forest.

My short flight is turbulent from Elwood to Elderberry Thicket. I feel unsteady, but I'm determined and the inner flames I feel blazing within my core keeps me from falling. As the broomstick dips, I force myself to think about the moment I realized River was dumping me for Dahlia. The memory ignites my jealousy—stoking my element, fire—and I ascend several feet.

Post tenebras lux.

I navigate around flocks of birds and dip below gray clouds. The blood from my injury has dried a muddy blue color. Several small jagged wood splinters poke painfully from my forearm. When I reach the yellow Victorian in Elderberry Thicket, I lean forward, steering the broomstick to the valley below. I land roughly, using my feet as brakes in the sweet-smelling, freshly cut grass.

Goblets and paper plates litter the ground from the Solar Solstice party. Children with sunshine golden hair and glittering lavender eyes are running merrily through the field. The young Widow-Tears kids pick up trash, restoring the yard belonging to the High Priestess and High Priest of their clan.

Banquet tables and seating has since been removed. The valley is devoid of solar lighting and lanterns. The land is empty but for a bench and a large iron cauldron that will remain until the next Sabbat in August, when Lughnasadh brings the annual Witches Fair on the Green.

With Dahlia's broomstick in hand, I exit the valley through a rusted old gate, onto a narrow gravel road where Widow-Tears clan members live. The street is bordered by large sprawling Elderberry trees that overhang the street, connecting over the street with the branches on the other side.

I pass through the enchanting tunnel-like space. Thick, cord-like branches scrape against one another above my head. Heavy blackberries weigh slimmer branches down. Native birds and squirrels feast on the dark purple fruit. The rodents issue high-pitched warnings as I walk below.

Spiderwort grows alongside the shaded thicket. Sprawling green fronds are dusty from the street, but the flowers are untouched, in vibrant shades of purple. As I pass a sprawling colonial, a large dog pokes his nose through the dilapidated fence, growling, barking, and scaring me half to death. I slap my hand to my heart and shriek crossing the street as the mean-looking dog throws himself against the pickets. The wood snaps behind me; I pick up my pace.

Widow-Tears children—out for summer break—play in their yards. I pass a pregnant witch gardening at the edge of the road. She's tamping down the soil around her annuals planted at her mailbox, then dowses them with a tin watering can. Birds sing and butterflies flap around phlox and other wildflowers planted roadside. I reach Aspen's current placement home and take a deep breath.

The house is an eyesore. It's missing half of the clapboard shingles—exposing the insulation—and the roof is covered in thick, green mossy growth. A fluorescent orange utility notice stuck to the door flaps in the wind. As usual, there are several street kids sitting out front on the old lady's stoop. Aspen is not one of them.

I'm finding it increasingly hard to believe that he would leave what is essentially a glorified summer camp for *this*.

As I approach the driveway, the boys leer at me, snickering and speaking in hushed tones. Weed laced with the autumnal scent of clove is heavy in the air. I call out from a short distance, "Aspen been around?"

"Nah," one answers, his eyes drowsy and hooded. "My boy's gone for the summer. Wanna hang?" He waves a blunt.

I frown, disappointed that Aspen isn't around. My gaze shifts to the smoldering blunt between his fingers. "No, I'm cool. That's a nasty habit for air witches, you know."

The group bursts into laughter followed by a series of hacking coughs.

"That wasn't that funny," I say to nobody in particular, shaking my head. I leave the driveway, feeling defeated. I hoped so badly he would be here, but he's not, and I don't know where else he'd be hanging out.

In a daze, I retrace my path back to Elderberry Thicket, numbly passing the barking dog, hidden beneath the intertwined branches of elderberry. Within the valley, I hop aboard the magenta broomstick, unsure of what to do next. A craving for caffeine hits me hard. I would kill for the dark stuff right now.

That's when it dawns on me… maybe he's been hanging out at the Witches Brew? I could always make a little stop before returning to Charm School and ask around.

Employees of the Witches Brew haven't seen their favorite customer in weeks. I'm tempted to flyer the entire city of Springfield with Aspen's face, headline *missing and missed* written in bold red lettering.

My stomach twists into a painful knot at the recent revelations. Deep down, I was hoping it was just Aspen being Aspen, possibly trying to get my attention by ghosting. Except nobody can account for him, leading me to believe it's foul play. As I'm flying over Elwood Avenue back to Camp Bitter Tonic, my anxiety again spirals out of control.

What if he hit his head and is walking around Springfield without a clue as to who he is? That only happens in the movies, right? That doesn't happen to people like Aspen. Does it?

What if he choked on his own vomit? What if he's lying somewhere, a stiff corpse with birds picking off his body like he's an elderberry? What if he's alive, but injured, and can't move?

What if my persistent nightmares are urgent warnings that I'm unable to decipher?

Is this how my mother felt when my father left? I wonder. No surprise she was a mess. The worry is enough to drive someone insane. The pain and anxiety from a missing friend to a missing spouse coupled with family abandonment isn't even remotely comparable. I've been too hard on her, I realize, frowning.

This has been a wakeup call. I could be in Aspen's shoes right now, wherever those figurative shoes may be. I drank a lot on the night of the Solar Solstice and I polished off the mead with a hypnotic tea that made me, like Rugosa said, *trip balls*. Fern blacked out. She complained about missing large chunks of time. It could have been any of us.

I'm haunted by the nightmare; the frightful images of Aspen inside the hollowed tree flood my mind. What does it all mean? It's scary to think how fragile we truly are and how every decision we make has a consequence. Did something terrible happen to my best friend?

I release the broom with one hand to wipe my tearing eyes. As I do, the broomstick dips slightly and I notice something unusual in the murky lake below, like a small yellow glowstick floating atop the water.

As I get closer, I recognize the yellow handle of a broom, split and moving slowly across the lake. Searing pain rips through my soul like a firestorm as a wailing scream erupts from my throat.

17

I zip back to Charm School, flying dangerously through the air at speeds that shouldn't be attempted by an *experienced* rider, never mind a novice like myself. Ahead a short distance is a shoreline. I speed over a sandbar as the picturesque setting of Camp Bitter Tonic comes into view. Sunlight strains through thick green foliage onto nature trails that wind up the forested hills. The rustic cabins look like sheds from up here.

If he's in the murky water, I haven't a chance of finding him myself. However, the Devil-Claw clan's connection with the element can no doubt be useful. The only problem is, the only water witches here are River, Azalea, and Dahlia.

So, basically, I'm screwed.

My feet touch down at the beach of Camp Bitter Tonic. I hop off and stash Dahlia's magenta broomstick within a thicket of trees, scratching myself as I release the handle. A stinging sensation in my forearm reminds me to care for myself before I move forward. The time I'm losing to help my friend pulls at my heart strings, but deep down, I know if he's been in the water all this time, it's way past too late.

Regrettably, I return to the shoreline and drop to the wet sand on my knees. Cupping my hands, I splash cool lake water on my hot, tear-stained face. I carefully lean forward to dip my bloodied arm into the water, letting the lake rinse away my blood. I examine my injuries, yanking out slivered bits of wood from my flesh with my bare fingers, wincing with each removal and clenching my teeth to bear the sting. When my arm is finally free of splinters, I rinse quickly and spring to my feet, on a mission to locate water witch Azalea Devil-Claw. She's my first and possibly my *only* choice.

I wish I could go to Headmistress Starwort or Mistress Aster about this, but to do so, I'd have to admit to sneaking out, and I'd risk graduating on time. Telling Spring isn't a possibility either. I could get her in trouble again because of her position as a Camp Counselor, and I don't want to do that. I felt terrible when Headmistress Starwort stumbled upon us in the forest. It was clear she wasn't pleased with Spring—like somehow it was her fault that Aspen was unaccounted for.

This time I have to step up and take matters into my own *trembling* hands, for the sake of my best friend.

On a trail leading to the common area, I run into Fern and Rugosa. She bounces along happily beside him, their arms interlocked.

"Where's Azalea at?" I ask when we're within shouting distance.

As they draw closer, Fern lifts a golden eyebrow. Her short, pixie hairstyle is messed up. Her hair sticks this way and that. Upon inspecting Rugosa, he isn't looking put together either. He shuffles down the trail, leaves crunching beneath his feet. Pine needles are on their wrinkled clothing and within Fern's hair. It only takes a few seconds for me to realize what they've been doing… Again.

Fern and Rugosa. Gross. I could vomit right here on this trail.

"Why are you looking for Azalea?" Fern asks, blinking her lavender eyes.

"It's complicated. Have you seen her around?"

"She's with Mistress Aster doing, whatever," Rugosa tells me, waving his hand dismissively.

"They went to the lake for a lesson in reflection because of all those selfies she took. Her task is to discover herself," Fern says, peeling pine needles from the sleeve of her shirt.

"Noo... That's going to take forever!" I bring my hands to my head, my fingers trembling as my anxiety kicks up. My scalp prickles with fire energy and I feel almost electric.

"Whoa, girl. Chill! What does it matter? Why're you lookin' for her anyway?" Rugosa asks, peeling my fingers from my face. He gets ahold of my wrist. "Um...What's up with your arm?"

He rotates my arm, inspecting my wounds with awe. Fern has a eureka moment—her lavender eyes light up and she stabs one finger in the air. She disappears around the corner.

I yank my arm away from him. "Show and Tell is over," I say, wincing from pain as his palm brushes against a thin cut. It begins to bead up with blood.

"Must have gone temporarily deaf during the *telling* part," he says, raising an eyebrow.

"I fell," I respond. Self-conscious, I hide my injured arm behind my back. My knee bounces as I anticipate my backup plan.

"Into a bear trap, or something?" Rugosa asks, his face twisted with confusion. Fern returns, bouncing up the trail, her hands cupped around a clump of purple deadnettle, roots intact. The vine trails to the ground and dirt drops with each step she takes.

"Give me your arm and hold still," Fern demands with a stern expression I've never seen. I glance at Rugosa, slightly apprehensive.

"She means business," he says. "I'd listen to her."

I offer her my arm. She plucks the small leaves of the purple deadnettle plants, pressing the soft greenery over my wounds like bandages. Her brow furrows as she concentrates.

"How'd you know about that?" I ask her. The small leaves are strangely soothing; her treatment is surprisingly helpful.

"I just know some things," she answers, pinching the leaves and separating them from their vines. "I guess I'm learning stuff. It's also anti-microbial, anti-fungal, and will stop your bleeding."

"Yeah, I see that. Like nature's Band-Aids."

"Something like that." She giggles.

"Okay, well thanks guys," I say, withdrawing my arm and squeezing between them. As I pass, Fern protests and waves the purple deadnettle in the air, demanding I return. I wear her remedy like a badge of honor as I weave my way around the forest to the common area.

Back at the cabins, Amaranth and Petal are talking at the picnic table. Hyacinth is sitting beneath a tree, quietly grinding something purple-colored using a mortar and pestle.

"Where's Dahlia?" I shout.

Amaranth and Petal's conversation stops abruptly; they snap their heads to the side and peer at me. Hyacinth looks up from her project and points at the boys' cabin. Her brow wrinkles in confusion. Hanging from the doorknob is a yellow sock.

I let out a long sigh. I don't care about that stupid sock or what it represents. I don't have time to wait around while they cuddle in bed all day. I have no choice but to interrupt them. I take a deep breath, clenching my fists as I muster up my inner strength and courage. The atmosphere fades around me until all I see is the boys' cabin and the symbol of the Horned God on the door.

I approach the cabin, my heart in my throat and my scalp tingling with electricity. I free the sock and toss it over my shoulder. Amaranth gasps. My courage wanes as I place my hand on the knob, and I'm hit with the urge to flee; I pull my hand back.

"Goddess, what is she doing?" Amaranth giggles. "You see this, Petal?"

"I'm thinkin three's gonna be a crowd," Petal responds, rising from the picnic table.

For Aspen, I remind myself. I twist the knob, pushing on the door with force. It swings open, cracking against the wall.

"Dahlia." I take a sharp breath. "I need your help."

18

Light floods the small, dim cabin from the open doorway. River is bare-chested. His shirt is bundled in a ball, crumpled on the floor beside his bunk. He rolls off Dahlia with a groan. She shields her eyes from the rays of Sunna's sun with her arm, cursing my intrusion.

Something amazing happens… I no longer feel that ping in my heart of longing or that stab of jealousy from seeing him with another girl. I feel nothing. Just the desire to grab Dahlia and bring her back to the lake with me. And it's so incredibly freeing. The only thing that worries me, is Dahlia's rejection. I fear she will tell me no, and I'll be screwed. I've been burned enough. I can't take another rebuff.

She sits up and swings her legs out of bed, tying up her hair into a ponytail. "Why do you need *me*?" she asks, the elastic snapping.

"I need her more right now," River bemoans behind her. "Trust me on that."

"Please, Dahlia," I plead. I feel a glimmer of hope when her face softens. She rises from the bed, agreeing to help me. I let out a deep breath, flooded with relief. River complains as I turn my back.

"Don't be mad, but I kinda stole your broom," I admit to her, as we step outside. Hyacinth's curious gaze dips to her mortar and pestle; she grinds away, and purple dust rises in the air. Petal and Amaranth rush back to the picnic table.

She sighs angrily as she adjusts her black clothing. "So, whatever you need me to do involves leaving the campground?"

I cringe. "Is that a problem?"

She thinks about it for a moment, her blue eyes darting to the side, then shrugs. "I guess not." Her cinnamon colored ponytail swings as she walks. She reeks of River's patchouli, a harsh scent that clashes with the gardenia oil she rolls on her wrists, ankles, and neck every morning.

We pass Rugosa and Fern—their curiosity noticeable to even the ants on the ground I'm sure—on our way to the thicket at the shoreline where I stashed Dahlia's broom. When we come upon it, I pull apart a tangle of branches, reaching for the brightly colored, eye-catching broomstick. Dahlia lifts a brow, her hand on her hip. She shakes her head. "Could you at least *try* to be careful with it?" As I climb aboard the broom, she adds, "Nuh uh, you're riding. That's *my* broomstick."

We switch positions and she takes us up into the air. As we fly over the water, I catch her up to speed on Aspen.

"So what exactly do you want me to do?" she asks.

"Remember when we made those chocolate cookies and you told me how water witches have the gift of clarity?"

"And? This helps you with Aspen, how?"

"I need you to clear the water, so we can see to the bottom, look for signs or clues. It would take a millennium to comb the murky water on my own."

"Oh. That's all?" she asks, her voice laced with sarcasm.

"Please," I ask. "You're my last hope."

She nods. "I guess I'm up for the challenge."

I sigh in relief. As we close in on the area I last saw his broomstick floating, my heartbeat quickens. As before, the yellow stick shines like a beacon from the murky water. I point it out over her shoulder, and she lowers the broomstick until we are hovering only feet above it. I snatch it out of the water. The handle is split, broken. The tangible reality of it is shocking. My eyes flood with tears as I roll it over, noticing a tell-tale mark on the end of the handle.

No. My Gods, it's his.

Dahlia lifts her ride back in the air. We zip over to the rocky edge and land. I sit on a large boulder, crying, with the end of a broken broomstick in my hand.

Dahlia paces the boulder. "Okay, so I agree, it doesn't look good, but maybe it's not what you think."

"What else could it be?" I wail. "His broom is in pieces. Nobody has seen him around. He was in an accident and now he's in the water, dead." I hug my knees, sobbing. Moments later, I'm interrupted by a splash of water.

I lift my head with a scowl on my face. Dahlia's underwater, her head close to the surface. How she can consider swimming at a time like this is beyond me. She's no better than her boyfriend. I rise to give her a piece of my mind when she breaks through the water and begins to quietly chant.

> *"Water dark, water light,*
> *I ask for sunshine, for clearness of sight.*
> *Sun above, shine below for me,*
> *it is the bed of the lake that I wish to see."*

I close my mouth and scrub my tear-stained face with my hands. Above, the clouds break apart in the sky and the sunlight streaks between. It shines down on the lake, reaching the small rocks on the bottom of the sandy floor. A school of minnows darts through the water. A bullfrog surfaces to seize a mosquito. The water is crystal clear. I blink my eyes and take a second look before scrambling up.

I point at the water. "It's working!" I say, hardly believing my eyes. "Let's go up and check!" I reach for her.

She takes my hand and I help her out of the suck of the water, pulling her up onto the boulder. We board her magenta broomstick, zipping over to the area where a piece of Aspen's broom was found floating.

"We only have so long," she warns as she lowers her ride. My heart pounds as we skim across the surface, searching the area before the lake returns to its former murky state. I stare into the water, but nothing out of the ordinary is visible.

There's decaying plant matter at the bottom of the lake and dark silt. Jagged rocks and debris.

The water gradually darkens as time passes. After an hour of searching the area, we find no clues to suggest that Aspen is in the water. We collect his broken broomstick handle from the boulder and head back for camp.

"On one hand, I'm relieved. On the other, we still don't know what happened. I feel like he must have been in an accident," I say to Dahlia as we lift up. Her clothing drips into the lake water below, falling in fat droplets.

"Here, though?" She gestures to the clearing above, devoid of trees. "There are no obstacles. What could he hit?"

"I don't know. That's what's bothering me. When I saw the broken yellow broomstick, I thought for sure he was in an accident and was in the water. I'm relieved to be wrong," I reply. "But I'm still worried."

"Right. That doesn't explain why it's in the water, to begin with. I don't think one can fly with half a broomstick." Her black clothing hangs on her, soaked from the water, and her wet hair whips in the breeze, smacking me in the face as we soar over the lake. The scene is vaguely familiar...

My eyes widen in alarm and I come to a horrifying realization...

Is Dahlia Devil-Claw the Night Hag?

19

"What's wrong? Why did you get so quiet back there?" Dahlia asks as we're nearing the shoreline of Camp Bitter Tonic.

"Nothing," I squeak. "Just thinking about Aspen... Thanks for helping, by the way. Sorry, I interrupted you, and *you* know."

"Oh, it's cool," she says, navigating the broomstick. We land smoothly on the bank. "So, do you still need this for any covert operations?" she asks with a grin, gesturing to her ride.

"You'd be willing to let me borrow it again?" I ask, genuinely stunned.

"Well, I never let you borrow it, to begin with. You kinda just stole it."

"True," I admit.

"How'd you get it, anyway?"

"It's probably better that you *don't* know," I respond, averting my eyes.

"You can just have it," she says with a shrug. "I'm getting a new one when I get home, anyways. A green and blue one," she says proudly. "My parents are bribing me, so I'll actually take this place seriously. That and a new freshwater aquarium!"

I nod, glancing over her, and barely listening as she goes on about her freshwater and saltwater aquariums at home. Her wet, cinnamon-colored hair is windblown. Her soaked black clothing hangs heavy on her small frame. She looks like the woman of my nightmares; the woman I see myself as, riding on a broomstick in a storm, and the one that loomed over me in a cloud of smoke, destroying Iris with black salt. Why do I see her from two perspectives? Is it important for me to humanize the Mare, to be able to understand?

I gulp, wondering if I really did summon the Night Hag at Iris Rose-Thorne's house. Perhaps I wasn't hallucinating— as Rugosa believes. Is Dahlia Devil-Claw the cursed witch who has been haunting my sleep?

"—the kids really like it," she says.

"What'd you say about kids?" I interrupt, stunned, remembering the odd comments from my nightmare.

"Oh, my little brothers and sisters!" She passes me the broomstick. "Anyways, do what you have to do. If you need help—"

Dahlia is interrupted by a woman clearing her throat. We spin around and are met with Spring Widow-Tears, camouflaged behind a thicket of trees. Her hands are on her hips and her lips are pursed. I drop the broken yellow handle and hide the magenta broomstick behind my back, but it's too late. She's seen and heard everything.

"We can explain," Dahlia says, her palms in the air.

"I don't want to hear it," Spring says back, throwing her hands up. "As a matter of fact, *please* don't tell me. Summer, no offense, but you've gotten me in enough trouble as it is."

"I know, but it's about Aspen," I say.

"Oh no. Not this again," Spring says with a groan, her shoulders slumping forward. "It's not that I don't care, I do, but I'm not sure what I can do to help. The Headmistress doesn't want to investigate it, and she's the boss. She feels he left on his own. We can't force people to stay." Behind her are two large mesh bags full of dirty clothing. As I notice it, she responds without me asking, "Oh, this is for you two. I told Mistress Aster that you both volunteered to do laundry since Aspen isn't here any longer. She was completely impressed that you both had given up lunch to do laundry." Spring retrieves the bags as we look on with horror. She tosses the bundles at us. "And here is as good a place as any, so start scrubbing, ladies."

We groan as we dump out the clothing on a rock formation by the shore. Piles of socks, underwear, and uniforms litter the boulders. "How did you know we were over here?" Dahlia asks while I hide the broomsticks in the thicket. Spring catches me and calls me back over.

"What's that small one you had? Bring it over here." She turns her focus on Dahlia and says, "I could see you coming from like a mile away. That broomstick is bright and sparkly. I wouldn't take it out again unless you two are *really* stupid."

I return to the rock formation with the broken broomstick. Spring blinks several times as she takes it, rolling it over in her hands. "Where'd you find this? It's like, rotten." She scrunches her small, freckled nose.

"In the lake," Dahlia and I answer together.

"It's Aspen's," I add.

Her deep lavender eyes widen in alarm. "Are you sure it's his, though? How can you tell?"

I take the broomstick handle back, rolling it over until I find the distinct scratch at the end where the buckle on my shoe scraped against the yellow stain, several years ago. I tell them the story, and they listen quietly, their eyes full of sympathy and understanding.

"So there's no doubt in my mind that this is his broomstick. But where is Aspen? We combed the water." I gesture to Dahlia. "She used a clarity spell. We spent over an hour searching the area before the water clouded. There was nothing. The area is clear of trees. There's nothing for him to crash into. It just doesn't make sense why his broom would turn up there. He wouldn't go swimming with it."

Without any answers or suggestions, Spring shakes her head, her expression troubled. She suggests we start laundry while we think it through.

We begin unrolling the socks and sleeves of clothing, to make it easier to clean, and we shake out the sandy clothes in the air. Spring joins in to help us, snapping a tee-shirt beside me. She taps her chin, then says, "You know, this could be totally unrelated, but when Oak and I went to Senior Prom, we were flying by broomstick, and on our way to school this woman came out from absolutely nowhere. Nearly ran us right outta the sky! It was awful. We never knew who she was, but I think she was of the Devil-Claw clan."

"Of course! Everyone always blames us evil Devil-Claws. The wicked witches of the west," Dahlia remarks, rolling her eyes and wiggling her fingers. "Ooh, so wicked!"

As Spring calms Dahlia down, I consider what she said.

My nightmares have all been about storms and broom wrecks—there has to be a reason for that. Coupled with what Iris said about the dream symbol of Aspen, and me being neglectful of an urgent situation, leads me to believe the dreamwalking episode *is* connected to the broom crash dreams. What if he had a collision with another witch while he was in the air? It doesn't explain why only a piece of his broomstick was found... but, it's the most I've had to go on.

Perhaps it would be a good idea to keep an eye on the sky tonight, in case someone is making a habit of wreckless flying.

The Dark Moon rises above the forest, its dim lunar glow guiding me through the woodland hills of Elwood's Camp Bitter Tonic. I navigate around thick rambling roots that support age-old trees, using the magenta broomstick as a walking aid. Pine needles and fallen leaves crunch beneath my bare feet as I climb. They release a sharp resinous scent that I wish I could bottle and wear. With one final step, I'm on top of the cliff where Aspen and I viewed the shooting star. The entirety of Elwood is within my view.

Leaning against a tall sturdy birch, I allow myself a moment to catch my breath and reflect. After dark, when I returned to retrieve my broom at the shoreline, I was shocked to see it where I left it. I thought for sure Spring would hide it, but she didn't, and for that, I am grateful. I may not need it, but if I do, I have it.

After dropping my backpack and blanket at my feet, I swing the shoulder strap attached to my canteen forward and tip it back, taking a much-needed drink of the cool water. As I sip, an owl hoots in the distance. A warm, humid breeze blows through the pines, carrying with it the familiar scent of campfire smoke from below.

The clouds obscure the moon. The darkness is perfect. The last thing I want is to be noticed.

I roll out my blanket on the soft forest floor of pine needles, coils of peeled birch bark, and fallen leaves. It's hot. The air is thick. I stretch my legs before me, leaning back on my elbows against the scratchy woolen blanket. I keep my eyes trained on the sky as I fidget nervously, peeling the purple dead-nettle from my arm.

It's quiet but for the owl hooting in threes. The silence is strange; I'm so used to being surrounded by people this past week. But right now, I'm all alone, hidden under darkness and surrounded by pines. As a Wormwood, I blend into these woods—with my hair as black as pitch, my eyes as green as the pine, and my skin the color of earth. On the mountain,

I have nothing but time to think, and besides Aspen, my mother is on my mind.

Her illness has robbed so much from her and from us, and I want to forgive her because I know it's not all her fault. I know that she did the best she could with what she had, just like I'm trying to do the best I can for someone I care about right now. I realize that sometimes the choices we make aren't necessarily the right ones, but that we do what we need to do... to survive. Yes, I'm risking not graduating on time, but not knowing if he's okay will kill me, spiritually and emotionally. I have to do something. Just like Meadow, who crafts expensive fake love charms and offers herself to lonely men to put food on the table and keep a roof over our heads. She ensures our survival.

"I'm sorry, Meadow. I get it now," I say to myself, wiping a tear from my eye. When I get home, I'm going to start treating her differently. I'm gonna help out more. Today I did a ton of green laundry, and I cook all the time now. I think my mother will be really proud of me.

As the hours pass, the air cools. My eyelashes flutter as I try to stay awake, watching for any unusual activity in the sky. I know this is a long shot, but I'm not sure what else to do at this point, and nobody is taking Aspen's disappearance seriously. I can't sleep. I don't want to sleep, anyways—my nightmares terrorize me. If Dahlia is the cursed witch who is haunting me, what curses her? It just doesn't make any sense. She has everything anyone could ever wish to have.

The sun begins to rise. The atmosphere lightens just enough for me to notice the sheen of a black velvet ritual robe—and the witch riding her broomstick erratically above.

I shoulder my backpack and straddle the magenta broom, rubbing my palms together desperately trying to create enough friction to lift off. I curse as the witch in the black velvet robe gets further away, but I don't lose hope. I can still see her; therefore, I can catch up with her.

As a fire witch, I *should* be able to generate sparks to power the broomstick, in addition to stoking my inner fire with emotions, but my lack of experience and past unwillingness to try is making that difficult. Air witches have it the easiest, they use their breath. Earth witches ground themselves by planting their feet firmly on the ground before lift-off. And water witches can use the sweat of their palms.

Most fire witches can lift a broom with a special touch. They brush their hand across the wood in a way that sparks the magic needed to lift the broomstick. You have to do it *just* right. My inexperience is slowing me down significantly.

I focus my intentions, but it's hard to concentrate with all the stress and pressure, coupled with lack of sun and sleep. I slow my mind down, remembering an old rhyme my sister used to recite:

Under darkness of night,
the fire witch takes flight.
There she rides, above the moon,
where I hope to fly my broom.

Finally, there's a small flash of light between my palm and the handle, and the broomstick lifts beneath me, raising me from the ground into the sky. I smile, sighing with relief. The wind tousles my hair as I speed away, chasing after a hunch.

I follow the dark-robed woman from a considerable distance. Even from back here, her erratic pattern of flight is noticeable. She often dips, her broomstick free-falling from the sky for several seconds before she corrects herself. She reminds me of my nightmares, and I wonder if I should alert someone for her safety, at the very least. She turns off a short distance from my public school, landing in the small neighborhood of Pine Point, home of the Devil-Claw clan witches. I circle above the pines while she parks her broomstick outside her house, oblivious to my presence.

The woman stumbles, staggering to her door. Her keys jingle for a good five minutes before she finds the correct one and pushes her way into the house. As the door shuts behind her, I swoop down in the gloom of her backyard.

I swat at the insects buzzing around my head, waving my broomstick. Bullfrogs drone in the nearby pond. The air is thick, like a swamp. Only a water witch could enjoy this, I think, as I creep around the perimeter of the house. Lights flick on from inside, shining out the glass panes. Several thumping sounds are followed by a crash and a moan.

Weird.

The broomstick is parked beside the entry door. The green grass-stained handle looks familiar, but I can't place it. I run my palm down the grain of the handle. Scratches and out-of-place paint marks mar the wood. A glugging sound from inside startles me, and I jump back into the shadows to avoid being seen.

Ice cubes crack from a tray on a hard surface and clink one by one. I peer into a window. A woman with cinnamon colored hair stands in her kitchen with her back to me, holding onto a countertop, while she plunks cubes of ice into a glass brimming with wine.

Oh.

Charm bracelets with tiny seashells and bottles of sand rattle around her wrists. She's shed her black velvet robe, wearing a blue paisley dress. Her hair is tied up on the top of her head in a messy bun. There's no sense in watching her any longer. She was flying erratically simply because she's had too much to drink. She's home now and no longer a danger to herself.

I'm no closer to discovering clues to Aspen's disappearance than I was before I had this crazy hunch, and the disappointment is real. And the worst part is that I don't know where to turn next. It's like I'm the only person who cares. Even Rugosa has given up. This is how kids like us fall through the cracks. I feel defeated and depressed.

As I'm brushing my hand against the magenta broomstick to leave, a woman's voice from inside the house distracts me. "Is she talking to herself?" I wonder aloud. My curiosity is enough to drive me to take another look.

I creep along the edge of the house, ducking under windows that shine light outside. The grass is tall and weedy, thick, and difficult to walk through in the dark. I follow her voice to the back of the house, where I find her leaning in the doorway of a bedroom, gripping the doorframe for dear life. Her head hangs low and her reddish-brown hair covers her face. I stifle a giggle with my hand and turn to leave when I hear a male voice groaning for help.

I pause a moment but take into consideration that he may be a bit wasted, like the woman. As I'm straddling the broomstick to leave, the woman pulls herself upright.

I drop my ride in the grass—possibly losing it forever in the tangle of weeds—shocked at her identity.

It's Priestess Anna Devil-Claw, my prim and proper magical studies teacher. I blink my eyes several times. I can't possibly be seeing this right. Priestess Anna is a wreckless drunk? Wow.

That's when I remember her face smashing into her plate at the Solar Solstice party. Maybe this is an ongoing problem?

I approach the window to get a better look. She's perched at the end of a bed. Knotted, sweat-stained sheets cover a mattress. A shock of blond hair spills across a pillow. A man's wrist is tied to the wooden bedpost with thick twine.

Whoa, okay. Freaky stuff. None of my business. I'm out. Too much information.

As I'm backing away, the man turns his face… and I'm looking straight into the lavender eyes of Aspen Widow-Tears.

The boy I've finally started to realize I've always loved.

20

My body numbs at the shocking sight of Aspen bound by rope. My ears ring sharply, momentarily quieting the never-ending chirps of insects and droning bullfrogs. Early morning birds are waking, singing merrily. Sparks of electricity prickle my scalp and arms.

Aspen's skin is pale and waxy. Bruises mark his body; there are too many to count. His leg is in a cast of some sort. He holds my gaze and blinks hard, twice.

I nod, acknowledging him, and duck under the window, waiting for her to leave his side. My heart pounds against my ribcage as I formulate a plan to free him. I wait for her to fall asleep, but as time slowly passes, she's still moving around inside the house.

He's weak. He's got a broken leg or something from the looks of it. I wish it were as easy as busting down the door, cutting him loose, then throwing him over my shoulder and escaping under the cover of darkness. But that would never work. Priestess Anna is clearly dangerous, and I'm no action movie hero.

A struggle from inside piques my attention. I bounce up and peer into the window, ready to bust through if she's hurting him, but she's not. She's poorly administering something to his leg wound. The whole situation is odd. I have no idea what's going on here. I know one thing… I can't do this myself. I need help.

The sun rises behind streaks of dark clouds. I speed back to Camp Bitter Tonic, landing at my familiar spot at the shoreline. My tongue feels gritty, like sandpaper, and my throat is dry. I cup lake water into my palm, taking a sip and promptly spitting it back out.

I'm physically exhausted but mentally wired. I'm on a mission to find a trusted adult, like Spring Widow-Tears, to confide in. She's getting involved whether she wants to or not. Isn't that what they always say to do when you have a problem you feel overwhelmed by? To go to a trusted adult and confide in them?

Moving quickly, I stumble on the trail, stubbing my toe. I cry out in pain, hopping as I tend to my foot. Moments later as I round the corner, I receive the unwanted attention of Headmistress Starwort.

Her absinthe-colored gaze is focused on the magenta broomstick, tucked under my armpit. She stares at in disbelief as she folds her arms over her chest, approaching me on the trail. My eyes instinctively drop. Her emerald green skirt dusts the forest floor as it swishes around her bare feet. Black crud is jammed under her toenails. The hem of her skirt is dirt-stained. She halts a couple paces before me and huffs.

Our eyes meet. "Before you get upset—"

"I'm already upset," she interrupts, sternly.

I nod and gulp. "I had a hunch about Aspen, and I followed up on it. I found him."

"And do you feel better now?" she asks, pulling the handle of the broom from my armpit. "Was it *really* worth possibly not graduating on time with the rest of your class? You had one week to go, Summer. That's it!" she exclaims, stabbing the magenta handle of Dahlia's broom into the dirt to further drive her point.

"You don't understand. Aspen's in a bad way. He's with Priestess Anna and—"

"Well, darling it sounds like he'll be okay. Aspen bounces around a lot," she says, physically turning my shoulders and changing my direction. She gives me a little shove on the trail, and I stagger forward, tripping on a sharp pinecone.

I protest over my shoulder, "Nothing looked okay about what I saw."

"Hush while your ahead, Summer. One more infraction and you won't complete Charm School. You've got one, young lady. Want to make it two?"

I bite my tongue, knowing I will see Spring soon. My only hope is for her to be a bit more receptive.

We part when I step into the girls' cabin. The old door *thunks* as it bounces against the log wall. I close it behind me and slide down the wood, my head in my hands.

I'm such a coward.

With Headmistress Starwort lingering around the common area, I haven't a chance to set off for the main building to find Spring. Coming back here was a big mistake. Now I've lost my broomstick, and once the Headmistress returns it, she'll notice the damage I caused to the broom shed. I have no way of going back to him unless I bust in it again and steal another one. And I can just kiss graduating on time goodbye. Oh well, I can't leave Aspen by himself with that deranged woman for a week!

Only feet away in the bunk by the door, Fern Widow-Tears snores. I shake my head, blinking away my tears. I still have an hour or so before breakfast. I feel exhausted and absolutely sick to my stomach.

I'm vaguely aware of a large shadow looming over me as I close my eyes, my head crashing against my knees as I fall asleep.

Winged black creatures flap their wings under a milky moon, spinning in a dizzying circle above. Two small ones swoop down and land between the crook of two branches. They hang upside down, staring at me through little eyes of black coal. I blink, and my blurred vision clears, reducing the creatures in half. I realize there is only one—a small, inquisitive bat.

A woman riding a broom zooms past me, high above. The branch holding me cracks under my weight, the wood splitting and weakening. Alcohol sits at the bottom of my stomach, threatening to rise any second.

The woman passes again, so close her broomstick stirs my hair. "Help," I shout.

She returns, hovering above me, fifteen feet or so. She's dressed in a black ritual robe. Her face is pale, her dark eyes round and terrified. I rub my eyes to clear my dimming vision and find myself staring into the face of someone I know well. Relieved, I call again for her help.

"Can I get a little assistance?" I say with a forced chuckle.

"Wake up, Summer. Get up," Amaranth drones from her bunk with little sympathy.

My eyes spring open and I take a sharp breath. I'm wedged between her bunk and mine, lying on the braided carpet on the floor. One leg is on her bed, and the other is bent over the nightstand. I couldn't recreate this move if I tried.

Amaranth gives me a helpful shove without glancing from her magazine. My body nearly splits in half. As I come to, I remember Aspen and get a sick feeling in the pit of my stomach. Last I remember, I fell asleep at the door. Not sure how I wound up here.

I pull myself up off the floor and peer out the windows, looking for any signs of Headmistress Starwort.

"Where is everyone? Who else has breakfast this morning?" I ask the room, frantic, walking quickly to the dresser for a change of clothing. I yank off yesterday's clothing and add them to the new heap forming in the closet.

"Just you, River, and Hyacinth," Amaranth answers with a smirk. "Have fun with that."

I yank my shorts over my hips. "Who's guiding?"

"Spring, I assume—"

Before Amaranth finishes her sentence, I'm out the door.

"Boy, someone's eager to start breakfast with River!" Amaranth shouts from the cabin.

I walk briskly to the kitchen hall, tightening my braids as I walk. I really need to shower, but there's no time. My small nap did little to refresh me, and the nightmare has left me emotionally exhausted. I'm now surer than ever that my dreams are messages. I push my way into the kitchen, yawning. I'm relieved to see Spring in the galley cutting bananas. I zip over to her and she startles, cutting her finger.

"Sorry," I apologize, cringing.

She pulls her finger from her mouth with a loud pop and glances at her small cut. I follow her to the sink, where she rinses her hand under cold water. "Can we talk?" I ask softly over her shoulder.

She jumps, slinging a spray of cold water at me, and shuts off the tap. "Damnit! Stop doing that! What's wrong with you?"

"A lot," River answers.

Hyacinth gathers bowls for cereal and looks on with a raised eyebrow. I find myself apologizing to Spring for the second time this morning. She retrieves a clean rag by the sink, pressing it against her cut, and I follow her outside to speak privately.

Other campers are beginning to wake up. Fern passes us in the hallway with her shower tote in hand. Her short blond hair is sticking up and she looks crazy. She disappears into the shower hall. Spring and I step outside. I close the door behind me. Her boyfriend Oak is walking up the trail. He waves as he sees us.

"Do you want me to get rid of him?" Spring asks, clutching the rag to her finger.

"No, he's cool," I say.

"Summer says I'm cool, so it must be true," he grins, feigning a snap of his imaginary suspenders. The smile falls from his face when he notices Spring's hand. "What happened?" he asks, his green eyes darkening with concern. He takes her hand, unrolling the rag to examine it. His act of tender love and concern reminds me of Aspen, and I burst into tears.

Spring and Oak's confused faces mirror one another's. "Spring it was just an accident," she says, turning to Oak and saying, "I cut myself when she startled me, but it's fine now." She squeezes her cut to illustrate her point.

"It's not that," I whine. "I'm just frazzled. Aspen's in trouble and he's in need of our help."

The volunteer counselors share a look.

I take a sharp breath. "This time it's different. I saw him—"

"Summer..." Oak says, trailing off. "I heard about this morning."

"What happened this morning?" Spring asks.

Oak fills her in on my run-in with the Headmistress and subsequent scolding.

"Oh," Spring says, averting her eyes and shaking her head. "I can't help you again. Not with a broomstick, anyways."

"Then maybe you could check things out yourself?" I suggest.

Oak sighs. "Where is he?"

"He's being held against his will at Priestess Anna's."

Spring bursts into laughter and slaps her hand over her mouth. Oak turns his head, sizing me up.

"You're kidding, right?" he asks.

"No, I saw it with my own two eyes," I respond.

"You didn't have any more of that tea at Iris Rose-Thorne's, did you?" Spring asks, placing her hand on my forehead. I swat it away.

"No!" My cheeks flame.

"C'mon," Spring says, stepping away. "Let's go back inside... Priestess Anna?" She stifles a giggle with her hand.

"I'm serious," I reply through gritted teeth.

Oak doesn't budge, his face curious. He opens his mouth to speak, but his girlfriend cuts him off before he has a chance.

"What? You believe this?" Spring exclaims, propping her hand on her hip. "Okay, I've had my laugh for the morning. Stay out here and entertain this if you want." She spins around and steps back inside. As the door swings in the doorframe, I'm left alone with Oak.

"Don't mind her. Spring looks up to Priestess Anna, but I have a good friend who's well respected and isn't so fond of her, so... I'll check it out this morning," he says softly. "First chance I get."

"Thank you," I say, sighing with relief.

"Don't mention it."

21

I barely make it through breakfast without having a mental breakdown. I feel like a caged animal, only the cage is the perimeter of Camp Bitter Tonic. I can't believe I could be so neglectful to just prance through the forest with that damn magenta broomstick tucked under my arm. In my haste, I completely forgot to stash it in the thicket.

If I could rewind time I would do so many things different. I wouldn't have left the Solar Solstice party because I was feeling rejected and bummed that he didn't kiss me. I can't help but feel this is partly my fault. I should have just *stayed*. It feels like my hands are tied. I'm powerless here to help him.

After witnessing Priestess Anna flying erratically last night I wonder if she could have hurt Aspen. What if they were in a broom crash? I just don't understand why she would keep him if it were only an accident.

After breakfast, I clean the galley kitchen floor with a besom broom, sweeping dirt and bad energies right out the door. A note was left on the chore board from Headmistress Starwort to use kitchen witchery today to prepare for the morning lesson.

The morning class on fire divination is held in the cramped confines of the galley kitchen to avoid interference from the winds. Our group has been split into two. Mistress Aster has brought Petal, Hyacinth, River, and Rugosa outside for cauldron fire scrying. Headmistress Starwort teaches Amaranth, Azalea, Dahlia, and me candle scrying before we rotate out. I'm thankful for a hands-on activity instead of a mind-numbing sit-down lecture. Candle scrying keeps my nervous hands busy and my scattered mind focused on something other than what's going on with Aspen and Oak.

After we receive a refresher on the basics, we move on to the fun part, foretelling the flame.

The lights are dim, and four white taper candles are lit. We stare at our candles, searching for any signs from the flame.

My candle flame burns brightly, sparking at the wick. It fizzles, slowly dwindling, then seems to turn in a circular motion.

I sigh. It's definitely not a good sign. This activity is doing nothing to soothe my anxiety.

Headmistress Starwort paces the galley, walking behind us as we stand at the counter. She speaks of fire magic and the history of scrying. Her speech is low and controlled. The monotony of her voice and the dimness of the room is enough to put us in a meditative state, open to receive messages from the flames.

The Headmistress halts in place and peers over Azalea's shoulder. The flame of her candle appears dim. "I wouldn't make any plans," she tells her, scrying the candle. She steps forward and evaluates Dahlia's candle. Her flame waves about, predicting a major change in her circumstances. Amaranth's flame is steady and bright, a sign of steady good fortune.

And mine twists like a hurricane, foretelling danger. When Headmistress Starwort gets to me in line, she confirms my prediction.

The smell of cauldron smoke is thick in my nose after smoke scrying. As I'm taking a nature trail from the lesson area, a crashing sound echoes in the woods, followed by laughter. I'd recognize Spring's cute giggle anywhere. She's with Oak. Upon seeing them, I duck behind a hemlock tree, letting an overhanging branch hide me. I peer through the curtain of pine needles.

"Girls can't steer brooms," he says chuckling, with a leg on each side of a vibrant purple broomstick. She giggles, slapping him playfully. She then pulls bits of leaves and debris from his clothing.

"This better be a real quick trip," she tells him as they lift off. "You know, I didn't want to say anything—"

"But you *are*," he interrupts.

"But I am, and her mom has some issues, you know."

"Whose doesn't?" he asks, hovering several feet above the ground. "Have ya met mine?"

"It's just, I think this is completely freaking ridiculous. You know about my struggles with ghosts in the past, and I hate to be hypocritical, but I worry about you. I know you love working with kids, but you gotta know when one's got a screw loose. Apple doesn't fall far from the tree and all. She has those nightmares and she's like, really imaginative. Point is, you can't go chasing every wild goose you see."

I gasp, but I should expect as much. She laughed at my accusation. It burns deep.

"Ah, quit yer bitchin. It gets us outta here for a few," he says with a dimpled grin. They lift up smoothly, their legs dangling over the broomstick. He looks below, scanning the forest; I step out of view, scurrying against the thick trunk of the hemlock tree, but a weak, willowy branch snaps behind my back. The sound is loud enough to draw Oak's attention. Without cover from the branch, the red coloring of my Charm School tee-shirt quickly gives me away.

He lowers the broomstick. Spring hops off, her hands in the air apologetically. "I am *so* sorry," she says, sinking her hands into the pockets sewn onto the hips of her green dress. "I shouldn't have said that," she adds frowning.

"It's not anything I haven't heard before," I admit, saddened, stepping out from under the hemlock.

Oak interrupts, speaking to Spring, "Why don't we let Summer have a look for herself, too?"

"I'm completely against the idea, but I think it's only right after what I said—whoa!"

I nearly plow Spring over, boarding the broom before she finishes her sentence. She squeezes between us and we set off to Priestess Anna's to save my best friend.

"For the record, I think this is insane," Spring reminds Oak, as we land in Pine Point. Dust clouds rise from the dirt street as our feet hit the ground. I hop off the vibrant purple broomstick.

He shrugs and twirls the broomstick like a marching baton as we walk down the center of the street. "Nothing surprises me anymore," he says with a sigh.

We reach Priestess Anna's house, and Spring steps into her yard, through yellow dandelions, pink clover, and weedy grass. Oak catches up behind her. He grabs her shoulder, spinning her around. "Don't you think we should have a look first? What's your plan?" he asks, pulling her behind a large yew tree. I dart across the lawn and join them.

"I was just gonna knock," she answers, stepping out from the cover of the tree. "Now c'mon. We gotta get back," she calls, waving over her shoulder. Oak and I share a troubled look, then we catch up to her.

Spring complains that the doorbell is broken when I reach the porch. Oak sprints across the lawn, heading around the house. She rolls her eyes and raises her fist to the wooden door, knocks three times, then steps back. I wait on the porch.

She folds her arms over her chest and confides in me, "I've always liked Priestess Anna. When I wanted to go to Prom, she hooked me up, and I was able to trade my science credits for Alchemy." She returns to the door and knocks again, giving up after a few moments. As she steps down, she says, "I'm going to find Oak."

Movement of the lace curtain on the door behind her catches my eye. "There's someone home," I say, urgently. Spring waves and identifies herself as a former student.

The door pops open and Priestess Anna steps out, closing the door behind her. She leans her back against it. "My former student?" she asks her. "You graduated all of a what? A week ago?" She smiles and looks beyond Spring to me. "Hello, Miss Summer." She squints, her brow furrowing. "Shouldn't you be in Charm School?"

Before I respond, Spring saves me as she says, "She has a special emergency pass. It's family related," she whispers, cupping her hand over her mouth and winking.

Priestess Anna nods in understanding, sharing a knowing look with Spring. "Oh. How can I help you, ladies?"

"Uh," Spring stammers.

I guess we really should have had a better plan than just knocking on the door.

Spring's boyfriend comes around the side of the house, trudging through thick grass and tall weeds. His eyes are wild-looking, and his forehead is etched with concern. I can only imagine what he's seen. I swallow hard. I hope we aren't too late.

He raises his hand, and slightly out of breath, he asks, "I need to use your bathroom. Do you mind?"

Priestess Anna's inky blue eyes widen in alarm. She crosses her arms over her chest. "You came all the way out here, from wherever just to use my bathroom? What were you doing in my backyard?" she asks defensively.

"I was gonna pee back there," he answers quickly, "but the old lady next door was looking out her window."

Priestess Anna squeezes her temples, closing her eyes. "Oh," she groans. "That's old Marjoram." She gestures to Oak. "Hurry just come in and be on your way... Teachers never get a vacation," she mutters under her breath, complaining about the downsides of her work.

From the porch I can smell the wine she drinks on her breath. Oak brushes past me, and he's in the door before she finishes her sentence. I step behind him and she stops me, pressing her hand into my shoulder. I blink.

"Are you going to hold it for him?" she snaps, her face twisted in an evil sneer.

I take two steps back, nearly tripping on the curled edge of the doormat. "No..." my voice trails off. "I just thought it'd be okay?"

"Is there a problem?" Spring asks, her lavender eyes rounding with wonder.

A commotion from the back of the house pulls the attention of the Priestess. She flees into her home, leaving the door wide open. I take the opportunity to follow, my heart hammering against my ribs. I chase Priestess Anna through the kitchen, down a dim hallway, into a back room.

"No!" the Devil-Claw Priestess cries, diving toward Oak. He raises his arm and she bounces back, tripping over an empty potion bottle. It rolls across the floor as she sails backward into the wall, collapsing on the ground in a sorry heap. She sobs quietly, banging the floor with her fist.

The scene is confusing and chaotic. Aspen is entangled in the thick rope around his neck and wrist, bound to the oak bedposts. I nearly vomit at the sight. His arm hangs limply, smacking the mattress as Oak frees him with a knife. I untie the knotwork at his neck while my camp counselor cuts the restraint.

He's bruised, pale, and his pupils are dilated. His leg bends unnaturally. Herbs, vials of oil, and empty potion bottles are scattered about on the nightstand, the small desk, and the bureau. Bloodied bandages, used compresses, broken teacups, and filthy vomit pails litter the floor. It smells like a hospital ward, sour and antiseptic. I'm horrified, shocked, and disgusted.

"I looked up to you," Spring says, towering over Priestess Anna. "I admired you. I just want to know one thing…"

"Why?" I croak, finishing her sentence. I clear my throat, then repeat myself louder, "Why?"

Spring nods, her lavender stare boring into Priestess Anna. Aspen groans as Oak piles him over his shoulder.

"The time for this is after, Spring," Oak says tightly as he passes us, carrying a nearly unconscious Aspen. "We don't need to play jury, trial, and execution right *now*."

"Bull we don't," she responds, stomping her foot into the ground.

Priestess Anna startles, then rises to a seated position. She dabs her eyes with one of the many tissues that litter the ground.

"Please, just get the broom. We need to get this kid to the hospital. It's around back," he calls from the hallway.

"You sicken me," she says to Priestess Anna, as she leaves the crude hospital ward.

I spin around when the floor creaks behind me. With a swiftness I didn't think she had, Priestess Anna hops to her feet and charges me, taking me to the floor with her.

22

My shoulder collides with the hardwood floor, my arm crushed beneath me. Spring knots Priestess Anna's clothing in her fist, yanking her with all her might from me. My braids are pulled, and I swat backward, connecting with the side of Priestess Anna's face.

Oak rushes to our side. Priestess Anna releases my hair and scurries backward, crab-walking to the corner of the room. She rises slowly, procuring an object from her book shelf beside her.

"I can't let you take him," Priestess Anna says. "I was only trying to help after what happened. It was a bad storm. I didn't see him! I swear!" Within her trembling hand, she holds a black handled, ceremonial double-edged dagger. We raise our hands. Aspen groans from the front of the house.

Sunlight glints off her athame. Sweat pours down my neck and trickles down my chest, dipping into my navel. The room is deathly quiet but for Priestess Anna's labored breathing. It's time for me to step up. I need to do… something.

"We know," I say. "It's clear you're helping him." I glance around the room. "But it's time to bring him to the hospital where he can be treated by a Shaman and a team of medical professionals who are equipped. This is too much for one person."

Her stormy eyes dart between us, mistrustful.

"We don't have to tell anyone where we found him," Spring suggests, her hands in the air in surrender.

She raises the knife, pointing it at Spring. "I'll lose my title," she says angrily, streaks of black mascara running down her cheeks. "My position at Springfield High. I will lose everything I've ever worked for!"

"You won't," Spring promises. "It will be our secret."

As Spring attempts to calm the distressed Priestess, a strange memory resurfaces from the night of the dream at Iris's house. I remember the witch I cowered beneath, and the odd comments she spoke about doing everything for us kids.

It was real. Those dreams were precognitive, from before Aspen disappeared. The Night Hag of my nightmares was Priestess Anna—cursed by alcoholism. The broomstick accident in a rainstorm, the ceremonial black robe, the peculiar comments made by the Devil-Claw witch—it all unfolded in my dreams.

It feels like the wind has been knocked from me. I'm not only a fire witch... I also have the gift of precognition. The answers have been there all along, amid a nightmare.

"But he'll tell if you don't," Priestess Anna says, gesturing down the hallway. She drops her head in her hands, her voice muffled as she says, "It was an accident. I should have left him and kept going. I thought I could heal him... It was a mistake! One blunder shouldn't cost my good name!"

As she speaks, Oak tiptoes from the room, down the hallway. I glance at Spring. Her pretty face is twisted with confusion, her eyes focused on a woman she admired only minutes ago.

A thumping sound from the hallway stirs my attention. I look over my shoulder. Oak points in the direction of the door, mouthing slowly, "I'm bringing him. I'll get help." I return my attention to Priestess Anna, inwardly sighing in relief.

We drop our hands as she sobs. She unburdens herself, sharing details from that fateful night Aspen went missing.

"I didn't see him," she says. "I had a bit too much to drink and I hit him on my way home. I wasn't sure it even was a person until I noticed the better half of a yellow broomstick in my lap. I swooped over the lake, numerous times, looking for any signs. I found him in a tree."

As she speaks, more pieces from my nightmares fit together. Just this morning I dreamt about being stuck in a tree and feeling relief when I saw someone I recognized. Little did I know, I was experiencing Aspen's tragedy.

"I was only trying to help," she reiterates.

She made a horrible mistake, and she didn't want to own up to the consequences. As Wiccans we are hyper-responsible. We have a responsibility to help, whenever feasible, but she didn't help him. She helped herself. Her actions were selfish and harmful.

"An it harm none, do what ye will."

She broke the most basic principle of the Wiccan Rede, a crime punishable by the Elders of all four clans.

Her insistence and emphasis on *helping* him get on my last nerve. I can't stand to listen to another second, but we have to keep her distracted while Oak brings Aspen to the hospital and sends back help. I don't understand why she is telling us all this stuff. Does she think she can manipulate us into believing her? Does she not realize the *only* reason we are entertaining this is because she's holding a sharp athame?

As my mind spirals with questions, the glass of the window beside the bed shatters, and a pink smoke bomb hits the floor. Spring and I scream as shards of glass spray into the room, followed by large puffs of billowy magenta smoke. The room fills quickly. It doesn't faze me as a fire witch, but Spring is struggling. An air witch, she begins to cough and becomes disoriented. As she steps in the direction of Priestess Anna, I reach for her, and her fingers encircle my arm. I pull her with me out of the smoky bedroom, into the hallway, and out the door to fresh air.

Emergency vehicles are parked outside, lights flashing. Shamans rush to us, ready to assist. The Elders storm the house to arrest Priestess Anna. She surrenders without incident but insists on her innocence. As she's boarding a broom to be brought to the detention facility, her hands tied behind her back with black ribbon, she glares at me. Her stare is dark indigo, almost black. I confirm the report Oak gave to the hospital workers to the first person who asks.

Spring is taken to the hospital for observation. As the ambulance doors close, Spring coughs, gasping desperately for breath.

This entire event is such a tragedy. It's going to be a shock to the community, especially everyone who loves her and her beloved students. If I've learned anything from her, it's to own up to your mistakes. I've been a bit in denial about the implications of my love spell—my only concern was the way it made *me* feel in the end—but I realize now, I was wrong to have done it. My actions were terribly selfish, like Priestess Anna's, just not nearly as disastrous.

Amid the confusion, I almost don't register someone calling my name. I glance around, spotting Oak, towering above everyone else. The sea of people part as he passes through and he calls out again, "Summer!" I wave to acknowledge him.

He waves his purple broom in the air, narrowly missing heads. "Aspen is asking for you… Where's Spring?"

Dread sweeps over me. He crumples to his knees when I tell him she was hurt, his hand in his hands.

Word travels fast. When Oak and I arrive at the hospital, I'm stunned to find Headmistress Starwort and fellow Charm School students in the waiting room. Rugosa approaches and we're updated on Aspen's status. He's injured but otherwise okay and currently getting X-rays on his leg.

Headmistress Starwort rushes toward us, throwing her arms around the both of us and thanking the Goddess neither of us was hurt. I'm surprised by her change in character. Oak excuses himself politely to check on his girlfriend, Spring.

"I'm not in trouble for leaving, right?" I ask, unsure if I want the answer. I cringe as I wait for her to respond.

"Certainly not, my lovely one. But we will be discussing the magical broom shed," she raises her eyebrow, placing a hand on her hip.

I smile awkwardly, remembering the hole I kicked through the rotten wood.

"I'm sorry for not believing you," she says in a hushed tone, pulling me to the side of the waiting room. "You had your sneaking suspicions, and I feel terrible for discounting you. I'm responsible for you *all* while you're in my boarding school, and I failed to keep you, Aspen, and my counselors safe. For that, I am everlastingly sorry." She grasps my hand and I squeeze it back. With a sigh, she adds, "And now your friends have a lot to ask you." She gestures them over, and they spring up from their chairs at once.

I'm bombarded by questions.

"What are those new cuts on your face and arms?" Fern asks. "Did the Priestess cut you?"

"Glass from when they threw in a smoke bomb and broke the back window," I answer.

"What did he look like?" Rugosa asks.

"Not great. He was tied up and stuff. I dunno, guys. Maybe you should just wait for him to tell it," I respond.

"Someone said it was an accident, and she was trying to heal him. That it was a big misunderstanding," Azalea says, her blue eyes dark and stormy.

"Priestess Anna could never hurt anyone, let alone a kid." River seconds her comment.

I try not to get angry—it's no wonder they're skeptical. They're Devil-Claw witches, and their Priestess has been disgraced. It's a hard pill to swallow.

"Did you not hear her say he was tied up?" Amaranth asks them, furious.

As Azalea and Amaranth bicker, I approach River. "Hey, can I talk to you for a second?" Dahlia looks on, her brow furrowed. He nods, and we step away from the group.

"What's up?" he asks, his confused expression mirroring Dahlia's.

"I just wanted to say I'm sorry about the spell." My gaze falls to the ground. "I should have never done that. It was wrong of me. I hope one day you can forgive me."

"I'm not upset with you anymore, Summer. We're cool. I'm glad you're okay. You're a pretty badass chick for what you did today."

My gaze lifts, and I brighten. "Thanks, River."

"You got it." We hug and step apart, rejoining the group.

The double doors open, and a nurse enters the waiting room. Looking past her, a gurney is wheeled out from an elevator by two medical associates. A flash of blonde hair immediately gives him away; it's Aspen.

I part from the group, walking swiftly toward the corridor. The nurse stops me as she helps a sick patient in a wheelchair.

"Whoa! And where do you think you're going?" she asks, her hands on the handles of the wheelchair. She pushes her patient forward, stopping as she reaches me.

"My friend—I mean, my brother, Aspen Widow-Tears. I need to see him."

She smiles, hunched over the wheelchair. She pushes the patient through the double doors and says over her shoulder, "That blond haired boy? Nice try but you don't look like those golden-haired, lavender-eyed witches."

"It's true," the Headmistress says, rushing forward. "They are *my* foster children." She winks at me.

The nurse turns and says, "Alright. Head to a nurse's station to find out where your brother is."

I smile at the Headmistress before exiting the waiting room. I find a nurse's station and gather his room number, taking deep breaths as I walk through the maze of hallways. Butterflies flap wings of steel in my stomach. I pause before knocking on the door; it's half-way closed and the lights are dim.

I knock twice, pushing open the door.

"Summer," Aspen says hoarsely, a weak smile on his face.

I rush to his side, planting a soft kiss on his forehead. Tears pool in my eyes as he pulls me close for a hug. I press another soft kiss on his cheek as we embrace. He cups my face with his bandaged, IV-ridden hands.

This time he kisses me back.

Epilogue

One month later...

Meadow tears the leg of a loaf of Lammas. She passes the bread across the table to my sister, Wisteria. "Mm, Summer. This is delicious," she adds, relishing it.

"Better be delicious," I say as I ladle a second helping of homemade barley mushroom soup into her bowl. "He's the God of the harvest, after all. I'd expect nothing less."

She picks up her spoon, her mouth quirked up in a half-smile. "I don't know what happened in those woods, but I'm loving the new and improved Summer. This is amazing," she says, gazing around the room dreamily.

The kitchen is clean and uncluttered, decorated for the Sabbat, Lughnasadh. A bunch of brightly colored corn has been hung on the entry door. A large wheat pentacle hangs on the wall. Fresh herbs from the garden have been tied and bundled. They hang in the kitchen, perfuming the air with mint, yarrow, and sage. I've done the best I can to have a nice Lammas celebration for my mother, at home, so she can enjoy our Sabbat too. Of course, I've had a lot of help today from Aspen.

"It's best you *don't* know," he says to her, winking.

"I'm sure you're both just glad to be out of there," Wisteria says, wiping her face with a cloth napkin.

"It was bittersweet," I admit.

"She cried when Headmistress Starwort hugged her goodbye," Aspen teases.

"Be quiet. You like her too." I shove him playfully. Wisteria looks on in confusion, her spoon frozen mid-air between the bowl and her face. A drop of cream drips onto the tablecloth, stirring her attention. She shakes her head, plunking the spoon into her mouth.

"I seem to remember you wanting to fly off on a broomstick, leaving her in a cloud of dust?" Aspen remarks with a sly grin.

"Was the accident a head-on collision?" I tease. "At least she canceled the remainder of Charm School and gave us all passing grades. Now we can graduate on time!"

"So, what happened today?" my mother asks, dipping her spoon into her bowl. "You kids gonna keep me waiting all afternoon, or what?" She drops her utensil and it clatters against the bowl. "Okay, that's it. This is incredible. From now on, you're cooking."

I smile, taking my seat at the table beside Aspen. "Priestess Anna was found guilty of kidnapping, FUI—"

Meadow's head springs up. "FUI?" she asks.

"Flying under the influence," Aspen answers.

"Oh, right," she says.

"Also bodily harm, obstruction of justice, and failure to report a broom accident. For the crime of breaking the Wiccan Rede, she was scourged on the ever-populated Elwood Ave, witnessed by members of the four clans. It was no big. She wasn't really hurt or anything. Nothing like what happened to Aspen. Anyways, her mother was there of course. She looked on in total shame as her daughter was taken away by Devil-Claw clan Elders," I tell her. "I think that was the worst part for her."

"What makes you say that?" my mother asks.

"Just a hunch," I respond, remembering my nightmare where the witch was worried about her mother's reaction to her damaged velvet robe.

"She was suspended from her teaching job, too," Wisteria chimes in.

"She wasn't fired?" my mother asks, surprised. Her gaze darts between us three.

We all shake our heads no.

"I wish I could have witnessed it," she says, her gaze dropping. "I'd like to scourge her myself."

"It's okay, Mom. You're doing better," I tell her.

She grins. "It feels so good to have you calling me mom again."

I return her smile and blow on my steaming soup.

I'm so proud of my mother. While I was at Charm School, she graduated from Blue Ivy Academy. She had been slowly working on her credits without anyone knowing and built up enough to graduate with a Medical Billing and Coding degree. It took her a year to complete a six-month course, but she did it. Tomorrow, she begins working from home doing medical billing and coding for the Springfield hospital that serves both witches and non-magicals. The best part, no more guys like Ash coming around. I haven't seen him once since I've been back. I love that she found a way around her agoraphobia to support us without using fraud or depending on guys like Ash. The Elder-approved computer and fax machine are so much nicer to come home to than heaps of fake charms and random dudes.

"We're all doing better," Meadow says with light in her eyes. She reaches to Wisteria and me, squeezing our hands affectionately.

"What's that old expression?" Aspen asks, snapping his fingers as he stammers for words. His eyes light up. "Oh! I know! We reap what we sow."

"Not always," I respond. "You didn't ask to be injured and held against your will. Or to have your leg broken," I add knocking on his cast.

"It's coming off tomorrow. Besides, it was worth it," he says with a sly grin, biting into a chunk of buttery baked bread and chewing it thoughtfully. "You finally felt sorry enough for me, and I if I do remember in my woozy state, I got *three* kisses out of the deal."

"And many more after that." I peck him on the cheek and nuzzle his neck.

Wisteria feigns gagging as my mother clears her throat, loudly. "We're trying to eat here," my mother says, breaking our romantic moment.

We apologize in unison, returning to our meal.

"So what are you kids plans for the evening?" my mother asks.

"We're gonna head back to Elderberry Thicket after we clean up here," I say, rising from my chair and retrieving empty bowls and plates. "The Witches Fair on the Green is already in full swing, I'm sure. Dahlia and Rugosa will be here any minute. We're gonna head over together. High Priestess Widow-Tears puts out a spread like you wouldn't believe." I rinse the dishes in the sink, running the garbage disposal.

"What ever happened with River and Dahlia?" Wisteria asks from the kitchen table, shouting over the roar of the garbage disposal.

"Yeah, she's with Rugosa now," I respond, silencing the roar. "Rugosa and Fern had a little thing going, but I don't think it was anything serious, just like a summer camp fling sorta deal. Dahlia broke up with River the night Aspen was brought to the hospital. They got into a big fight about—I don't even know what—and she told him she was gonna put a mirror on the bottom of the lake, so he'd drown." I pause as Wisteria spits out her soup.

"Because he's so egotistical and narcissistic?" she asks, wiping her chin.

"Right," I say with a grin. "I've never seen him pass a reflective surface without staring at himself, so it could work. Anyways, Dahlia is with Rugosa now. They seem happy together."

"So who's Fern with now?" Wisteria asks as I return to the table.

"River!" I respond, chuckling. "They switched off."

"Oh no. Are you mad?" my sister asks.

"Not at all." I reach for the bread plates and pause as my mother places her hand over mine. Her jade ring is tight around her ring finger from the ten pounds she gained over the summer. She's never looked better.

Her hair is clean and combed, and I've introduced natural deodorant to our household. Wisteria wasn't impressed. My mother's bathrobe was burned in the cauldron out back, and she wears pretty dresses every day made by the Stitch Witch, seamstress Iris Rose-Thorne. Graduating from Blue Ivy and receiving a diploma gave her back her confidence. My sister and I framed her certificate and hung it over the mantle in the living room, where it's displayed proudly.

"Leave it. We'll clean up. You two run off with your friends, and Wisteria and I will take care of this. Have fun at the Witches Fair on the Green," she says with a smile.

Wisteria huffs beside her. "Why can't I leave too?"

"Because they cooked. It's the least we can do to show our gratitude." My mother pulls the bread plates from my hand, and juggles the bowls in her other, making her way to the sink.

"That's cool, Meadow. Thanks," Aspen says, reaching for his crutches. "Can't wait to get this damn thing off," he adds with a groan, rising stiffly.

"You can call me *mom*," she shouts over the roar of the water at the sink.

"Um, noooo," I say, embarrassed, my cheeks heating.

"Yeah. Let's not make things any weirder," Aspen remarks, cringing. "The nurse at the hospital transferred out after she saw Summer, who identified herself as my *sister*, kissing me."

I giggle. "It was the only way I could see you. And we were, you know, at one point. So technically, it wasn't a lie."

He sighs, rounding the table on his crutches. "It was *temporary* foster placement. Why can't anyone remember that part?"

"How's your new foster placement, Aspen?" my mother asks. "You getting along okay?"

"Oh, it's going good. Lilac Wormwood is really nice. Plus, it's right down the road so I can see Summer a lot."

"That reminds me. I need to compensate you for mowing the lawn," my mother says. "Let me just get my purse—"

"No! Please don't, it's okay. I'm happy to help out. With the amount of time I spend here, I think it's only fair that I pitch in," Aspen replies. "If you need anything else done, just let me know."

"Well, okay then," my mother responds with a shrug. "Summer, hang on to this one. Don't let him get away."

I smile, retrieving Aspen's specially designed handicapped riding broom from the adjoining laundry room.

The magical community presented it to him while he was in the hospital. The broomstick is larger than most, with hooks on each side of the handle that carry his crutches. It lacks the fancy frills of Aspen's old broom—sadly there is no smoking sage when he accelerates, nor is it stained by the skins of onions—but it's reliable and safe for him to fly on while his leg heals.

"When are you going to make one with an herbal tea cup holder for me," I ask him, holding his handicapped broomstick at a distance.

He laughs, his lavender eyes sparkling. "I could do something like that. But if you come near my next broomstick with buckles on your boots, it's a deal breaker."

"Deal. Absolutely no buckles." I grin. "And when you're feeling better, I'm steering my sparkly magenta one, freshly fashioned with the aforementioned tea cup holder you promised."

As I hand Aspen the broomstick, he nods in the direction of my mother. I spin around. My mother dabs at her tears with her cloth napkin.

"What's wrong?" I ask, bewildered by the change of her mood.

"You look so beautiful in your late grandmother's dress," she says, setting the napkin on the counter. She plucks garden-picked ruby-red poppy flowers from a vase on the counter, braiding the thin stems into my hair behind my ears. Her touch is gentle and tender.

"That dress belonged to your grandmother?" Aspen asks, hobbling toward me. "Wow," he adds, his eyes feasting upon me.

"Well, Iris made some adjustments," I reply. A soft knocking at the door interrupts our conversation. I squeal, "They're here!"

I throw open the door, delighted to see Dahlia and Rugosa on the other side. She's clutching her brand-new broomstick, speckled in the colors of emerald and ocean blue. She wears tiny seashell clips within her hair and a stunning, short aquamarine-colored summer dress. We squeal and hug as Rugosa and Aspen fist bump and greet each other.

"You look amazing, Summer!" Dahlia says as I do a little twirl to show off my dress. "That's the dress Iris made you, right?"

"Kinda," I reply with a grin, running my hands down the soft black fabric. "Just before you knocked, we were talking about it. It was my grandmother's. The Stitch Witch made some alterations to make it a bit more modern."

"Your Grandmother Rose was beautiful," my mother says, after greeting my friends. She tucks my hair behind my ear and adjusts the floppy flowers within my hair. I brush her hand away.

"Okay, Mom. You're embarrassing me," I say with a nervous chuckle.

"Oh, stop. You're my baby!" She turns to my friends and says, "Summer looks just like she did as a teen, actually. Hold on, I organized old photographs the other day. Let me find the picture of your grandmother wearing the dress."

While she retrieves the photograph, and everyone chats in the kitchen, I excuse myself to grab my handbag from my bedroom.

My walls are no longer bare, nor plastered with relics of my relationship with my boyfriend. Instead, they're covered in beautiful tapestries—my favorite displays twinkling stars and a round, full moon. I've painted my stark, white walls purple, the rug is vacuumed, and laundry doesn't sit in heaps on my floor. Twinkling fairy lights are strewn above on the freshly painted ceiling, and pastel-colored beaded curtains cover my windows. There are images of Dahlia and I hanging on the wall—chocolate smeared on our noses from a recent cupcake eating contest—and a gift from Aspen, a dark stained wooden wall plaque he created that reads, *I love you to the moon and back*. I had to make *one* exception.

As I grab my purse from my dresser, I check my reflection in the mirror, barely recognizing the girl staring back at me.

I've changed so much this summer…

I've learned not to tie my identity to a romantic relationship. I've been spending a lot of time with Dahlia and other girls from Charm School, fostering those friendships instead of devoting all my time to my boyfriend. We hang out as couples, and it's so nice—we go to the Witches Brew for herbal tea, go for walks on Elwood Avenue checking out the shops, and joyride together on our broomsticks. I've developed new interests that don't include Aspen—like writing, there's a romance novelist within me—so I don't get sucked back into old codependent patterns.

I consider myself blessed for the magical women in my life. For Fern Widow-Tears, who bandaged my arm with purple deadnettle, but especially for Dahlia, who used magic to gain clarity, clearing the lake water, despite the problems between us. She is no longer a frenemy. I've gotten to know her better over the summer in ways I never thought I would know her.

Like water, she's reflective and treats others how they treat her. She seems to go with the flow. She's a powerful water witch, with the gift of clarity, and I think sight and intuition; it would explain how she swooped in so fast after River broke up with me. But I'm not mad at her for it; if anything, I'm grateful.

I'm familiar with her morning rituals, like how she rolls gardenia on her ankles, wrists, and neck every morning. Her favorite colors are green and blue, and she enjoys her freshwater aquariums; it's all she ever talks about. She's at her happiest when she is in the water, no matter if it's rainwater, the river, or the lake. Like the sea, she is always in motion, full of energy. I can't believe it, but Dahlia Devil-Claw is my best friend. My jealousy of her was only a reflection of the hatred I felt for myself for not being as perfect as I perceived her to be. The flames of envy have transformed into an inner aura of shining light, love, and acceptance. I could learn so much from her and the other women in my life.

I've learned how to *witch* properly. I've aligned myself with the lunar cycles and balances of Nature and have been gardening. I've put all my kitchen witchery skills to the test in our home, and I've replaced sugary coffee drinks with teas that hold magical properties—and I will never, under any circumstance, drink one of Iris Rose-Thorne's teas again, even though I am grateful for her help and think of her as my adopted grandmother. I've been to her house once since that fateful night. She's trying to teach me how to sew and become a legendary seamstress like she pictures herself to be. I don't know if I'll ever get the hang of it, but I love that she's trying to foster that in me.

I've healed the complicated, tumultuous relationship with my mother by forgiving her and making more of an effort to aide her with her limitations. I even call her "Mom" sometimes. I feel lighter without the weight of anger on my chest.

I realize now that my witchiness isn't tied to trinkets and clothing. My fears of not being witchy enough were unfounded. I shunned my inner witch because I believed I wasn't good enough and feared my own growth. It's okay not to float around in velvet robes, wearing semi-precious stones. Denim is perfectly acceptable; it's not the clothes that make the witch.

My passions have been rekindled, my future is bright, and I'm ready for whatever is next.

Meadow hollers from the kitchen, her voice high-pitched and excited, eager to show me the picture she dug up of my late grandmother when she was a teen. I adjust my black dress, stepping out of my bedroom.

Aspen leans over his crutches, his gaze lifting from the old photograph and falling on me. He smiles, his lavender eyes twinkling under the soft lighting of the kitchen.

"Come, look at your twin," he says, to my mother's delight, winking. Dahlia giggles and Rugosa shakes his head. Wisteria bounces past them, clutching a handful of dirty utensils.

I join them. Aspen balances on one crutch, wrapping his arm around me as I gaze down at the photograph of a young woman who looks *nothing* like me.

I glance at him and he smirks. He looks over my shoulder between my mother and me. My heart warms as he rubs my back. Butterflies flap their soft wings within my belly.

We are of air and fire. He's the oxygen to my flame and I burn brighter with him by my side. I've found romance… with my best friend.

Because love is friendship, caught on fire.

The story continues with Autumn's End: The Final Harvest...

Summer Wormwood's No-Bake Cocoa Bombs

Ingredients:

1 ¾ Cups White Sugar
2 ½ Cups Quick-Cooking Oats
1 Stick of Salted Butter
½ Cup Unsweetened Cocoa Powder
½ Cup Milk
½ Cup Creamy Peanut Butter
1 Tsp Vanilla Extract

Prep:

Line baking sheets with wax paper.

In a medium saucepan, bring sugar, milk, butter, and cocoa powder to a near boil, stirring carefully for two minutes as it bubbles.

Remove from heat and add peanut butter, oats, and vanilla extract. Stir until fully combined.

Drop Tbsps. of cookie mixture on wax paper and pop into the freezer for 30 mins.

Check with your finger to see if the cookies have set. Nab one regardless—because they are *oh so good* and who has time to wait?

Once firm, remove from freezer and enjoy, you little kitchen witch!

Season of the Witch the Book Series:

Winter's Curse I

Spring in Summerland II

Amid Summer's Nightmare III

Autumn's End: The Final Harvest IV Coming Soon!

Acknowledgements

As always, I'm grateful for my publisher, Prince and Pauper Press. Especially to Jennifer Carson and Trisha Wooldridge. Trisha, you push me to be a better writer with your thoughtful comments and constructive criticism. You truly are a "Novel Friend".

I am thankful for my family—especially my mother, Robin, who is always available to offer a sympathetic ear and words of support and encouragement, and my father, Jeff, who reads my stories despite his failing eyesight and argues passionately with me about who the *true* villains are, and then proceeds to quiz me ON MY OWN BOOKS! I love you both so much. Thank you for everything, you both are so appreciated.

For my sister, Crystal, and nephew-of-awesome, Josh, and my in-law parents, Thomas and Elizabeth. I'm blessed to have such a loving and supportive family.

For the book world, as a whole, but especially Tiki Kos—who named my sugar-laden, chocolate cookies and has been my favorite part of Facebook since I've met her—Ali Winters, Tricia Beninato, Kristine Schwartz, Michelle Fritz, Laura Jones, and countless others who have cheered me on throughout this process. To book bloggers and reviewers. What would I do without you amazing people?

For my wonderful husband, Benjamin, who anticipates my coffee refills, donut needs, and supports my dreams and goals. Thank you for being my story book "hero". You are so loved.

And last but not least, for my readers! I'm delighted you took a chance on my story. If you feel so inclined, please consider leaving a book review from the retail site where you purchased my work. I'd love to hear your thoughts!

About the Author

April L. Wood is an author of magical, YA mystery-romance, and a book blogger for A Well Read Woman Blog. When she is not glued to her computer or pressing her nose in a book, she is busy obsessing over her gardens to the point of insanity, feeding wildlife, and propagating her ever-growing collection of African violets. She lives in a beautiful historic Tudor-colonial with her rock star husband and their beloved black cat.